Bittersweet

JANAY BAKER

Order this book online at www.trafford.com
or email orders@trafford.com

Most Trafford titles are also available at major online book retailers.

© Copyright 2014 Janay Baker.
All rights reserved. No part of this publication may be reproduced, stored in a
retrieval system, or transmitted, in any form or by any means, electronic, mechanical,
photocopying, recording, or otherwise, without the written prior permission of the author.

Printed in the United States of America.

ISBN: 978-1-4907-4347-9 (sc)
ISBN: 978-1-4907-4349-3 (hc)
ISBN: 978-1-4907-4348-6 (e)

Library of Congress Control Number: 2014913975

Because of the dynamic nature of the Internet, any web addresses or links contained in
this book may have changed since publication and may no longer be valid. The views
expressed in this work are solely those of the author and do not necessarily reflect the
views of the publisher, and the publisher hereby disclaims any responsibility for them.

Any people depicted in stock imagery provided by Thinkstock are models,
and such images are being used for illustrative purposes only.
Certain stock imagery © Thinkstock.

Trafford rev. 08/04/2014

www.trafford.com
North America & international
toll-free: 1 888 232 4444 (USA & Canada)
fax: 812 355 4082

Chapter 1

TAMIA

As I sat and listened to the preacher explain how short life was, everybody crying. Some harder than others, some not at all. I wondered, how did we get here...how is that so many people are now dead. My best friend Sidney sat to my right or Sidney Rose as everybody called her. She was named after her uncle who's name was Sidney Mac respectfully so. She was silently going through her own drama, wondering if she was pregnant or not. I told her to take the test this morning but noooo. She felt that the longer she held off finding out for sure, that it was ok for her to continue to smoke and have some spirits. She would then begin the game of Who's my baby's daddy. Don't get me wrong, on paper it looks bad, I know. But she's really not a bad person. She just got caught up in loving more than one man, or three. I couldn't tell if she was crying because of the occasion or because of her soon to be reality. On my left sat my fiancé Lance. He always smelled so good. He looked good too in his black Armani suit and fresh haircut. I had to wonder sometimes if I really loved him for him, or if I liked the way he completed my look. We were the perfect couple on the outside.

On the inside, Lance is very spoiled with multiple personalities. He's always gotten everything he wants. He's never had to work for anything he's had so when we first met, I had to make him work really hard to get any of my attention. He figured that because he was fine and had money that that was enough. Little did he know that I had my own money, and was not impressed by his.

We had a whirlwind courtship. We went on every island from here to Jamaica. On my birthday last year, he proposed while were in a cabin

with my cousin Reece, her husband DJ and Sidney and her boyfriend Rickey. Roc, Lance's best friend came the next day with some big boned girl. She had a pretty face and just as much confidence as Sidney Rose. I liked her, Sidney Rose didn't. They went back and forth with snide remarks that whole day. If Lance hadn't proposed that night they would have ruined the weekend. Lance always had to be the big man on campus, so everything he does is in a big way. We were on boat in the middle of lake when he got down on one knee and asked me to marry him. He presented me with a 5carat diamond ring. I was in total shock. He surprised everybody. I expected my girls to be happier for me than they were. Maybe it was just me. but before they said congratulations, they looked at each other with raised eyebrows. I never understood why Sidney Rose and Reece act like Lance was an intruder. Just because he didn't drink and smoke all the time, he was lame. **Or because he preferred Khaki pants to jeans and only wore tennis shoes when he worked out or played ball with the fellas. He just wasn't a thug, he was a Princton graduate who was not street smart at all.**
    They both could have all kinds of men in their lives and even marry them, but as soon as I got a man of my own and we were progressing forward they were tripping.
    Lance was never too crazy about Sidney Rose anyway especially since Roc came to town and started sleeping with her. He never wanted to be around her, she never wanted to be around him either. I was always caught in the middle. I kept trying to explain to him that I have been the only constant in Sid's life. Her mother worked all the time and was never ever home and her older brother was never around either, even before he left for the military. She was alone most nights, when she wasn't at my house. It was hard for her to share me now. He bought that story for a few months then went right back to keeping his distance. If he came home when she was there, he'd find a way to leave or stay in the back. I moved in with him shortly when we returned from our trip. It wasn't easy for me to give up my first house and move in with him in a condo in Midtown. I wasn't used to city living. Although the view from his condo was priceless and there was a fitness center, cleaner service and restaurant on site. I must admit, it wasn't that hard to get used to.
    Once we're married we plan to move into our dream house. It's in the northern suburbs in Gwinnett. Sidney and Reece had a fit about that. They've always lived on the East side of Atlanta, between Lithonia and

Stone Mountain. Me moving an hour away did not sit well when I finally told them.

In the beginning Lance wasn't very experienced in the bedroom. We had missionary sex most of the time. When we did explore other positions, it's because I usually initiated it, or he was drunk. He had all the right size materials, his body was amazing. He put Tyson Beckford to shame. His personal trainer made sure of that. He used to be a very selfish lover. I had to train him to please someone else. He said he was used to just laying there and being pleased, he never had to make much of an effort, before me that was.

From the way I see it, this all began a couple months ago. I woke up that morning with Lance licking my breast. I think his mother breast fed him for an unusual amount of time because he woke me up like that almost every day, even if we don't end up having sex. I don't think he can start his day without it. He was very good at it so he got no complaints from me. I was so used to it now, that sometimes I could go back to sleep when he did it.

This morning it was turning me on though and he knew it. As he laid on top of me just about to make his entrance the phone rang. From the ringtone I knew it was Sidney-Rose so I answered it, she would just call right back if I didn't answer, Lance went back to work on my breast. Good Morning she sings in her I know I'm waking you up tone. Before I could even respond, she began giving me the rundown of the day. She hated her car, and always wanted me to drive, the only problem with that was her errands were usually deep in the hood.

Our last official summer barbeque was today. Sidney Rose and I have lived together since we graduated high school. I bought the house when we graduated from college and we've lived there up until recently. When I began staying over Lances, we went through a rough period. You would have thought I stabbed her in the back by becoming engaged. I all but gave her the house. I left everything, but my bedroom and that was only for the guest room of me and Lance's new house. After a lot of talks, name calling and accusations, we got back to a good place between us. Today she was especially tense. She was sure that two of her current lovers would soon be at the same place at the same time. Sidney Rose lived for drama; one man has never been enough for her. No matter how good the man was, she had to have a man on the side. Her boyfriend Ricky cherishes the ground she walks on. He's one of those big country boys who got him a pretty city woman and done lost his mind. He has forgiven her, so many times after catching her with different men that they don't even break up anymore. When they first met, he had an innocence about him that was cute. Now he looks like the walking dead sometimes. She has really changed that man. I mean don't get me wrong, I believe that she really loves him. She just can't have just one man. Ricky is not what you would call book smart, but he can build and fix anything. He's also not what you would call a looker, but what he lacks in physical appearance he compensates in being a good person. He has a heart of gold. Man #2 would be Terry, he was a fireman she met about a year ago. He was a tall fine chocolate brother with the ego to match his huge pecks. She loved him for that confidence; he loved her for the same thing. She didn't follow him around like most of the women did when they saw Mr. June on the public servants calendar. She treated him like just that, a public servant. He saved her life once. Pushed her out the way of a moving car. He went flying through the air like in he was in an action movie scene. They both fell in so called love on the spot. Sidney Rose had that effect on men, her latte color, coal back wavy hair and hazel eyes were a shoe in to a mans heart, her looks alone made them give up everything they had just to be with her. it was either that or the way she dressed. she never left a lot to the imagination. They soon found out she was a lot of pretty work. Terry didn't know about Ricky, he thought Sid was just busy all the time with work. She was a social worker and although that did keep her busy, what Terry didn't know was that she worked from home, a home that she now shared with Ricky.

  After she let me know that she would be at my house in an hour she hung up. I don't think I even spoke two complete sentences in our entire 12 min conversation. I was preoccupied with Lance licking me all over by now. And I was more than ready to be taken to the promise land.

  30 minutes later we were both panting trying to catch our breath when the door bell rang. Sidney was early, I thought as I wobbled to the door. To my surprise it was Roc, Lance's best friend and Sidney's #3 not so secret lover. Roc introduced me and Lance. We went out once and decided that we were more like siblings than lovers especially since I knew we never would take it to the lovers stage. I was never really into the gangster type.

When I first saw Lance I couldn't believe that he was hooking me up with someone or even knew someone so opposite of him, perfect for me.

He always said that Lance was the only one besides him that could have me. I never really knew exactly what he meant by that, but I just let it sleeping dogs lie. Now here he was standing at the door looking like a hip hop ad straight off rap beat magazine. He didn't grow up fortunate like Lance. Roc found his riches in the street. What's up Ma, he said with a slow drag. I could tell he had had more than just his cereal this morning. It was a wonder him and Lance were so close, Lance didn't do most things that his brother from another mother did.

Roc's father worked for Lance's family ever since before they were born. Roc had all of the same opportunities that Lance had, he just chose to go the street route. He said he had the looks, Lance had the brain. No one had the heart to tell him that Lance had the looks too. The only thing he had was the crazy. He had a short fuse and was as bold as they come.

Money however helped him out a lot. This brother was fine and very well put together today. He walked right past me kissing my forehead.

Where's L?

In the bedroom?

He sleep?

He probably is now, I laughed.

Just as I turned to go in the back, the doorbell rang again. In walks in Sidney. She had on shorts a half top and stiletto heels, her hair looked perfectly done I didn't understand her need to go to the beauty shop today. She always wore the best weave jobs, that paired great with her own texture and it really did look just like hers. I had to admit that even dressed like a hooker, she did look very cute. Although I would never wear that, I've always admired her for her confidence; she had enough for us all.

Roc must have thought the same thing too because he went and hugged her up off her feet. While they got reacquainted I went to get ready before she got on me for not being dressed. I was now very glad Roc came when he did. He was the one thing that could take her mind off everything else she had going on in life. She thought she was being slick sneaking off with him every chance she gets. She got thug passion written all over her. Rock didn't care that she had a man, he got all of her he wanted.

When I went back into the room, Lance was coming out the bathroom. Your making breakfast before you leave aren't you? He asked

Lance I told you I was taking Sidney to the beauty shop this morning before going over Reece's. She just got here. Can't you just grab something out today?

Why do you need to take her? See it's this type of shit I'm talking about Mia. She always needs you to do something and you run like a little dog every time. You do realize that your going to have to get a better class of friends.

Don't start Lance, She dropped her car off at the shop this morning. Aren't you about to leave with Roc? why can't you just grab something out, or how about making something yourself.

My mother said that a good women should always make sure a man never leaves the house on any empty stomach. It's about time for you to know your role He said.

Here he go with quotes from his mother again. My role, I said ready to let him have it. before I got fired up, I just turned and went into the bathroom. I was not in the mood for his antics today. When I came out, he stood there looking at me while I dressed and said you're so beautiful, I do love you.

Thanks, I said blushing. I love you too

I'm hungry, are you going to make me something to eat?

What do you want to eat I said exhausted, he wasn't going to give up. I had nobody to blame but myself. When I moved in, I told him he no longer needed a housekeeper, he had me. Now I know that he really does need a housekeeper, or his mother.

Maybe just some rye toast and scrambled egg whites, oh, do we have anymore of that turkey sausage?

No Lance, and we don't have any rye bread, we have wheat maybe even sourdough. Lance never ate Rye bread, he was only asking today to be difficult.

Never mind…he said in a huff, make sure to get some while your out. and you need to change, I don't like what you have on.

What's wrong with what I'm wearing? I asked. You were with me when I bought this dress.

I think it's a little tight don't you. Your going to be my wife, I can't have you going around lookin like your trying to catch.

Lance, this dress is not tight and the only thing I'm trying to catch is you, I said trying to lighten the mood. He could go from I love you to I hate everything about you in a matter of minutes.

By the time me and Lance were dressed and joined the other two, they looked to be in deep conversation. You ready I asked Sidney. She got up, gave Lance a quick hello and was out the door. There was some obvious tension there between her and Roc that I would be getting to the bottom of. I'll see you later baby I said to Lance giving him a kiss. I knew had I not kissed him, there would have been trouble later. We had to show PDA especially in front of any of his boys. I don't think he truly believed that me and Roc never had relations. He couldn't prove it and we both denied it, so he really couldn't do anything but get over it. I couldn't wait to get out of there and hear about the tension with Roc.

As soon as we got into the car, Sidney lit a blunt and started her story. As I sat there and listened to what I thought was another one of her Ricky caught her slippin she may be losing him stories. She had that same drama going on all the time. This time however, she began with two detectives showing up at her door. What did you do I asked in total aw.

I didn't do anything really she responded.

What do you mean by really?

Well, Roc asked me to deposit these checks into my account and wire his boy half of it and I could keep the other half. He said they were legit

Are you out of your freaking mind. You know better than doing some shady shit like that with Roc. Sid, you know what he's into. I don't even know what made you think you were going to get away with something like that.

I know girl, he just kept coming at me and it sounded like fast money.

What do you need the money for so bad. I would have given you money I began to yell.

I don't want to always need you to take care of me. I'm grown. I can take care of myself

Ok, miss grown lady, but now you got the police on your ass.

Shut up Mia, I don't need you coming down on me. I don't have an inheritance. I can't just go to the bank and get out as much money as I need.

Why every time you do something it always comes down to me and my inheritance? I recently found out that I indeed had a father and he didn't die in the war in Iraq. He was a married business man that didn't want anything to do with me or my mother once she got pregnant. He took care of me though. We never wanted for anything, I just assumed that my mothers nurses salary afforded us all the things we had when I graduated college my mother told me the whole sorted story and handed me a check for. half of my inheritance. The other installment I am set to receive when I turn 30. It totaled a little over two million dollars that was left to me by the man that never wanted me, who died before I could even tell him how much I needed him. The money was bittersweet

But now every time something in Sidney world didn't go as planned, she blamed the fact that I have an inheritance.

Its so easy for you Mia. I don't have it like you do. My reality ain't as pretty. She said as she pulled on the blunt. I thought if I cleared enough of these checks that I would be able to pay off some of my credit cards or get ahead of my student loans. The detectives want me to give up Roc and the dude I wired the money to, and if not then I may be looking at 3-5 yrs.

In prison I yelled

Yes, Tamia in prison, and these people are not playing, they have been eyeing Roc for some time and need me to testify against him. Mia I can't do that. I can't betray Roc. I can't send him to jail….

But you can't go to jail either Sid.

What is Ricky going to say, how am I going to tell him, he's bound to find out. Terry is coming down on me to move in with him. He said that since I'm always working and never home anyway, I might as well spend what time I do have with him. I love Ricky and don't want to hurt him again. He's talking about buying me a new car next week and everything. Girl you know I need me a new car, she said blowing smoke out of her mouth.

I almost bought her woe is me spill until I began to think. What reality do you have? You don't make any house payments, you live with a man who pays all of the bills. You have a man on the side, that takes care of all of your personal grooming needs and you have another man who spoils you with the best clothes and jewelry money can buy. And… your making your own money. What else do you need? This ain't about you needing the money.

Well what is it about miss know it all she spat. Passing me the blunt

As I smoked I thought how this was classic Sidney, she was never able to accept responsibility for anything in her life. We rode in silence until we reached Ms Lo's house of style. With my wedding coming up, the last thing I needed to deal with was Sidney possibly going to jail.

I was no longer in the mood to deal with Ms. Lorraine and her cussing every two minutes talking about everybody's business in town. If it happened in SW Atlanta, she knew about it. Before I could get in the door good I could hear her yelling about Patrice who was one of her best customers, she got caught with her baby daddy again. Her husband decided this was the last time he would allow her to sleep around and shot them both. She lived, but Tyrone, Lil bits daddy didn't.

"It's all that Bitches fault" she said. She ain't nothing but a Hoe always been a hoe and gone always be hoe. Now she gone be a crippled hoe.

Although I thought how Ms. Lorraine is as ignorant as they come, I couldn't help but to laugh at her display of what a women shouldn't be.

I looked over at Sidney who apparently had the same thought as I had and got up and walked out. I followed knowing that we would be the next talk of the shop. I made a mental note to never come here again. There was only so much ghetto I could take in one day.

As we headed back towards the East side, my phone rang. It was my cousin Reece. She grew up with up with us too, she was more like my sister than a cousin. Reece who's full name was Clarice but she dares to be called that after the silence and the lamb movie. It scares her to this day.

I thought you were going to come before the party started

Well hello to you too Reece, I told you I was taking Sid to the shop first and would be over there afterwards.

Why do she still fool with Ms. Lorraine ghetto ass you know all she gone do is talk about you when you leave?

I know, Sid had to go there, I was certainly not in the mood to be in nobody's hot shop today especially that one. But we're on our way now, do you need anything before we get there? I knew I was pissing Sidney off talking about her beloved beauty shop.

Oh yea, she answered that's why I called bring lots of ice.

As we hung up and I agreed to it, I already knew that I would calling Lance to bring the ice.

Sidney wasted no time pulling out another blunt. Damn Sid, how much higher can you get?

Girl, I don't know, but I'm sure gonna find out. I'm trying to not think about all the bullshit I got going on today, she replied.

As I looked at my friend my heart went out to her. She spends so much time trying to please so many men, that she has lost sight of what's important in her own life.

Pulling up to Reece's house I couldn't be prouder of her. She has come along way from where she started. Today's party was to be extra special because her little sister Rhonda was leaving to go to college. It took us all to get that girl to this point.

They mother ran out on them when Reece was 14 and Rhonda was only 10. They stayed with me and my mom until Reece was grown and started working two jobs and got them their own apartment. She stepped right in and became Rhonda's mother. And me and Sidney stepped right in as the wise aunts. Raising a teenager is not easy. Keeping that girl out of trouble, without a baby, and not on drugs was a full time job for us all. She was a mess from the beginning, but who could blame her. She had seen so much from Karen her Mom that she grew up faster than she should have. She began to develop at an early age as well. We always wondered if she lost her virginity before she actually admitted to it. Karen was a old hoe. She danced most of her life, she was always very beautiful even when she began to age from hard living. She was a free spirit and raised her girls to be just so. None of them were shy with there bodies and would get naked for any occasion. Thank goodness they were blessed with a her body type.

Reece has gained some weight since getting married and having DJ. She had a complex that I never thought she'd have before. I guess having a baby will do that to you. She don't even dress the same. She would normally wear a halter dress or something else skimpy, even if she was just going to the grocery store. I thought the older the baby got, the more she would come around and start to once again care about her appearance. She would be the first one to talk about other women for letting themselves go after they get married, the last time I saw her she was looking about 10 lbs heavier than the previous time I'd seen her and her hair was still in that awful pony tail. I felt bad for her. Her husband DJ or Darryl Johnson looked good as ever. We have known him since we were 10 years old. They've been together since High school. Now he was about 6'2, mocha brown, he had a clean cut beard. With a body like Tyrese including the tattoos in all the right places. He came along way from the scrawny little boy in elementary school. He opened the door with huge grin on his face.

"About time, yo girl is about to drive me crazy" DJ said moving aside for us to walk in.

Everything ready, I asked walking past him into the house, Sidney dragging in behind me. She was enjoying the grin on DJ's face. She get on my nerves, she never understood that she don't need to have every man who smiled at her.

He had on some heavily starched polo shorts with a polo linen shirt. He had on just enough jewelry to know that he had money, but not too much so that he was flashy. He held onto little DJ who had just turned 2 and was dressed just like his daddy, even down to his little ring he had on. Reece didn't even look like she belong. She walked in with a big tee-shirt on and some extra long blue jeans and some $5 flip-flops. I made a mental note to myself to have a heart to heart with her, something was going on and I would have to get to the bottom of it. I went and greeted her with my usual hug. Today she held on for a few extra minutes.

The house looks great I said, breaking the ice.

Thanks, everything is ready, people should start arriving any time I guess, she responded.

I'll be back DJ announced, go give yo mamma a kiss he said to little DJ.

"bye mommy" DJ said running into Reece's arms. He was on his way over DJ's mothers house for the weekend.

As soon as they were out the door, Reece looked to Sidney and said I need some of what you got.

Without hesitation, Sidney pulled out another blunt out of that magic bag of hers and lit it up.

I sat there wondering if Reece was going to change clothes, not really wanting to ask her and hurt her feelings, since she appears to be kind of fragile these days.

After about an hour, the house was packed, she still had on that same outfit, but now she was barefoot.

I thought about pulling her aside and talking right then, but before I could complete my thought about her, in walks Sidney's uncle, Sidney Mac. Now this man was the icing on the cake, he was a big shot in Atlanta back when me and Sidney were in high school. I had heard some stories about him and different women back in the day that make me blush just thinking about it. He was one smooth cat. He looked Spanish, even though no body else in their family looked it except for Sidney Rose a little bit. He had this wavy coal black hair that is never out of place. He always has on something that looked dressy, even if it is just some pants and a shirt like today. He has always been a secret crush of mine. When me and Sidney were little girls I would love to go over uncle Sid's. Just to look at him and imagine a life where he was my husband and we had pretty Spanish babies. I never understood why he lived with Ms. Lorraine, she was much older than him, she was so tacky and she had a foul mouth. She owned a couple beauty shops in SW Atlanta, so her hair stayed laid, and she dressed in the latest fashions, even if she was too old for most of them. She was only some good up until around 5 or 6, after that you could bet the bank that she would be drunk out of her mind. Rumor had it that she has some information on Sidney-Mac that could put him away for a very long time and she made him stay with her. They've been together for so long now that I don't know if anyone would still care about what he did.

Ms Lorraine and Karen were best friends growing up, which is why she was Reece's and Rhonda's God mother. And she was very proud of that title, especially when it came to partying. It was like I couldn't get away from this lady today. She walked in making her famous Ms. Lorraine entrance

"Is this a Muthafuckin party or what" she screamed as she walked in moving to the music. I couldn't do nothing but shake my head. To know Ms. Lorraine is to ignore Ms. Lorraine especially as the evening progressed.

Two hours in, the party is jumpin. It was people everywhere, weed smoke filled the air, and the Dj was doing his thing. I had had a few drinks and was now ready to eat. I went into the house and who do I run into but Sidney Mac, he was looking at me as if I've had a secret and he wanted to know it. I began to look around to see if anybody else was noticing this look that he was giving me. Especially Ms. Lorraine, who would for sure cut me if she even thought that he was looking at me. He almost glided to me, maybe it was the alcohol, but it was the coolest move ever. I thought. He leaned in and whispered in my ear that he wanted to set up a time to talk to me. I was so confused as to what he could have wanted to talk to me about. His cologne was intoxicating, more than the 3 glasses of wine I had drank, combined with the rhythm and tone of his voice and his body heat was making me slightly moist. So much so, that I just stood there taking it all in. I guess too much time had gone by because he stroked my cheek and asked if I was all right. I snapped out of my trance and just looked at him. At that moment, I wanted him, I didn't care that he was my best friends uncle. Or that my man was there Or that his women was crazy or that he was much older than me. I was in that moment when nothing or nobody matters, that moment when you've wanted something for so long and now it stood right in front of you for the taking. We stood there making love to each other with our eyes. His eyes were deep black in color, he had wrinkles around them when he smiled. That was the only indication that he had any age on him at all. he'd aged perfectly and he knew it. he undressed me ever so slowly with his stare. At the point when I felt his facial hair on my cheek, I knew it was about to be on. My tongue was all ready to explore what this man had to offer. We were Goin in….

We need some more ice yells Rhonda twitching in the kitchen flinging her micro braids. Sidney Mac did a sexy cool little chuckle and kissed me on the cheek. We'll talk later. And with that he glided out the kitchen. I stayed there trying to get my heart rate back down, when I felt a light kiss on my neck from behind. He couldn't stay away I thought as I turned around ready to give this man a piece of my candy.

There Lance stood, drunk, with this crazy look on his face. I wondered if he'd seen the show with me and Sidney Mac. I hated when he drank, he always became some super thug wanna be. His family owns half of Mississippi, he comes from old money and has always had nothing but the best. He wouldn't know how to spell thug if he hadn't went to some of the best schools in the country. But tonight he was Tupac. As much as his thug routine got on my last nerve, it did make him a love genius. That is the only reason I still allowed him to drink. In one swift motion, his lips were on mine and he had picked me up and now we were in the bathroom. He wasted no time in taking off my thongs and let his fingers roam in my hot spot, the wetter I got the more turned on he got. He dropped to his knees and his tongue continued the job, as he devoured me, it was all I could do to balance myself up and keep one leg posted on the wall. As I began to feel myself climax, he got up and turned me over and started to go the hardest he has ever gone. Our sex life was just that. Sex, nothing special, unless he was in his Tupac zone. That is.

Tonight he was in overdrive. He had so much passion. He kissed everything like he longed for it. He handled me like he hadn't just had me that morning. Like this was our first time after years of waiting. Our bodies met each other with force as he went in and out with so much power. When I felt him about to release, I really gave it to him. He began to moan louder with each powerful stroke. As we both reached our peak I looked up at him through the mirror and saw a look that I had never seen before. I couldn't tell if it was love. Hate, passion or sheer exhaustion from some of the best sex we had ever had. He washed himself up and walked out without saying a word. 15 minutes later after getting myself together I was out the bathroom and now extremely hungry.

In the kitchen, I ran into Rickey, Hey Mia, he said coming to give me a hug, this party is jumping huh.

Yea it is, I hope the food is too"

Where's L? he asked

You just missed him, I guess he's outside somewhere. I had to wonder how long we had been in the bathroom, because it had gotten very dark out.

Rickey and Lance had become close over the years, out of everybody they had the most in common and now they have a lot of business dealings too. The one thing they didn't agree on however was Roc. Rickey didn't trust him and it had nothing to do with Sidney Rose. He would surely try to kill him if he knew that Rickey was having his way with his precious Rose. Rickey was just a good dude. He has an old soul He was raised in the country by both of his parents who had been together for over 30 years before they even had him. Roc probably wouldn't want Sidney rose so bad if he didn't think he could hurt him like he's hurt by Rickey and Lance's relationship. And Sid, was so caught up in his bad boy image that she couldn't even see that.

As I made my plate and ate I began to wonder just where Sidney Rose was now, she had to be really drunk at this point. She was always the one that you had to watch at the club, because she always gets too drunk and either wants to fight or she gets way too friendly with everyone she comes into contact with. I guess that's why I never really drank. I always had to be Sidney Rose's keeper.

Chapter 2

SIDNEY ROSE

I was hoping that when I woke up this morning that my life these past couple of days were just a dream. I looked in the mirror and saw the condition of my eyes and knew that it was all real.

How could I have been so stupid, fuckin around with Roc, I knew he wasn't any good from the day he got to town. We'd met earlier that day at the gas station, and I blew him off. It was to my surprise that we were being introduced when me and Rickey went to dinner with Lance and Mia. I don't know how I got wrapped up in that Fifty cent reject. He ain't even as cute as fifty cent, although his body is. And he has this way about him. He commands respect, I find that so sexy, especially since Rickey is so timid.

I was so glad that Ricky had business to take care of this morning, I don't think I could take him and all of his questions that he's had lately. He ain't as simple as I thought or maybe he just tired of dealing with ma shit. I know I shouldn't cheat on him, that's my boo. He has everything that I want in a husband and plan to say yes to his constant marriage proposal one of these days. He is my rock. He is always there for me no matter what. All he know is to work and he wants nothing more than to give me anything that would make me happy. He would just die or kill me and Roc if he knew we were fucking around and that I may be going to jail for doing business with him. What the hell am I going to do?

I need to call Tamia so we can get our day started, I needed her to take me to the shop, since my car was on the fritz again. The barbeque was today and since it might be my last one for awhile, I need to make it a good one.

Before I could dial out, my phone rang. ugggh, it's Terry. He is starting to get on my nerves. His sexy fireman thing he had going has started to get old. Now he wants me to move in with him. Is he crazy? He has no idea that I live with my boyfriend. He fine as hell, he good in bed too, if only we had more than a few great stolen minutes together, if only he wasn't so clingy he'd be perfect. I think I'll ignore his call and deal with that later. He at work anyway and won't be off until tomorrow.

I know Tamia was doin it. she barely said two words, but made a lot of sounds, she ain't slick.

Her and Lance stayed doin it. Lance thinks that if he sexes her crazy that she won't have the energy to have sex with anybody else. As fine as he is his self esteem is shot to hell. I don't know how she do it. He's such a baby, she act more like his mother sometimes than his fiancé.

He got it goin on and all, but he lame as hell. He don't really drink or smoke and he walk around wearing khaki's and expensive suits. He's just a little rich boy who wants to be hard so bad. Tamia always wanted that fairly tale life. Married with kids and shit. With the perfect house, perfect husband two kids and a dog.

Growing up she would never step out of her perfect little box to have any fun. It was always business with her, she always stayed in passing up the parties to study in college. I had to work a part time job and managed to get my party in. she didn't have to work. Turns out she's a freakin millionaire. Only me her mom know exactly how much she was left, and of course Reece. She didn't want people to treat her differently. I don't even think Lance know's exactly how much little Miss Dubois is worth. Hell, I wouldn't be livin here in Atlanta if I had all that money she got. I'd be traveling around the world. But not Mia, she's my rock too. I wish I didn't resent her so much for having that money. She don't know what it's like to want to live a certain way, but can't afford it. I was made for money. Not her, she don't even enjoy it like I would, she still cleans her own house. Of course everything, down to her hair is always perfect, her sense of style is right out of a fashion magazine. Growing up I always felt like her poor friend. My daddy and Uncle Sid were some of the biggest hustlers at that time which made my mom want nothing to do with him. She would have preferred to work day and night to support us, she wouldn't' take his devil money she called it and when my mamma did let me see him it was because I insisted. They would both sneak me money and I would get to buy some of the same expensive clothes Mia had. We always thought that her momma tried to compensate for working so many hours at the hospital by buying so many expensive things. I loved to go over her house, they had everything. She was the only girl our age that had a big screen TV and a vcr in her bedroom. When we turned 16, her mom bought her a silver Mitsubishi eclipse. She had the nerve to pout because she didn't want a silver car.

As I went into the kitchen I called Reece. I hope she had snapped out of her funk. The past couple of weeks, she done really let herself go. Reece had to grow on me, she has always been such a downer. She would be that girl to get drunk and take off her clothes out of no where. I don't know how she married such a babe like DJ. She better be glad she snagged him in high school when he looked like a geek. That brotha done came into his own. He do a lot of business with Roc. Reece think don't nobody know her man is a drug dealer. She try to act so better than everydody cuz she married now. She better get herself together or she gone lose him. That childhood puppy love gone only get her so far. She was never the cutest thing to me anyway, now she all fat. That's my girl though.

Hey miss thang I tried to say in the most cheery voice I could. When Reece answered. What's up?

Girl tryin to get up and get little DJ ready to go over his grandmomma house. She gone have him for the whole weekend. Thank goodness. I need a break.

I bet girl, babies are a lot of work.

Yea, and so are they daddy's she said in a quieter tone.

What's going on, is everything alright? I asked

It will be. She responded loudly. Have you spoke with Tamia, she asked changing the subject and what time are you going to get here.

I'm on the way to her house in a few. We got a few stops but will be there way before party time.

Before she hung up I got the impression that she had something else to tell me. We just recently became tight, we've always been friends because she was always with Mia, but ever since Mia got engaged and moved downtown, me and Reece and have grown very close.

As I laid the phone down to get dressed it rang again. Damn, Terry again. I hit the ignore button, hoping for a fire somewhere in the city, so this man would stop calling me.

I knew Mia wasn't gone be ready when I got there. She gone end up pregnant, before this lavish wedding their planning. Between his parents and her mom, this was sure to be the wedding of all weddings. They were sparing no expense.

Damn, Roc sexy ass was there, even though I could be going to prison behind his bullshit, he still makes my panties wet when I see him. I was glad he was there because I needed to say some things to him that I couldn't say to him over the phone about this case looming over the both of us. He was facing more time than me, so I could imagine how he was feeling right now. I hope he knows that I would never betray him. I'm a ride or die chick, I hope he knows that.

You know the folks came to my door again, I began

Damn for real ma. What they say this time? He asked.

They want me to give you and the Kansas connect up or I'm going to do some time. I had hoped to see a look of regret on his face. He just stood there looking blank.

Did you hear what I just said Roc. I said demanding some sort of response.

Yea, I heard you, what you want me say?

I want you to tell me what to do.

What do you wanna do?

I don't wanna go to prison

Look ma, I understand that and I can't tell you what do about this. We all knew the risk. You made me cut you in on the Kansas deal, I didn't want you getting in that shit.

So, what does that mean for me now, I asked getting an attitude.

Now, you need to let me hit this right fast. I see you got all my ass out and everything. He said as he bought me closer to him.

I could smell the liquor on his breath, he had been drinking already. Later I said in a dry tone. How could he want to have sex at a time like this.

He was about to insist when Mia and Lance come walking out of the back looking like Ken and Barbie, the perfect couple. I know Lance don't like me. He thinks I'm trash. Ever since he found out I was messing around on Rickey, he would barely even look my way. I know he thinks I will taint his precious Mia to cheat on him too. She so sneaky, even if she was cheating on him, I don't even think she'd tell me right away.

I couldn't hold it in any longer telling her about this police drama I had going on. I tried to keep it from her with the upcoming wedding, she had enough going on. I knew she was gone flip out. She don't think it's ever worth it to break the law. She don't even like to jay walk. She don't know I was making some good money, I wasn't gone need nobody no more. Make my own way. Maybe even get me a fly condo overlooking the city.

By the time we got to Ms. Lorraine's shop I had had enough of Mia's mouth and the last thing I wanted to do was hear Ms. Lorraine's. Getting Mia to come here with me was already a task but I needed her bring me, since my car was in the shop again. She got her hair done at some spa like place. She hated the beauty shop especially the hood shops even though nobody did weave like Lo's house of style, she didn't understand that, she never had to wear weave. Her mom was Creole and black and her mystery dad she was told was I think white or Italian. She was a mixture of it all. but you better not tell her she's not black though.

I skipped getting my hair done, if I had to see Mia turn her nose up at one more person, we would probably have to fight to get out of there. And it was so hot in there. I started to get quizy I knew I should have eaten, I thought. I had already had 2 blunts this morning and now needed some food. I looked down at my phone once we reached the car and saw two missed calls. Both from Terry. I'm gonna have to tell him it's over. I just can't deal with him right now with everything else. I needed to smoke or something because I didn't feel so hot.

By the time we got to Reece's house I was feeling pretty good. Reece's house was not the biggest house on the block, but it was the most welcoming by far. She had planted flowers all around the house, the grass was always perfectly manicured and they had a party perfect back yard. There were balloons and decorations everywhere. It looked like she had spent a lot of time making this happen, and it paid off. It made me a little envious of her life. Especially when I saw DJ fine ass. I know he wanna hit this. He always making little hints when nobody's around. Reeces is my girl though, I couldn't do that to her. But damn, she looked busted. Her hair was still in that dumb ass pony tail, and she had gained some more weight too. I made a mental note to talk to her later.

As the party progressed me and Reece began doing Tequila shots, me trying to escape my problems and her just trying to get as drunk as possible. I looked into the house and saw Uncle Sid up on Tamia, I couln't tell what kind of conversation they were having, she just stood there lookin at him with those baby doll eyes. Uncle Sid knew he was too old for her I thought as I watched them in deep conversation with their eyes. He spent more time with me than my daddy did. I was always his favorite. Before my brother Paul went to the military he used to say that I was really Uncle Sid's daughter just to taunt me. He was always jealous because I was daddy's little girl.

My daddy and Uncle Sidney was as close as two brothers could be. they grew up in a foster home along with my mother, and they were all best friends, after my parents split up, uncle Sid still came around all the time. It was my dad who named me Sidney after my uncle, Uncle Sid gave me my middle name. He used to say that when I was born, I looked like a perfect little red flower, that's why they named me Sidney Rose.

I looked over and saw Lance looking at Tamia and Uncle Sid the same way I was. He didn't look to happy about it either. For some reason, that pleased me even if it was my Uncle Sid. Rhonda walked in just in time. It looked like he was about to kiss her. Would he really do that I wondered. Would she let him?

Rhonda ole fass ass. I know she wanna fuck Roc, she was always up in his face rubbing on some part of his body, she just don't know. She ain't even ready for a nigga like Roc. He will chew her up and spit her out.

Lance went from looking crazy mad across the room, to kissing her neck, what was that about. Oh now they goin in the bathroom. He such a lame, I bet he about to fuck her again. Sometimes I think it turns him on to see men sniffing up under her. He always watches from a distance and then take her off somewhere. He think I don't notice. There is something about him that I just don't like, there is a side to Lance that he's hiding. No man acts the way he does all the time. It was only a matter of time before his true colors would show. That I was sure of.

In came Rickey, I hadn't seen him all day and surprisingly had missed him. If only he had Terry's looks. He wasn't ugly, he just wasn't polished as Mia would say. He didn't care about nice clothes and material things. He was just a good ole country boy, so his jean shorts and polo top that I had bought him was as in fashion as he got. He looked good though, he had just got a haircut, his bald head was shiner than usual. His size made him intimidating. He was a big boy, with big arms, big legs, big hands and...a big thing, that he knew how to use when I let him. Not many would even try to mess with him. I loved that about him. I felt so safe with him.

As I got up to hug him, I see Roc and Rhonda in the corner, she's laughing like he is doing standup comedy. Once we caught eyes, he pulled her closer. He just don't know. I don't care about him feeling up that teenage porn queen, he better try to get it all in before he goes up the river. From the look I shot back at him, he knew he would regret that move. I know he was just trying to make me jealous. And I hated that it was working. Rickey hugged me so tight, we've been arguing a lot lately and I could tell that he was ready to call a truce. And from the bulge in his pants I could tell that this month I haven't given him any was about to come to an end.

Have you eaten I asked him

Naw, not yet, I am pretty hungry, he said kissing me on my neck.

I must admit that he was turning me on. And the look on Roc's face was the icing on the cake. Miss hot in the pants had nothing on me and I knew it and he knew it. I stood there and let my man kiss on neck while I rubbed his back ever so seductively. If Roc had a lighter skin tone you would have seen him become blood red, I know I saw smoke coming out of his ears like a cartoon.

Baby, I don't feel so good, I think I need to eat. I whispered in his ear.

Go sit down boo, I'll get you something.

Thank you baby. I needed to get rid of him for just a couple of minutes As soon as he reached the inside of the house, Roc made his way over.

"What's up with this lame ass nigga" he says

What's up with Rhonda, you know you too old for that girl. Roc had a way about him that made you just want to do things when he was in your presence. So I completely understood Rhonda's crush.

I looked in the house to see Rickey talking to Lance and knew that I had a little more time to play. Next thing I knew Rickey was pulling me to the other side of house that was completely secluded. He grabbed my face in his hands and kissed me so hard with so much force that we were both left breathless. I knew kissing him right there was dangerous, but I just couldn't stop, he had some kind of hold on me. I guess that's why I let him push me up against the house and slip his finger in my wet place. I was so wrapped up in it that I didn't even realize he was unzipping his pants. I was so turned on that I wanted all 12 inches right then. But I knew I couldn't get down with this right now and besides that, he never wanted to wear condoms. I knew the dangers of having sex with that fool raw, but he persisted so much and I be so turned on that sometimes it was easier to just give in. "We need to talk about this case, I panted

Not now, right now we need to talk about you bending over so I can hit this right fast.

My man is in the house, Roc, I can't do this right now.

Fuck that nigga, ain't nobody thinkin about that country ass muthafucka, now turn this ass around. You know you want some of this dick.

Baby, I'll get out and meet you later I promise. Telling Roc no was a gamble, catch him on the wrong night and no was not even an option. He always had a way of making people do things they might not otherwise do.

You think you slick, you don't be answering yo phone an shit. Now let me get in this and quit playin. He says as he was trying to pull my shorts down.

See, this is what I was afraid of. I should have never came around here I thought as I struggled with this fool. He was not hearing no for an answer.

Chapter 3

REECE

I laid in the bed wondering if I was going to bring up the fact that DJ's phone went off at least five times throughout the night and that was after getting home at 4am. Business huh? Yea right I ain't stupid. I got too much to do today to be fighting with this stupid ass boy. I'm tired of him doing whatever in the hell he wants to do.

He act like he don't hear his son crying, he's the one who insisted I have a baby so soon. We weren't even married when he began his plight to get me pregnant. We used to have sex several times a day. He couldn't get enough. He wanted a son so bad, I think he would have loved a daughter just the same, but he wanted a son more than anything. At first I thought he was just making up for all the times in high school that I told him no, that once he was able to have me, he couldn't get enough. After I had his son, I can count the times on 1 hand that we've had sex. I know I've gained some weight, but it ain't easy to keep up after a baby, deal with his verbal abuse, clean this house, take care of Rhonda and deal with mamma who keeps calling, asking me for money.

I hate that Rhonda gave her my new number, she's been calling me every day with another reason to need some money. She keeps selling Rhonda the dream of getting clean and off the streets. That has not happened since before Rhonda was born. I took care of her since day one. Rhonda wanted so much for her be a normal mom like Auntie Marie. If it wasn't for her we would have been on the streets when mamma left the last time. We were used to her disappearing for a couple days, but when she was gone for 1 month, the neighbors got concerned. Child Protective Services were just about to take us and put us in separate foster homes. But Auntie Marie came right over and got us. She didn't want us to bring any of the little clothes we had or anything else from that house, she said she'd get us new things. And she did just that and raised us as her own. Her and my momma were like night and day you have never known they came from the same household.

I feel like I could never repay her and Tamia for taking us in, they never treated us like our mother was a dopefiend or a whore. We were family. Even though we could have lived there forever and Auntie would have let us. As soon as I could I worked and got me and Rhonda our own place. I felt like it was up to me to raise her, not my auntie. She is still there for us though. She paid for my wedding and she's helping Rhonda with college. Tamia was so lucky growing up with a mother like her. She worked hard for Tamia, she loved her. She loved all of us.

Reminiscing about my past made me forget that DJ was waiting on his breakfast. He was as demanding as his daddy. Sometimes I wish that he would leave and take his mini me with him. Mommy's coming I yell.

After getting him all settled with some pancakes and applesauce I went back in the bedroom to get my phone so I could make some calls. DJ was hanging up his phone as soon as I stepped in the bedroom, he make me so sick, I wonder who the bitch is he's messing around with this week.

Why can't you come in this house at a decent hour, I am your wife and I'm sick of the phone ringing at all hours of the night when you are here.

Don't start Reece, it's too early for this shit he responds rolling up a blunt.

I'm sick of this shit D, you don't care about me. Ima take my baby and...

Bam. the back of his hand hit my face so hard that I lost my balance and hit the floor. I was in total shock, lately he thought he could push, slap and punch me around whenever he felt like it. My arms and legs were so bruised up that I couldn't even wear shorts the day of the party as hot as it was. This was going to have to stop. What is wrong with you I screamed. Before I could say another word, he was up in my face talking real slow. "If you ever take my son from me I will kill you."

The look in his eye and his cold demeanor made me suddenly afraid of his next move. Don't hit me no more, was all I could say. When did

I become of those women that allowed a man to hit me? What have I done to myself? I wondered.

Or what, what are you going to do? Bitch Yo fat ass can get out, you not takin my son. I don't need or want you here noway. Look at you. You don't even bother to comb your hair no more., where the hell you gone go. I'll tell you what you about to do, and that's go get me some breakfast.

As I sat there listening to my husband disrespect me, I wondered who he had become, he has never been so mean and hurtful to me before I had DJ. I didn't know whether to get up and fight this man or put it off till another time. I decided I just couldn't get into it right then, but he would regret hitting on me. All in due time. I thought. God don't like ugly.

Sidney called and broke my concentration, I could tell she was already high. She had been smoking all the time lately, I wondered what that was about. She's always been a party girl, my nickname for her in high school was loosy goosy. She had sex with more dudes before she was even 18 than I've had my whole life. She's one of those pretty girls, if you like the tall slender light skin type. She dresses like she's going to the club all the time, even when she goes to work, I guess that would explain her revolving door of men. I think Rickey has been her longest relationship yet. He's too good for her though. Don't get me wrong, she's my girl and all but she ain't bit more faithful to that man than a fat lady in a bakery. She thinks nobody knows about her and Roc but me and Mia. It's so obvious. I don't know what she sees in that boy, he's got a nice body, but that gold tooth he got on the side is played. And he is way too flashy, he look like a walkin poster child for drug dealers. Sidney like that bad boy type, she been around hustlers all her life, that's all she knows I guess. Rickey would kill them both if he ever found out. That nice boy act he puts on in just a front. Them shy ones be the killers. I just heard that one of the girls Patrice from the old neighborhood got shot messing around on her man, and he was a good dude too. He never had a mean thing to say about nobody. Now he's about to spend the rest of his life in prison over her cheating behind. The man she was cheating with died. So he's going to do some major time.

I started to tell Sid about DJ hitting me, but every time I start to tell somebody, it just don't be the right time. I know she gone think I'm stupid, and Tamia, I hadn't even thought about telling her, she would kill me for sure if she even knew that he calls me out of my name, less and only hits me. I have got do something about this though. He had been hitting me almost every day now. Today, I am going to have a good time. I needed to party, and celebrating Rhonda going away to school was the perfect reason.

Don't get me wrong, I love my baby sister like she my own, but raising her has aged me more than I was ready for. Had it not been for DJ stepping in the father role in the beginning I don't know what I would have done with her. It was touch and go for awhile, I knew for sure that I would kill her little ass sometimes, her and that mouth of hers. And she so fast, I stop trying to make her keep her legs closed along time ago and I started making sure that she took her birth control pill every day. I had to pick my battles with her for sure. She was a good student, always did get good grades. She didn't drink or smoke that I knew of. She loved men though, always has since she was a little girl. She always ended up in some mans lap. I needed her to go away to school. I need some me time. I don't know what me and D's future is and it would be easier if she was hundreds of miles away while I figured it out.

I looked in my closet and thought about what I was going to wear that day, I was interrupted by little D calling me to come get him from his high chair, I guess his daddy didn't hear that either, so off I went. I had to hurry up and get him dressed so he can leave. I hadn't had a break for the whole weekend since he was born. His mother constantly asked, but I don't really like her, she's never thought I was good enough for her precious son. DJ was one of 6 sons that she'd birthed. She had chosen wives for all of them except for DJ who chose me and his brother John, who chose to marry a man. She almost died behind that one, but now they are as close as a mother and son could be. She now claims she has 7 sons. I wonder how many of them beat on their wives and what ole mother hen would say if she knew that her son was abusing me on a regular bases. I was determined to enjoy this day despite my husbands abuse. He will not spoil my day I kept repeating to myself.

One good decision I made that I was proud of, was getting "This is It" to cater. They had some of the best barbeque in Atlanta. I had decorated and set everything up last night, so all I had to do today was set up the bar and go get some ice which I called Mia to bring. Knowing her she would just have Lance do it. That boy know he love him some Mia, I know he gone try to move her to his home town when they get married. I don't blame her either, if I had a man like Lance I would follow him anywhere. I know she gone be on me to lose some weight before this wedding of all weddings she having. I'm sure it'll be nothing like mine and DJ's, we were married in Auntie Marie's back yard. It was beautiful and very tasteful, but I know it won't compare to Mia and Lance's wedding. Lance's mother has all but put an advertisement in the local Mississippi newspaper. I swear that lady has nothing to do with her life but plan social events for her town.

When I got out the shower, I looked at the true damage of my scars. Being dark brown had it's advantages at times like this. Who knew that one day I would be glad that I was chocolate. I hated it growing up, especially being around Mia and Sid. I was known as the dark skin friend. Never just Reece.

DJ walked in as I was examining my battle scars and I almost saw a look of regret in his eyes. Was it regret for hitting me, or regret for marrying me. I couldn't tell because he just walked right back out the room. I wish he would look at me the way he used to, with love in his eyes, he chased me from 6th grade until we reached high school. He was the one that got me through living with my mamma. He was the only one I had ever slept with. I don't count my uncle Harry who came into my room when momma was out on one of her binges, he started when I was 13. Uncle Harry was the only one who had ever shown me any attention, he called me pretty all the time. I thought he was just being a good uncle, later on I found out that he wasn't even my uncle, but my mother's supplier. When I told her what he'd done to me. She told me that sometimes as women we had to endure certain things to survive. She didn't even make him stop coming around, or raping me. I ran away after that, but came back at the thought of Uncle Harry taking Rhonda's virginity like he did mine. If she wasn't going to protect her, than I had too. We never had enough food to eat or clean clothes on our back. Mia gave all of her clothes she didn't want to Rhonda, I was always bigger than Mia and couldn't fit her clothes. I was glad that Rhonda could though, it was hard for her. The best thing my mother ever done for us was to leave. Our lives officially started for us when we moved in with our aunt.

My only rush to move out of Auntie Maries was DJ. He wasted no time moving into our apartment. I remember our first night there. He held me all night and told me that no one would ever hurt me again.

Who knew that five years later, we would be married with a child, he would be cheating on me with any and everybody, he would be a drug dealer, and to top it off, he was the one hurting me. I was at an all time low.

I grabbed the first pair of jeans and t-shirt I saw in the closet that would cover up these hideous bruises. I had plans on going to get my hair done yesterday, but me and DJ got into it and he didn't give me any money. I missed the days when I had two jobs and didn't need his ass for nothing. He needed me to give him some money. I never should have given him my whole tax return that year that put him on to the drug game. He gave me some stupid line about our futures and I bought it like a fool in love. Some future.

I was at the bedroom door about to go in but overheard him talking on the phone referring to himself as daddy. Ole bastard, I wonder which one of his hoes that was. The next thing I heard almost made me throw up. He asked whoever that was what if his baby was woke and he would be on his way to bring the milk. I couldn't believe this shit. He got a baby. How could he do this to me and DJ? and who was the momma?. How old was this baby? How long was he planning on keeping this from me? I had to get away from this hell I was in. This is not what I signed up for. I just turned around and went into the hall bathroom, I really was going to throw up. Before I knew it I was crying and couldn't stop. I don't know what hurt worse. My husbands betrayal, the fact that he had a child outside of our family or my entire existence as a whole. I looked at myself in the mirror and thought about a life away from this one. Death had to be better than the hell I was living. I would somehow make him pay for hurting me, I thought as I got myself together.

I heard voices in the living room and walked out to see DJ grinning like a fool at Sidney. She and Tamia walked in looking blowed. Tamia never smoked weed until recently. Sidney finally broke her down I guess. I wondered if Lance knew of her recreational hobbies. She didn't even look right high. Sidney with those tiny shorts on and 4inch heels, I don't how she wore heels with everything, she was the only girl in high school with super high heels and skin tight jeans. She always made a statement wherever she went. Men could never get enough of tall light skin girls with long hair. Even if it was fake. Tamia had on a little polo jean dress that fit her like it was made just for her. I could swear she got all of her clothes tailored, she had on the cutest sandels with a low heel. She hardly ever wore heels over 3 inches she said you don't have to be uncomfortable to be cute.

DJ is really looking at this girls ass right in front of me. I know giving the opportunity he would sleep with Sidney. Knowing her she wanted to sleep with him too. I was all to anxious to get this party started. I was determined to get the thought of my husband having another baby out of my mind.

Chapter 4

TAMIA

As I made my way through the crowd I passed Lance and Rickey who appeared to be in deep conversation. I passed by Rhonda who was sitting on some boys lap. I passed DJ who was talking to some young girl way too close for it to have been a friendly chat. I walked through wondering who all these people were, there were so many faces that I had never seen before. I ran into Spencer, my old boyfriend from high school. He used to be a handsome church boy who lived in my neighborhood. He always wore dress shoes with everything and was the first one to preach the word of God to anyone who'd listen. He was the only one in high school who had full facial hair, on the count of him being kept back I guess. But tonight he looked a hot mess. Life had not been good to him.

Hey there pretty lady, he said smiling at me with those teeth that had turned a nasty shade of yellow. His hair looked like wool, it hadn't been combed in so long. He had on a dirty grey jacket with holes and some filthy slacks on that were 3 inches too short for him. I couldn't tell if they were brown or if they were just that dirty. Seeing him almost brought tears to my eyes.

Hey Spence, how you been. It's been a long time.

I see you still looking good. Your man must be taking real good care of you.

Thanks, have you seen Sidney Rose?

Yall still tight huh. You was two peas in a pod back in the day. Naw, I haven't seen her yet. Can I get a hug for old times sakes though?

Oh hell no, I thought, he looked like he had not bathed in weeks. I stood there trying to get out of it when up comes Reece. thank goodness I thought.

Spencer Jones, it that you, she slurred.

Yes it is Ms. Clarice, how you been. You look like you feelin real good.

I knew that as soon as he said Clarice, he'd blown it, he knew it too. He'd made that mistake back in high school. She went off on him then, it was sure to be worse now, considering her drunken state.

You look like you lookin for rock she slurred. We don't have none of that shit here.

Bitch!, who you talkin too, you don't know me he yelled.

I got yo bitch you raggedy ass dopefiend, you better get yo two tooth ass off my property before you get fucked up.

I was stunned, never had I heard Reece talk like that. What was she going through I wondered. She always had such a calm spirit. She stood there looking deranged and super drunk. As she spoke, she swayed a little bit which let me know that she had reached her limit a couple drinks ago.

Hey hey hey I said, standing between them. Spencer your going have to leave I said trying to keep them apart.

Before I could say anything else, Reece had picked up an empty bottle of Hennessy and hit him over the head. He went crashing down on about 3 people dancing, making the whole crowd scatter. Once he landed on the ground blood was everywhere. DJ, Lance, and Rickey ran over to where we were standing, all shouting "what happened?" in unison.

Reece was standing there cussing, her hair all over her head, spitting everywhere, the music was still going, people were scattering around either trying to get a better look, or trying to find the nearest exit out of there. I just stood there stunned at what she had done. Just then my thoughts went back to Sidney Rose whom I noticed that I still haven't seen, I knew she was up to no good at that point.

Rickey also thought about Sidney Rose, because he started looking around, I knew that I had better find her before he did. I couldn't take more blood that night.

I turned around and saw her coming from the side of the house, Roc following closely behind her. She gone get caught one of these days I thought to myself. Tonight I decided not to have any parts of it and went back over to check on Spencer. Shouldn't we call an ambulance I asked. Hell naw DJ answered, ambulance means police.

As Spencer began to wake up, DJ had some of his boys escorted him out of there and gave him just enough incentive to keep his mouth closed or so they thought.

About twenty minutes later,. The party had started to wind down due to the earlier events, but the people that hung around got right back in party mode including Rhonda who had started doing a dance that she really should have been getting paid for, her mini shirt she had on began to rise and you could see the bottom her of behind during her sexy routine. It was really obvious she had had way too much to drink as well. On my way to get her, gunshots came tearing up everything in their path. I first thing I saw was Reece falling to the floor. DJ and Roc and 5 or so of their boys had guns drawn shooting back in the direction of the gunshots. Lance reached over grabbed my arm and ran towards the house, Reece, I have to get Reece, I began shouting with tears in my eyes.

After all the shots had stopped we walked back outside to see the damage of the evening. The police were in a distance we could hear the sirens getting closer. It looked like a bloodbath in Reece's once very nice backyard.

Reece laid there not moving. Tears began to once again flow down my face at the sight of her.

I looked over and saw Ms. Lorraine laying there in her own blood. She looked like she had been shot in the head. Sidney Mac sat near her with a blank look on his face.

On my way to Reece's side I thought about Sid.

Sidney Rose I tried to yell, it but came out as an exhausted whisper. Sidney Rose... Lance held onto my hand not letting go

Mia. Mia I heard very faintly, I saw Sidney walk towards me with blood on her face.

Are you ok? I asked, my heart was beating so fast that I was sure it was going to beat out of my chest.

I think so, she said right before she started screaming at the sight of Reece who was on the ground. We both bent down to see if she was still breathing. She started to move slowly moaning something. I got closer so I could make out the words. Rhonda she said, where is Rhonda. I looked around and didn't see her but thought that I'd better go and try to find her. Before I could get up, Lance read my mind and said he'd go find her.

Rickey came from the front with the ambulance and police that had arrived on scene. They went to work on the survivors and began loading them and transporting them to the hospital. While the police questioned everybody that was still there.

When It was all over with, 5 people were killed from the party including DJ, Ms. Lorraine, two of DJ's boys and Rhonda's best friend Monique. Rhonda was alive, but was shot in the arm. Reece was also shot, the bullet went right through her shoulder, but her blood pressure kept rising to unhealthy levels and her breathing was erratic so they were keeping her in ICU. One man was killed whom nobody knew, so he must have been one of them.

When Reece woke up in the hospital we had the terrible task of telling her that DJ didn't make it.

How you doin Reece? I asked walking into her hospital room with Sidney, Lance and Rickey. Rhonda was in there with her. Her wounds weren't bad and she was released from the hospital that morning. I noticed that Reece's arms were covered with bruises that didn't look like they were related to the shooting.

Where is DJ, Reece asked groggy from all the medicine she was on.

Tears began to run down my face as I sat on the bed beside her. Reece, DJ didn't make it. He died last night, they couldn't save him, he had been shot in the back.

She laid there looking at me and what blood she had left drained from her face. She didn't say a word, she just laid there looking at me not even blinking.

Reece, Sidney whispered, are you ok? Do you want us to get the doctor. Reece turned on her side and went to sleep without ever saying a word.

We stayed there just in case she woke up and didn't remember what we had told her. After a few hours and she was still asleep, we all went out to get something to eat.

Rickey and Sidney seemed to be happier than they've ever been. They walked arm in arm whispering in each others ear while we waited on the elevator. No one had seen or heard from Roc since the previous nights events. I could tell that Lance was worried. He had been quiet all day, except to fuss at me about my appearance.

Rhonda was suppose to leave for school the next day, But had just announced that she was going to be putting school off until next semester.

Rhonda I know with everything going on you feel like you should be here. But I think that the best thing you could do right now was go on to school.

Mia, I can't leave now. I have to take care of Reece. I can't leave her now, she would never leave me if I needed her.

Even though her argument was true, Rhonda had just lost her best friend and the only man that had been a father to her, besides her sister being in the hospital. I still thought the best thing for her to do was go on to school. If she didn't go now, I feared that she would never end up going. And Reece wanted nothing more for Rhonda than for her to go to school. She never went to college and wanted that for Rhonda more than anything.

Baby I know this is hard. But you know that Reece would have wanted you to go on to school. It's her dream too. And we'll all be here to take care of her. How about I call the school and see if you can come late with all that's going on I don't think it'll be a problem, and you can go next week. That way you can be there for Reece, help her get through this rough time and not miss out on your first semester.

She sat there for awhile trying to come up with another reason not to go to school. But I was not hearing it. We all worked hard to get this girl to school. She was not going to blow it. Everything had already been paid for.

Ok. She said slowly, I guess I do need to go to school.

Lance and Rickey left saying that they had some business to take care of. They were going to take Rhonda over my moms. We promised we would call her if there was any change in Reece's condition. I couldn't help but wonder what business was so important that he had to leave right then, but I didn't question it. I just gave him a kiss and watched them leave. We were all going off naps. I don't think none of us had had more than an hour of sleep.

On our way back up to Reeces room, Sidney admitted to sleeping with Roc outside at the party. Why Sidney Rose? I regretted asking because I was exhausted and didn't really feel like hearing about Sidney and her love life.

He made me, was all she said. She didn't go into it and neither did I.

By the time we'd reached Reeces room, she still wasn't awake. I went to find a doctor to get an update on her condition, while Sidney stayed with her.

The doctor said that Reece had slipped into a sleep induced coma. The news of DJ was just too much for her to take. And it would be up to her to come out of it. I asked if him if the bruises on her arms were in any way related to her injuries. He said that they appeared to be old bruises, not at all related. He asked if she had been a victim of domestic violence because of the various wounds all over her body. I didn't know how to answer that, she had never mentioned anything about DJ hitting on her. But that would explain her mood and appearance. I thought I would go and talk to Rhonda to see if she knew of any problems between her and DJ.

When I went back into the room to share the news with Sidney she was talking to Reece and crying. In that moment she looked like a little girl again with the world on her shoulders. Her once beautiful face, now had bags under her eyes and a scar from the evening when she fell and hit her face on the ground. When she heard me walk in she just looked up at me and shook her head. What are these bruises on her arms. The doctor said that they were all over. What's going on.

I don't know Sid, I think DJ may have been hitting on her.

Why didn't she say anything to us? She asked

Maybe she was too ashamed.

What happened tonight she then asked? Who shot up the party?

I don't know Sidney, I guess it was Spencer. He was the only one with an obvious motive.

I wasn't sure, but that's what I had told the police when they asked. He was no where to be found afterwards, but come to think of it. I hadn't seen him any more after he was escorted out. So I really wasn't sure who had done this or why.

Reece is in a coma? I blurted out. They said it's up to her to come out of it. it can be today, tomorrow or next month. I'm going home I said to exhausted to go on. We still had on the same clothes with blood on them

The next couple of days were very emotional. Me and Sidney took Rhonda to Monique's funeral and her God mothers Ms. Lorraine, they were both held on the same day, Ms. Lorraines later on in the evening. I wore a knee length Donna Karen black dress, my hair pulled to the back in a bun and a black hat just for effect. Sidney wore a two piece mid thigh black suit. She wore her hair hanging in curly locks and had covered up her scar with makeup. and of course 4 inch heels. We both wore our oversized Gucci glasses, with all the crying talking place on that day. They were a necessity. Rhonda wore a short red dress, she said it was Ms. Lorraine favorite color, her arm was in a black sling that she'd worn to match the dress. Her braids hung straight down her back. She looked very feminine and grown. My mother had to make her wear a bra. Rhonda always wanted on the least amount of clothing possible. That drove my mom nuts who thought that ladies were always supposed to wear undergarments no matter what.

Ms. Lorraine's funeral was like a who's who of Atlanta, everybody who was anybody was there. Sidney Mac sat in the front row looking humbled. He had on a expensive black suit with a black shirt underneath and a red tie. He looked so good, his wavy black hair in place as usual. He looked like El Debarge back in the day. We went over to pay our respects. He insisted that we sit up front with him. I didn't really want to, I mean I knew Ms. Lorraine, but I didn't really like her. The only reason why I came was to bring Rhonda and support Sidney Rose, who felt obligated to go as well.

After the two hour funeral a lot of people went over to Sidney Mac's house to eat the food that people bought over. I thought that I would be able to slip away and miss that part, but Sidney Rose insisted that I stay there with her and Rhonda. So I did. I tried Lances cell phone for the 3rd time and still just got his voicemail. I hung up without leaving him a message. He never missed my call before. I was starting to get pissed, but figured I would put my anger on hold for now.

Sidney Rose, her father, whom I referred to as Uncle Pete and her Uncle Mac were sitting at the kitchen table, Mac surprisingly looked upbeat. I hadn't seen Sidney Roses' father since our college graduation. He looked like Ving Rhames to me. He had invested his drug earnings wisely and now owned several houses and business office parks. He was the older of the brothers but didn't look it. Life had been good him. Besides Uncle Mac, he was the smoothest man I had known. He came with his new wife, who was expecting their first child together. She had to be all of thirty years old. Sidney didn't care for her much either. But that was no surprise, being that young, she made Sidney feel like she was no longer daddy's little girl. And with the arrival of the new baby Sidney's thrown was sure to be overshadowed.

As I looked around the house I noticed that I there was no longer a trace of Ms. Lorraine there. I thought that it was kinda fast that he'd changed everything, Ms. Lorraine had just been gone a week. She was always the animal print kind of woman. Their house used to look like a leopards den at the zoo. Now however it was very tasteful. Everything leopard had been replaced with black. The picture of her that hung over the fireplace was now replaced with some very nice African art. The two round leopard chairs that were in the living room were replaced with an expensive black leather recliner that matched the black leather sofa that replaced the hideous white one with the leopard throw. He even had the red carpet replaced with some plush dark grey carpet. He put silver accents all around the house. He must have had an idea in mind for some time, because he wasted no time redoing the entire house. We knew he never really loved her. But what we never knew was exactly how much of a hold Ms. Lorraine had over him. And now that she was dead, he looked as if he were reborn. I realized that the upbeat look on his face before was that of relief. The house was downright sexy just like him. I felt guilty for even having those feeling for him, while I was there paying my respects to his dead wife. But the look he was giving me from across the room told me that in his mind Ms. Lorraine was long gone.

Rhonda came up to me and told me that she was ready to leave she was tired and wanted to go back to the hospital to check on Reece before going back over my moms house. No one could handle going over Reece's house yet, but we knew that we would soon have too. DJ's mother needed some things for the baby and some clothes to bury her son. They were trying to hold off on his service just in case Reece woke up. She would never be able to forgive Reece if she knew that she may have been the one who had caused the commotion that led to her son's demise.

Rhonda being ready to go could not have come any sooner for me. I jumped at the chance to leave. I knew had I stayed that I would no longer be able to keep my distance from Mac and could not deal with those emotions that night.

Sidney was all too happy to leave as well, she jumped up, gave her father and uncle and hug and kiss and was out the door. I was left standing there with the two men looking at her speed out the door.

Where is the fire? Uncle Mac asked

Uncle Pete had gathered his wife and said their goodbyes too.

You know how Sidney is I replied, not knowing why she flew out of there is such a rush. What I thought was going to be a quick hug goodbye turned into something much more. There were only a couple people left at the house and they were already outside, so we found ourselves alone in his sexy house.

I've been thinking about you, he said

Really, I said needing to clear my throat. I felt like a love struck teenager.

You look beautiful tonight.

Thank you I said. I'm sorry about Ms. Lorraine.

It was her time to go, he said flaty. My eyes got wide, I didn't expect such honesty.

Oh, was all I could say. Well we're going to go on and leave now, we have to get to the hospital.

How is your cousin doing? He asked

She's still in a coma, but we're praying that she comes out of it any day now. Before I could complete my sentence Lance was calling my phone, I knew it was him before I even looked. His ringtone on my phone was Usher's 'there goes my baby. I have to take this, I said walking away toward the door. Uncle Mac turned me around and took my face in his hands and kissed me. As my phone continued to ring. I knew I needed to answer it, but for the life of me could not pull myself away from the kiss I had waited my whole life for.

We kissed softly at first then it got more hot and heavy. He had pulled my bun apart and now my hair hang with his fingers running through it.

The thought of Lance snapped me out my trance. I was about to get married why was I here kissing this incredibly handsome man that smelled like heaven.

I reluctantly pulled away. I can't do this right now I said out of breath.

Yes, you can Mia'amore. Some things are just meant to be.

Not like this, I said walking out the door without looking back.

What happened to your hair? Sidney asked when I reached the car. You look like you been running a race, why are you all out of breath. What did you do with Uncle Mac?

Nothing!! I said loudly. I just took it down ok.

Rhonda you doin ok. I asked getting off the subject.

Yea, I'm just ready for all this to be over with she said. She sounded like the little girl who had come lived with us so many years before.

I know baby, it'll be over soon I told her. I couldn't even imagine the pain that she was going through. All I could do was be there for her the way Reece would have.

After we found out there was no change in Reece's condition, I dropped Sidney off. And proceeded to take Rhonda to my mothers house. On the way there, Rhonda told me that she saw Sidney and Roc on the side of the house having sex. Although I already knew that I acted surprised but asked her why it bothered so much.

Why should she have Roc too. She already got a man. She ain't nothing but a hoe.

Rhonda, I said, first of all don't use that language. It's not becoming of such a pretty young lady. Secondly, Roc is much too old for you. You don't need to waste your time with the likes of Roc, he ain't no good. As far as Sidney Rose, she's a grown lady and the decisions she makes about her relationship is her business. I wouldn't worry about them Rhonda your going to college in a couple of days. Let's just focus on that ok.

I was so tired. All I wanted to do was go home, take a bath and sleep for a week. Talking about Roc and Sidney was not in my plan. Rhonda, I asked, have you ever seen DJ hit Reece?

They fought all the time, but I never saw him hit her. why?

All those bruises on her had nothing to do with the shooting. Is it possible that they were having physical fights?

I guess so, I never wanted to stay around long enough to hear. I always left when they started. But if he was hitting her, then I'm glad he's dead.

Well we'll know for sure what was going on when Reece wakes up.

Rhonda didn't respond, she just sat there looking straight ahead. I could tell that what I said to her about Sidney and Roc went in one ear and out the next. I got to my mothers house as fast as I could. When we arrived my mother was there with her new friend Mike. He was an older man very tall. 6'5. He had salt and pepper hair and light brown eyes. He was dressed like they had just come from a date. I could tell that by my moms reaction when we arrived that she was going to be desert.

Rhonda went right over to her open arms and just cried. Looking at the scene made my mother cry as well. Although Rhonda was now grown, she was still just a little girl. She had never had to deal with all the death she's dealt with these past couple of days. They stood there until my mother walked Rhonda to her room and put her to bed. I stayed behind so I could get some love from my mother that I needed as well. I had met Mike before and thought that he was very nice, but tonight I couldn't think of anything to say. So we just sat there in an uncomfortable silence. How's the wedding plans coming he asked breaking the tension.

With all that had been going on I had forgotten that my wedding was less than two months away and I still had so many things to do. I starting thinking about putting the wedding off with Reece being in hospital and everything, I had planned on talking to Lance about it when we were alone, but that hadn't been since the bathroom rendezvous at the party.

It's going fine I said, you two coming back from dinner?

Yea, we went to Copelands, we bought some food back if your hungry. As I began to go over my day I remembered that I hadn't eaten. But I declined on their leftovers, I really just wanted to hug my mother and go home.

Hey baby, my mom said coming from Rhonda's room. That girl went to sleep as soon as her head hit the pillow. My mother looked so beautiful. She had recently cut her hair that hung almost to her butt down to a short spunky hair do. It made her look younger. Her long legs were one of her great assets. She could have been a rockette with legs like that. Tonight she wore a green dress that was v cut showing a little cleave that I'm sure Mike enjoyed. She had on the house slippers that I had bought her for mother's day last year when I'd sent her to a spa for the weekend. She was the best mother a girl could have. I knew I was very lucky to have a mom like her. I thanked God everyday that I was so blessed to have been born to a women with so much love in her heart. As I rested my head on her shoulder and she stroked my hair. I felt like everything in the world was once again ok.

She worked at the hospital where Reece was at and said that she stirred around earlier, but never woke up. That's a good sign though baby she said. She may be coming out of it soon. You look tired, have you been to sleep yet she asked.

Not really momma I responded. It's been so much going on the past couple of days that I'm really running on fumes.

Bittersweet

Why don't you go to your room and get some sleep she asked. She had never changed our rooms from when we moved out. Before me and Lance were engaged I used to go over there and stay with her on the weekends. But not so much lately, and besides that she now had a man and I didn't want to intrude. Much like tonight which was why I told her that I couldn't and needed to go home, which was actually the truth.

On my way up the elevator to where me and Lance lived. I thought about the call from Lance that I had missed and the 3 calls of mine that he missed. I hoped he was there so we could talk about the wedding. My mind went to Mac and the kiss we shared earlier that night. A feeling of guilt came over me that would not go away. I'm getting married in two months and I'm over there doing the tongue tango with a man who just lost his wife. I would defiantly be in church this Sunday trying to get forgiveness for tonight.

Lance opened the door before I got a chance to unlock it. Where have you been he asked? Bringing me into his arms.

Two funerals and the hospital baby, you know that. I said tiredly Where have you been I questioned, turning around so he could undo my dress.

I've been looking for Roc, he said like a little boy who had just been caught with his hand in the cookie jar. I'm sorry I wasn't there with you today. I think Roc was hit that night, but now he's not answering his phone and nobody has seen or heard from him since that night.

I could see the worried look on his face. Roc was Lance's brother in his eyes. I didn't have any words of comfort. I wanted to, but I just didn't have any. Roc got on my nerves, his bad boy image was not at all as appealing to me as it was to my best friend. He'll turn up, he's strong is what came out. I'm starving, will you order me some food from Mr. Wong's while I take a shower. Mr. Wong's was my favorite Chinese restaurant; they delivered to us at least a couple of times a week, whenever I didn't feel like cooking. Lance usually gave opposition, he thought that I should cook no matter what.

As I undressed my mind again went to Mac. The way he kissed me sent my body on a whole new trip. The way he ran his hand through my hair was even sexy. I could still feel the way he touched my back. The thoughts of him made me wet. I stepped in the shower trying to think about anything but that kiss.

Lance joined me in the shower to my surprise and went to work right away; he kissed the back of my neck and down my back. I stood there with both of my hands on the shower wall until I turned around to face him and looked him into his eyes. He was so handsome; his chiseled features were flawless along with his caramel toned skin. I had asked him to let his beard come in just a little bit and now it was a full shadow making him even more handsome to me. I loved men with hair on their face.

You know I love you don't you I asked.

I know baby, I love you too he said as he stroked my face. What's wrong he asked. Is something bothering you.

No, I just wanted you to know that I love you very much and with so much going on, it just brings me back to reality and I don't know what I would do if I lost you.

Don't talk like that baby, your never going to lose me. You know I can't wait to make you my wife don't you.

I wasn't sure if now was the time bring up that I wanted to postpone the wedding, so I chose not to. I didn't want to ruin the mood.

I know, was my response and with that we kissed for what seemed like forever. I straddled my legs around his waist, while I kissed his face and neck. He leaned me up against the wall for better traction and he went to work on me. His lovemaking had certainly improved. We were interrupted by the doorbell. As hungry as I was I was not ready for this to stop. As Lance went and paid for the food, I slipped into something sexy. I used my Victoria Secrets lotion he bought me for sweetest day or something, that I knew he could not resist the smell of it. I was not done with him yet. Thoughts of Mac swirled through my mind, which made me even more horny. After we ate we made love around the entire condo. We started in the living room by the fireplace, the dining room, we went into the kitchen on the counter, we even made love on the balcony under the stars. By the time we got to our bed, we were both too exhausted to do anything but sleep.

The next morning, when I woke up, Lance was in the living room reading the newspaper. I went right to the kitchen to start his breakfast, what do you want to eat I asked.

Did you know Roc fucked Sidney at the party the other night? he asked coming into the kitchen.

I heard. Who told you?

I don't know why you insist on hanging around that piece of trash. I told you she's no good. We don't want her in the wedding.

Lance, don't call her that. Roc is just as wrong as she is, I don't see you calling him names. And who is we?

Me and mother think my cousin Tammy should take her place. I was hoping that your friendship would have run its course by now. But I see that you don't have enough sense to know that someone is not good for you.

Lance, I have been friends with Sidney since we were kids, there is no course to run. I don't know who this Tammy is but you and your mother can forget about that. I wanted to talk to you about the wedding anyway.

Just as I was about tell him I wanted to postpone the wedding, his phone rang and he was out the door.

I stood there thinking about him and how all of our decisions were made by his mother. I knew if I heard "Mother said" one more time, I would scream.

I filled the first part of my day refilling the kitchen with anything Lance may want to eat, and with taking his clothes to the cleaners and making sure that he had all of his beauty care needs. I had turned into his mother day by day. the second half was filled with making myself beautiful. Lance expected me to look my best at all times. There was no such thing as a bad hair day in his world.

Chapter 5

SIDNEY ROSE

I woke up this morning much like I had woke up for the past couple of days, nauseas.
    This stress is starting to get to me. I thought. I rolled and smoked a blunt in hopes that it would make me feel better. I reminisced on the past couple of days. I should have never started fuckin around with Roc. We did end up having sex on the side of Reece's' house the night of the party until we heard all of the commotion. I know Rickey saw us come from the side of the house together, but he hasn't said a word about it. That made my uneasy. He has been an angel these past few days. Which made me feel even more guilty. Guilt was not a feeling I was used to. I always felt like I what I did to men, was what men have been doing to women for years. But now I had this great guy who loves me and here I am taking every chance I can to sleep with someone else.
    Boo, I'm on my way to Lance and Mia's do you want to go? He asked.
    The thought of Mia upset me today. I know she did something with uncle Mac last night, she didn't have any lipstick on when she got to the car and her hair was down. Aint' nobody stupid. She acts like she and Lance are so perfect and I'm so wrong for cheating on Rickey and here she is cheating on Lance with my uncle of all people. I felt betrayed somehow. Partly because she chose not to tell me about whatever was going on. We're drifting apart by the day. I could feel it. I used to be the first one she called whenever anything happened in her life. Ever since her and Lance got engaged we talk less and less. Every time I called her, she's either busy and says she'll call me back, which she never does or she just doesn't answer her phone. I need her more than ever now, can't

she see that. Growing up she seemed to always know when I needed her and she was always right there. Now my life is in an uproar and she's over there playing house with her Ken doll. He'll never love her as much as I do.

Boo, did you hear me, Rickey asked walking in the room, snapping me out of my trance.

Yes Rickey I heard you, I think I just want to sleep in today I don't feel so good. I'm going to the office tomorrow to get my work. I've used up all of my sick days.

You been feeling sick alot lately. Don't you want to go to the doctor? I'm starting to get worried bout'chu

I will. I love you for worrying about me boo. I'll be ok, I just need to get some rest. I'll make an appointment if I don't feel better after today.

You want me to stay here in bed wit'cha he said, winking at me.

Yes, baby can you. I asked. I knew he couldn't that boy didn't know how to lay in bed without working.

How about if I go take care'a some biness and come back and get in the bed wit'cha later?

You've had a lot business to take care of lately. What kind of business are you doing?

I'm trying to to make us some real money, so you don't have to work if you don't want to. He replied.

I sat there thinking that as much as I loved my job, a life where I didn't have to work would be a dream come true for me right now. Even though I worked from home and only went into the office when I needed to. I would love to be able to just focus on me. It has always been a dream of mine to open a group home for foster children. Being a social worker enabled me to see a lot of terrible things and a lot of kids out there needed somewhere better to grow up than a cold building with a lot of beds.

Some of those kids I could have bought home with me. And I came really close on occasion, but was warned that that was not allowed by the staff.

Not that I would know what to do with a kid anyway. I don't even know how I got into social work. Some people just aren't the motherly type and I'm one of those people. You don't have to like kids in order to want to help them is what a lot of the other social workers say.

Well get back soon boo. I'll be waiting for you. I said blowing him a kiss. I thought it was a good answer even if it was a lie. He bent over to give me a kiss which turned into a quickie which was all I could really stand with him lately, afterwards, he was out the door like there was a fire.

That thought made me think about Terry, I still hadn't talked to him yet. My hope was that he had gotten the hint. I did like his sexy ass, he always made me feel so protected. Like noboby or nothing could touch me while he was around. He had gotten me out of so many tickets and trips to jail. He did it and made sure that my daddy never found out. Daddy seemed to always know everything.

I can't believe that daddy came with that slut of a wife. I can't stand her. She is younger than I am. She used to be a waitress at some hotel downtown and she now she waits on him hand and foot. Don't he know that he ain't nothing but a sugar daddy to that girl. Now she about to have a baby. I hope they don't think I'm about to treat that baby like it's my kin. As far as I'm concerned me and Paul will always be daddy's only kids. He gone ask me to try to include her more in family functions, how dare he. I will never include that girl in my life. He pissed me off. I was so glad when it was time to leave last night, I couldn't get out of there fast enough.

On my way to the bathroom my phone rang. it was an unknown number so I decided not to answer it, I was not in the mood for whoever it was. When I came out the shower, my phone rang again. Unknown number again. I answered it this time ready to cuss whomever it was out for calling me private.

Sid, Roc said fast like he had been running. Sid he said again before I even had the chance to answer him.

Roc, is that you? I asked

Yea it's me, can you talk

Yes, where are you?

Never mind about that, I need you to do me a favor.

Roc, you got everybody looking for you including the police. Why did you run?

Bitch did you hear me, I don't give a fuck about all that right now, I need you to go to my crib.

Roc on several occasions has called me out of my name. he thinks that word bitch is a term of endearment. And truth be told unless I'm around Tamia I really don't mind, Reece always says a man is gone be a man, but with Mia, you might as well have stabbed her in the arm if you call her out of name. she overreacts about things like that in my opinion. It's just a word. Men have been calling women that for years.

Roc, I'm not going to your apartment. I'm in enough trouble behind messing with you.

Man, shut the fuck up about that shit. I need you to go to my place and get me a couple things.

What are you gonna do?

What the fuck does that matter? Are you going or what he yelled.

I can't go, my man saw us the other night and now he got me on a short leash, I lied.

I don't care about that country ass muthfucka. Man, I need you go to my place. You know I'ma take care of you. I miss you baby he said suddenly calm and gentle.

Roc, I really can't. although right now I really did need the money for the attorney that was charging me an arm and a leg. Did you know DJ was killed and Reece is in a coma, Rhonda got shot, Ms Lorraine is dead. its too much going on right now for me to even consider this.

Hell naw, ma man's is dead. Damn man, you said his ole lady is what? In a coma? He asked.

Yea we don't know when or if she's going to wake up.

Who else got popped?

Two of DJ's boys. James and Black I think was their names.

Black got popped? He said interrupting me

Yea I think his name was Black, I didn't know him.

That was ma homeboy from Philly. Rhonda got it the arm huh? She alright though right?

Yes she's fine now. I still had the feeling that their relationship was more than any of us knew about. How did he know she was alright? She's been short with me lately and at the party I think she saw us on the side of the house.

Damn man what happened? Do anybody know who them niggas was that came shooting anyway?

Nope, all I heard about was this dude name Spencer. Reece got into with him right before the shots started. You know Lance has been going everywhere looking for you.

Man, I don't wanna get brah in no trouble. He don't need this shit. He would be better off if he don't know where I am right now.

The tone in his voice confirmed that Roc really cared about Lance. I didn't think he loved anybody outside of himself. But it was obvious that he really did consider Lance to be his brother.

What are you gonna do?

You got a lot of fuckin questions, you tryin to set me up or something.

Roc, shut the hell up. If you thought I'd do that then why are you even calling me.

See, there you go with that mouth again. You must need me to give you some more of this pole ova here. Man, go to my place and get my shit for me. I'll tell you where to get the key. I need you to do this for me baby, you know I ain't got nobody else I can count on. You it baby. You all I got.

He sounded so sad. I guess he was right too. No body else knew where he was. He trusted me and only me. I don't know why that made me smile. Ok I said. Where is the key.

I'm gonna call you back at 12:00 on the dot. That should give you enough time to get over there and get the key ok? OK. He said louder

Ok Roc, damn you don't have to yell at me.

Man, I don't have time for this shit you talkin. Get up and go get my shit man ok.

Reluctantly I got dressed and went to where Roc told me to get the key and then to his apartment. It was 12 and just as he'd said, he was calling.

You there yet? He asked

Yep, just got here I said walking around the mess at his place. You ain't cleaned up in a minute huh? I asked

IT'S MESSED UP he yelled. Who the fuck been in my crib. Go to the bedroom in my closet, look under the floor board on the right under my black shoes.

I did just as I was told and pulled out a black bag. It was full, whatever was in it made it heavy because I had to struggle to get it out of that little space.

Is that black bag still there? He asked

Yea it's right here.

Ok. Now look on the other side of the closet and grab that duffle bag in the corner. Is it still there?

Yea I got it. damn is that it I asked. I hadn't signed up to be carrying all this stuff.

Man, you always complaining. Meet me at that place we went to last month. Do you remember.

The place in south Georgia? I'm not about to go all the way there. That's almost a two hours drive. Are you crazy? Roc I came here, this is it. I can't do that.

Damn Sid, just meet me at the place man. I told you boo, you the only person I got right now. I thought you had my back Ma. Ride or Die remember. I guess you was just popping off at the mouth wit that shit huh? Now that a nigga need you. You can't do this and that. Man you ain't no real G like I thought.

Roc, I do have your back, you know that. But I can't come today. I may be able to come tomorrow.

I knew that this was just too much. How do I get this knucklehead out of my life. Why do I let him control me. These were all the thoughts I had even though I had just agreed to what he wanted from me. Again.

Man tomorrow, I need that shit today Ma. What do you have to do?

Roc, I can't do it today I said walking to the front door to leave. Someone was turning the door knob. At that moment I prayed that I remembered to lock the door back. I ran back into the bedroom to the closet. Roc, I whispered, someone is trying to come in.

Damn, man where you at. Go to the bedroom in the closet. It's a heater in the bag. Loaded. Take it out.

I am in the closet I whisper yelled as I pulled out the 9mm. Their in the living room. Oh shit here they come. I laid the phone face down so they couldn't hear Roc's background, he must have been on the street, because it was loud. I held the gun shaking the entire time. I wasn't really sure if I could actually shoot them or not. My first thought was that it was the police, but once they reached the bedroom I could tell from their language that they weren't. They walked around not really touching anything from what I could see through the slates in the door, they had on gloves and both of them had guns. I thought I would pee on myself for sure.

The smaller of the two men was the first to speak. Where this muthafucka at? He can't hide forever. He gone have to show up sooner or later.

Yea, he done fuck'd with the wrong one. The bigger one said.

He got family? The smaller one said

I don't know him like that. I think I heard the nigga say something about a brother one time.

Remember that little chocolate bitch he was bangin that day over Rico house? I heard she just got shot in the leg or some shit. I bet she know if he got fam or not.

Rhonda, they were talking about Rhonda I sat there thinking. Suddenly furious, he had been with that little bitch. I knew it. her fass ass. Now here I am risking my life for his ole lyin ass.

If he don't turn up soon, we'll have to smoke this nigga out of his hole. Replied the bigger one. Let's be out. I got some other business to tend to right now.

When I heard the door shut I picked the phone back up. He had hung up. Ain't this some shit. Here I am sitting in a closet trying to get some stuff for him and he can't even hold on to see if I got out of this situation alive. He make me sick I thought as I walked out of his place bags in tow. When I got back to my car I threw the bags in the back and headed back home. I defiantly needed a drink and a blunt at this point. As I drove home I began to wonder what was so important that Roc needed that I could have gotten killed for. So I pulled over in the Walgreens parking lot by my house and looked in the smaller one first. It was full of money, looked to be about 10 stacks. Under the money though was two white flat bricks. Dammit Roc you got me out here carrying around drugs knowing all the trouble I'm already in over this shit. What I had not told Tamia was that the police said they saw me making some deliveries for Roc too. It was only twice, that he asked me to do it. and he'd given me $500 both times which hardly seems worth it now. In the larger bag was clothes. Looked to be about 2 pair of jeans, a couple t-shirts, some socks, a box of bullets for the 9mm that was now in my purse and a silencer. There was a plastic bag on the side with a toothbrush, deodorant, a razor and some toothpaste. This was obviously his get away bag. It's something to be said about a person that keeps a bag packed at all times. Complete with a loaded gun and silencer. And who were those boys back at his place, he must owe them some money or something. It became apparent to me that Roc was in over his head right now and I didn't want to be anywhere around him when shit hit the fan. As I sat there in the car looking at the bags, I thought about what kind of choices I had at this point. My phone began to rang. Terry, damn, him again. This time I decided to answer it.

Hey baby I say picking up the phone, trying to sound cheery despite the fact that what I had in my car could send me to prison for a very long time.

Hi you, where have you been, I've been calling you like crazy.

I know baby, I'm sorry I've been going through it. Have you heard about the shooting in Lithonia, I was there and a lot of people were killed. I said giving it the dramatic effects.

I heard about that, and I heard you were there. Baby you ok right. What happened?

I don't know boo, somebody came shooting. My cousin Reece, the one you met. She's in a coma.

Man, I'm sorry to hear about that. When can I see you?

Baby I want to see you too, but I'm going back to work tomorrow, so I know I'm going to be swamped for the rest of the week.

Have you given any more thought to moving in with me? He said sounding irritated.

Baby, I don't know about that right now. I told you I've got a lot going on. I don't want to pull you into my drama.

What drama could you have?

plus, I told you that I don't believe in shacking up. It's either marriage or nothing with me I said ignoring his question. I knew the mere mention of marriage to a man was an instant red light.

I hear you baby. So when did you say I was going to see you?

As soon as I can. I promise. I want to make sure that when I do get to see you, that we can spend some quality time together and we can make up for lost time. I knew that I had to throw him some kind of bone, he would never let me get off this phone without a promise of some sort.

That sounds good baby, I got you a present he said sounding sexy.

You did... I said smiling from ear to ear, he gave the best gifts. Last time he said that he had surprise present for me it was one of those GPS systems for my car. I would now be lost without that. What is it? I said in my baby voice.

It's a surprise, I know your going to like it. When are you going to come get it.

Before I could answer my line clicked. I looked at the phone to see it was an unknown number. Roc, I thought good just the person I needed to talk to. Baby I need to get this call I'm going to have to call you back I said to Terry.

Sweetheart just stop by and get your gift, I won't keep you.

The line beeped again, before I could hang up from him. I agreed to stop by for a few minutes.

Why in hell did you hang up I said answering the phone starting my car so I could head to Terry's house.

Because man, some punk ass police kept driving by, I had to bounce. Who the fuck was that at my place? He asked irritated. Like I knew.

I DON'T KNOW WHO THAT WAS. YOU TELL ME I yelled. Real slowly. Whoever it was is looking for you to bring you pain, and is now looking for any family you got, including your brother I said.

What! That's what them niggas said. They don't know me. He said very seriously. You did get the bags right?

Yes Roc, I got the bags. I didn't want him to know just yet that I had been through the bags even though he probably knew I would.

I need you to meet me. I need those bags Ma.

Now knowing what the contents of the bags were. I knew he really did need those bags. But I just didn't see it happening today. I was pulling up to Terry's townhouse, but remained in the car to finish this conversation without Terry all in my mouth. Before I could tell him no again. My phone rang, it was Rickey. Hold on Roc I gotta take this I said clicking over.

Hey boo what's up I said to Rickey.

Where you at? He said

Ummm at the store, why?

You said you were going to stay home all day, and now you in the streets. What did you need at the store?

Baby, why you sound mad. I came to get something to cook you for dinner. I wanted to make something special. It surprised me at how quickly I was able to come up with a lie.

When you coming home, he asked not impressed

Baby I'll be there in a few I said remembering that Roc was on the other line I know he was pissed to still be holding. Terry had noticed that

I had driven up and was now standing in the doorway waiting for me to get out the car.

Rickey was still trying to protest, but I cut him off told him I love him and I'd see him in a bit. He can be such a baby sometimes.

Roc, I said clicking back over you still there.

Bitch why the fuck you keep me on hold that long, you know I'm out here on these streets.

Roc, do you think talking to me like that is going to make you get your stuff any faster? I asked very calmly. I was now in the driver's seat for once. He needed me. He needed this stuff, so he was going to have to wait, and he wasn't about to talk shit to me either.

Man, here you go with this ole bullshit again. Baby I really need those bags, you don't understand how bad I need those bags. You know I love you man, I just be talkin shit

Oh now you love me huh I bet you do. I know what's in the bags Roc.

Man, see there you go. I tell you I love you and you don't even care. Is you gone bring me the bags or what Sidney Rose.

Roc never called me Sidney Rose, I was Ma, Boo, Baby even bitch but never Sidney Rose, he said it sounded like a Disney character. Maybe he really does love me I thought.

Terry was now looking agitated and was about to come to my car any minute. I knew I had to wrap this conversation up.

Roc, I really gotta go, call me back later on tonight and we'll talk about where we're going to meet.

You better answer the phone Ma, I need those bags.

Ok Roc I said before hanging up. I got out the car and was glad that I had put on my pink Express sundress, I hadn't seen Terry in awhile and this dress hugged me in all the right places.

The agitated look on his face had now softened up and was replaced with a sexy smile. His perfect white teeth with the gap in the front greeted me as I walked up. He had on a wife beater and some shorts, his brown skin now sweaty from the heat. His arms were sheer perfection too, they were so big that they poked out even when his arms were down. His chest was begging to be released from the confines of that shirt.

He walked up and gave me hug lifting me off my feet making my short dress rise. Baby you gone let everybody see my goodies I said returning his hug. I had missed being in his arms. He smelled so good, he must have just gotten out the shower. He didn't put me down until we were in his house.

His house was so immaculate. I always wondered if he'd gotten it professionally decorated or if he'd done it himself. He was border Metro sexual, so I knew he had it in him. Everything was white. He had white furniture, white carpet a lot of big leaf plants and, there was beautiful art on the walls. His loved to cook, his kitchen looked like a kitchen off of a Food Network show. Although it was so clean that it was a wonder that it was even used.

He closed the door and wasted no time walking up to me kissing me on my neck. Baby I don't have a lot of time, I said. I need to get to the hospital to go see Reece.

This ain't gone take long he said bending over pulling my dress dress up all the while. Wait baby, I said. I had just had sex with Rickey this morning, and although he and Rickey had overlapped before, I never felt good about it. come to think about it I had overlapped with them all at one point or another. Roc and Rickey had overlapped the most. And on occasion Roc and Terry and Rickey. that was a bad day. I had never shared that with Tamia she would never understand how I could do such a thing. I could hear her now, telling me that I need to talk to somebody. I don't need nobody telling me how to live my life. I like sex. And I ain't married yet, so why not enjoy it every chance I get.

With that thought in mind. I let Terry take off my thong and play with my hot spot with his tongue. He really knew what he was doing when it came to oral sex. He loved doing it too, he would do it anywhere. One time we were at the Walmart at like 2 in the morning when he decided to make me his late night snack, in one of the try on rooms. He made me call to the heavens three times in that room. The thought of that night made me close to climax this time. he picked me up threw me over his shoulder and was up the stairs in two seconds flat. That fireman training sure does come in handy. I thought as he threw me on bed and took my dress off. He continued to feast on my body, until I couldn't take it anymore, he then entered me with a sense of urgency. He went hard on me like he held a grudge against me. He took one leg and held it over my head and went in even deeper. I had no choice but to scream out in ecstasy. And that was all he needed to shoot him up in overdrive. I didn't think it was possible for him to go any harder or faster, but he found a way. He went on like that for at least 30 min.

without ever slowing down, which was not like him. At the point when I felt him near his peak, I too went in overdrive. He picked me up so that I was straddling him, it was when he turned me over that I knew he was ready to reach his peak. Doggy style always made him release, just like Rickey. When we were done, despite that we were dripping with sweat, he wanted to spoon.

Baby, I'm hot move… I say to him pushing him gently off me.

Yes, you are boo, he said kissing my neck giving me some room.

I looked at the clock he had on his nightstand and saw that it had now been almost 2 hrs since I talked to Rickey. I gotta get home I thought, but first I still had to go to the store and buy something to cook. Which was the reason why I was out anyway let me tell it.

I jumped up and started looking for my clothes, I knew taking a shower over there meant some more lovemaking and I just couldn't risk that. So I had to just get dressed and shower as soon as I got home.

Baby I gotta go, I said bending down to find my panties. Have you seen my panties? I asked him, now looking under the bed. They were nowhere to be found.

Every time I left there I left without something I had when I got there. I think he was keeping my stuff. I didn't have time to deal with that then. I had to leave.

On my way to the door, he had gotten hard again. This was probably the only man that I had met who could hang with me sexually I thought as I looked at him in all his nakedness.

As I opened the door the first thing I saw was a police car then I see my car up on a tow truck about to drive away. In all my haste, I had parked right up on a fire hydrant and they were towing my car. What the hell I yelled as I ran towards my car. With all the stuff I had in that car. There is no way that I can let that car leave my sight I thought, And then how do I explain to Rickey that my car was towed all the way over here when I'm supposed to be at the store. by the house I can't let this happen, my heart started racing so hard that I thought I was about to pass out. The tow truck driver dropped something and stopped to pick it up which gave me enough time to reach him. Please sir, don't take my car, I'm leaving right now I said to the officer. He didn't look phased. Ma'am it's illegal to park this close to a fire hydrant. Your car was chalked and when it was not moved for over an hour a tow truck is called out. Terry had went in the house and put on some shorts and was now outside with us. Oh what's up T, the police officer said greeting Terry as he walked up.

Steve, why are you about to tow my woman's car, Terry said smiling this is your old lady man, I didn't know. Replied the officer

They stepped away and exchanged a few more pleasantries before the officer motioned for the tow truck driver to let my car down. See this is why I keep him around I thought as I looked at Terry handle this situation. The way he was able to get me out of yet another situation so quickly made me appreciate him even more. Not only did he just rock my world, he probably saved my life. I gave him a hug and kiss and was off to the store. On my way there he called me to remind me that I had forgotten my present. Dang, I thought, all this and didn't even get my gift. Oh well, I'll have to get it another day, because there was no going back now. Rickey was gone be pissed off as it was. I had a voice mail on my phone from my attorney. I had a hearing next week to discuss if there is enough evidence to charge me. He reminded me that I still hadn't paid my 2nd $500 installment. This case was going to cost me. I don't know how I was going to keep this away from Rickey. Especially since I was going to need him to give me some of the money. I had yet to even think about my daddy and Uncle Sid finding out. They would kill me and then kill Roc. Somehow I needed to find a way out of this mess, without giving up Roc. It was now officially time to pray. I rushed in Kroger to get something to make for dinner. When I got done and sped home, Rickey wasn;t even there. I decided against taking Roc's bags in the house, so I put them in the trunk and parked my car in the garage. With Rickey not home yet, I had time to go take a shower and get dinner on hopefully before he came back. I raced in the house up the stairs into our bedroom, and to my surprise, he was there sitting on the bed. I thought I would pee on myself right there where I stood.

Ha Hey baby, I said nervously. How long have you been here and where is your truck?

Where have you been Sidney? He said very seriously

I thought about telling him I was at the hospital, but didn't know if they had been there or not. So I decided to go with my 2nd excuse I had up my sleeve. My car wouldn't start at the store. I tried to call you, but your phone kept going straight to voicemail. Where were you I said in an accusatory tone. Before he could answer I went on to say. See I told you I need a new car.

Sidney I called your phone and you didn't answer. I got worried so, I went up to the Kroger and your car was nowhere to be found. So I'm going to ask you again. Sidney, where were you?

BaBaby, I told you, my car wouldn't start. I wasn't at the Kroger, I was on my way to the office to get some paper's I needed.

Rickey what are you trying to say. You don't believe me. Why are you always giving me the third degree anytime I'm not in our face? You don't trust me, I thought you were going to work on that. I screamed trying to turn this scene around in my favor. Yelling usually worked with Rickey, he hated loud talk.

No, Sidney I don't trust you. You ain't to be trusted. You ain't never where you say you are. You always coming home late with no excuse, a lot of the time you don't even have on everything you left with. Trust you Sidney Rose. I saw you the other night coming from the side of the house. And I know that your screwing around with Roc. So trust you I do not. The look in his face was one of pure sadness.

I didn't know how to respond. Should I just come clean about everything, lie about everything. I needed to talk to Tamia, she would know what I should do. I decided to lie. He didn't have any proof of anything. He only thought I was screwing Roc, he didn't know shit for sure, I thought.

What the hell are you talking about I yelled. I'm sick of you always accusing me of something. Anytime I'm not right in your face, then I must be messing around. It sounds to me like you have some self esteem issues that have nothing to do with me. You need to work on yourself before you go always thinking the worst of me. I said, storming out the room downstairs to the kitchen. I wasn't sure if it had worked, but it would buy me some time to think of another excuse if I needed one. To my surprise he stayed upstairs. He never came down to finish our conversation. The next time I saw him, I was in the kitchen finishing up with dinner and he was walking out the front door. I went to the window to see where he was going because his truck wasn't there, but to my surprise it was right outside still running. I couldn't see who was driving because of his tinted windows, I was sure trying to though, when he got in. They sat there for a few minutes, then drove off. I sat there eating alone not knowing what was going to happen with me and Rickey. On one hand, he is the best thing that ever happened to me. He is kind and sweet. he's gentle and loving and would make a great husband

and father some day. I really wanted to loved him with everything in me. But on the other hand, trying to be perfect is too hard. I've never been faithful to him from day one. We barely ever slept together, I just wasn't attracted to him at all. And I don't think he'll ever be enough for me in the bedroom. Did I even care if we broke up? I sat there pondering about my relationship with Rickey, when my phone rang. It was Tamia, see she knew I needed her. That's why she's my rock. I thought.

Hey Mia, I said picking up the phone, you must have felt I was going through crisis over here.

Hey Hon, what's wrong? Before you start, Reece woke up. she's going to be ok. She said happily.

That's great girl, why didn't you call me. How is she taking the news about DJ I asked.

Well as good as can be expected I guess, she didn't really want to talk about it. and I did call you, what were you doing earlier that you couldn't answer your phone.

This was the second time someone had told me that they called me. I never did look at my missed calls after all the police drama over Terry's. oh, I had some errands. I replied. I didn't feel like getting into the whole Terry story.

Well, what's going on with Rickey she asked.

Girl, same story. Rickey think I'm messing around on him. He said he knew about me and Roc. This time, he walked out without saying a word. Somebody came and got him in his truck. I think he's gone for good this time Mia. Saying it out loud made it real and I was now regretting our conversation earlier. Maybe I should have just told him everything and promised to stop, if he loves me then maybe he would understand.

Well Sid, you are messing around on him. And you had to know that he would find out about you and Roc sooner or later. You weren't exactly discreet.

What do you mean by that? I asked.

Rhonda also saw you and Roc on the side of the house, and I think she saw a little more than just you two talking.

Damn, you think she is the one who told Rickey? I think she been fooling around with Roc too.

How do you know that, she asked

Shoot, I can't tell her that I was over Roc's in his closet hiding out trying not to get killed while trying to get his money and drugs.

I know somebody who said they saw her with him. Was all I said. I figured that was the safest answer.

Saw her with him where Tamia said loudly.

I don't know where they were.

Oh, I told that girl she needed to stay away from that boy, I'll sure be glad when she leaves this weekend. She's going to get herself in some trouble she's not ready if she stays here I'm afraid.

Yea I know what you mean.

Im going back to the hospital later, do you want to go? She asked

My line clicked and I saw it was the unknown number. Damn, It was Roc. I think I need to go give him his stuff so I can be done with this. Having all that money and other stuff in my trunk made me uneasy to say the least.

Yea I'll meet you there I told Mia. What time are you going I said quickly. So I wouldn't miss Roc's call

I don't know, she said, I'll call you back.

Ok, I said hanging up.

Hello.

Sid, I need my shit man, meet me at the spot.

Just then, I heard Rickey unlocking the door. I hung up the phone and laid it down beside me.

Chapter 6

REECE

I remember waking up in the hospital not really sure what had happened. I knew that I was in a lot of pain. I knew that something was not right, I just didn't know what it was. It wasn't until Tamia walked in and told me that I my husband was dead that I remembered why I felt dead myself. When she left, different parts of that evening started to become more clear the longer I stayed awake. By the evening I knew exactly what had happened. Although no one knows for sure that it was Spencer, I knew it was, who else would have done that? I remembered the look on his face when I hit him with that bottle. I was so drunk, and for a minute I saw DJ's face on Spencer. I wanted to hurt him for sure. and because of that, my husband was dead. DJ had become a monster to me. God don't like ugly I thought I hated him for what he did to me. For making me become a victim in my own house. I hated him for making me feel ugly and fat. I hated him for making me feel less than. For not loving me anymore. For creating a child with someone else. I hated him for not touching me in over a year. I wanted him dead myself on a daily bases. But now he's dead. Because as much as I hated him for all of those things, I also still loved him. We had been in each other's lives for more than 15 years and together for at least 10 of those. He knew me better that anyone except maybe Rhonda and Tamia. And there were even things that I was able to share with him that not even those two knew He was the only one who knew about how I had lost my virginity. Me and DJ became adults together. We shared everything. I loved him with everything I had. I didn't know life without loving him. I couldn't even cry. I didn't know why, was I not sad that he was killed and I didn't have to be the one to do it. or I so overwhelmed with grief that it would hit me later? I laid there trying to figure it out until I drifted back to sleep.

I remembered that later on that night they bought my son to see me. He seemed like he'd grown so much since I'd seen him last. Looking at him reminded me that everything would be ok. It had to, I had a son to raise. I promised myself that, I was going to raise him to be a different man than what his father had become. As the time went by I think I went through every emotion possible. Thank goodness Aunt Marie told me to go get life insurance on him after we got married. We had them on each other. One hundred thousand dollars, ain't that something, he was worth more to me dead than alive. Everybody tiptoed around me like I was about to break at any minute and maybe I was. It wasn't until the funeral and I looked at him that it became real. The doctor didn't think it was a good idea for me to go to the funeral, but under the circumstances signed off on it. it became clear why he thought it was too soon, I felt like I was about to faint at any minute. My heart would not catch up with my breathing. His face didn't even look real with all the makeup he had on. They put him on a grey suit with a blue shirt underneath. I knew that had to be his mothers doing. He never would have worn that. As I looked at him, I saw the little boy who gave me his coat because it had gotten cold outside and I didn't have a jacket of my own. I saw the boy that tried to make our first time together special by making us a candle light dinner on our patio. I saw the man that got down on one knee and proposed the night after we moved into my new apartment. I saw the man that began to beat me on daily bases. I saw the man that told me that I disgusted him. I saw the man who had fathered another child. As the tears ran down my face, I could feel Tamia at my side making sure I didn't fall over. Goodbye my love I said as I walked away. I grabbed my son from his grandmother and walked out the church. I wanted to go home. My heart was broken into so many pieces that I didn't even know how to begin to put the pieces back together.

When I arrived to my house I didn't know what to expect. This was my first time back since the shooting. When I saw that my family had gotten everything cleaned and my house was spotless, was the start of my many days of unexpected tears.

It was my first time I had been in that house for days on end with no one but my son. If DJ wasn't there, than Rhonda was. I had never lived alone before. I was scared and excited all at the same time. Rhonda had left for school finally. She wanted to take the entire first semester off. I was not hearing that. I needed for her to just go to school as planned. I told Tamia and Auntie Marie and Sidney that I needed some time to myself with little D. They wanted to come over and stay with me all the time. I loved them all for that. But right now what I need more than ever was to be alone. My shoulder was now almost completely healed and a lot of the weight had begun to come off. When the stress was not there, surprisingly neither was the urge to eat everything in sight. I started taking Little D on long walks. The first couple of days, he and I needed a nap when we got back. After a couple of days I ;put him down and used that time to read the bible and began to work on me. I still cried myself to sleep every night, and at least once in during the day.

One day after our walk, after putting DJ down for his nap. the door bell rang, I opened it to see Kim one of Rhonda's friends, holding a baby seat. I hadn't seen her in a long time, I heard she had gotten pregnant and had to post-pone going to school. I felt bad for her, I know like Rhonda she worked hard to get into college. She was only about 5'2, but with her heals on she stood to be my height. she had really bigs hips and big breast that looked to have gotten even bigger. Her hair had gotten longer since the last time I'd seen her. The outfit she had on was much more conservative than what she used to wear. She appeared to be doing very well for herself. When she saw me she smiled to reveal the cutest dimples.

Hi Reece she said, how are you?

Hey Kim, I'm fine, you know Rhonda went to school don't you.

Oh yea, I talked to her before she left. I came to see how you were doing, I heard about DJ, your uh... husband getting killed she stammered. Can I come in.

Sure I said, can I get you something to drink. I just got back from a walk and your just in time for my famous smoothies.

Sounds good. She said following me into the kitchen.

So, what have you been you been up too? I heard you had a baby. Is this her? I asked looking at the pretty brown baby in the seat.

Yes it is, she's 3 months today.

Awwww, I said what's her name?

Deanna she answered. She looked to have dimples just like her mother. She's been a blessing to me. I never knew how lost I was until after I had her and I know what it means to truly love someone other than yourself.

I know girl, kids will do that for you. She's beautiful. Are you going to go on to school I asked.

Well, right now I'm just trying to make things right, get my life together.

Oh I said handing her one of the two smoothies I had just finished making.

We sat there talking for about an hour about everything under the sun. She told that she was raised with a dope fiend for a mother as well and that she had experienced much of the same heartache growing up. She said she guessed that's why her and Rhonda had become such good friends. We were enjoying our conversation so much that I invited her and her baby to stay for dinner. While we ate we continued to talk about the old days and about recent events, she gave me the rundown on Ms. Lorraines funeral and who all was in attendance. It felt like I could talk to her. She wasn't my cousin, or my cousins best friend who had no other choice but to befriend me. Our friendship was so easy.

She came over every day. We did everything together. If you saw me, you saw her and vice versa. She had practically moved in. I expected to get more opposition to my new friendship from Mia, but she had so much going on, that our conversations were limited to five minutes or less. Sidney too had a full life going on. She's so jumpy, and she looked as though she'd aged so much in just a short amount of time. She must really be going through some heavy shit. The last time I saw her she didn't even have on heels. And Sidney always had on heels. I think they were both probably relieved that they didn't have to constantly check on me. I was now back down to my weight before I'd had DJ and I was feeling good about myself. That ponytail was a thing of the past. And without those battle scars, I could once again wear whatever I wanted. I was even looking into going to college. I was never able to go before, because I always had multiple people to care for. Now I could get the teaching degree I've always wanted. Kim urged me to apply to school, she was the one that went walking with me everyday even though she didn't need to. She was the one that did my hair. I don't know where I would have been had she not come to my door that day. Even after several weeks we would still stay up till all hours of the night talking, there was never a shortage of topics of conversation with her. On most nights she would end up sleeping in my bed or we would be on the couch together. I never even thought about it twice when we would wake up in spoon position.

One night after we'd put the kids to sleep, we were sitting on the couch drinking margaritas and smoking a blunt. She always had a couple of blunts on hand. When Kim turned toward me and said Reece, I've never met anyone that I felt so comfortable with. I want you to know how much you mean to me.

Oook, I said wondering where she was going with that.

I don't know, she said maybe I'm just drunk but that's how I feel right now. Haven't you ever just been in the moment and went with it.

No I haven't I said. After thinking about it.

You need to learn to relax Reecey she said.

Oh I am relaxed right now, I said getting up to pour myself another margarita.

Kim came up behind me and started rubbing my shoulders, telling me how tense she could feel I was. After I poured both of us another drink and got ready to hand her one of them, she took mine and put them both on the counter and kissed me. I didn't know right away what was going on, but when I figured it out, I kissed her back. It was the most tender kiss I had ever had. She took her hands and began to run them up and down my back bringing me closer to her. without heels on she was shorter than me so I was kinda bent over. I pulled away finally coming to my senses and went to the couch to sit down before I fell down.

Kim, what the hell was that about? I asked trying to wrap my head around the fact that I had just kissed a girl.

She came and sat on the couch beside me and said Reece, I have been wanting to kiss you for so long now. I hope you don't hate me. I'm sorry she said sadly.

I don't hate you Kim, I just didn't expect that from you.

Don't you feel this, she said stroking my face. Don't you wanna touch me like I want to touch you she said while she kissed my neck.

It had been years since someone kissed my neck and told me that they wanted me. even though she didn't have the package that I expected the next person that kissed me to have it still felt good in that moment. I let her continue to kiss me and take off my shirt. I wanted to say no, get up and tell her to leave for even thinking I would do such a thing. But I just kept looking at her, the way she looked at me, her dimples shined with even the slightest of smiles. Her skin was so smooth, she looked like a smooth cup of coffee. I let her suck on my breast, each time I interjected she would tell me how much she loved me, and how beautiful I was. She told me that she has never felt this way about anyone in her life before.

My head was spinning with all the new information, on top of everything else I had consumed that evening. I still wanted to tell her to stop. I didn't know if I wanted it to go that far. Although her kisses felt good, she was a girl I kept thinking. I'm sorry Kim, I can't do this I said pushing her off me. I'm sorry, I can't handle this right now. I just lost my husband I'm still trying to find me again. This…You…I just can't do this. I put my shirt back on as I spoke.

Tell me you don't feel this she said kissing me again. And again, I wanted to stop, but there was so much passion in our kiss, that I grabbed her pretty round face and kissed her back.

No, I'm sorry Kim I had too much to drink I said getting up to go my room. I really can't do this.

When I woke up the next day, they were gone. I went on about my day trying to forget about the night before. Trying to not call her, wondering why she hadn't called me.

I sat wondering all day why it had to be all or nothing. We were friends, just because she took it there and I'm not ready for anything like that means we're no longer friends? I called her but got her voicemail.

I had gotten a call from Tamia telling me that they had found Roc, dead in a Motel room in South Georgia. Somebody had shot him in the head. From what Mia said, Lance was not taking it so good. They had decided that with everything going on they would probably be putting the wedding on hold for a couple of months. I think Lance's mother was going to be more devastated than anyone about that. She said she knew Ms. Chapman would do every thing she could do to get them to stick to the date planned. I'm getting myself ready for the fight she said.

As she spoke she sounded sad and relieved at the same time. I'm sorry you had to put off your wedding Mia, I know much this wedding meant to you. When is the new date?

It's ok, it'll happen when or if it's supposed to. I was going to suggest it when you were in the hospital anyway, I could never find the right time. Now we have to go to Mississippi and deal with mother Chapman in person. We're supposed to discuss a new date then. I guess, she said under her breath. This is going to be fun. Don't you want to go?, she asked. I know you could use a vacation, even if we are going for a funeral, she said trying to talk me into it. And I'm going to need all the support I can get. I'm pretty sure Sidney's coming but she's been such a mess lately. I don't even thinks she knows if she's coming or going right now, with all that's going on with Rickey and now with Roc's death.

As I sat and thought about what she had just said, I really could use a couple of days to get away. And if nothing else use that time to get Kim off my mind. When do we leave, I asked

Friday morning, we're flying out. I'll get your ticket today. Rhonda called and said she was going to try and come here first, but if she couldn't she would meet us there.

Rhonda, I said. Why is she leaving school for this?

Well apparently she and Roc had a thing.

A thing I said, what kind of thing? That boy was too old for her and he wasn't no good, being around him could be dangerous with the deals he was into, I had overheard DJ on the phone talking about some of the things Roc did. What did she think she was doing. As I began to go over things in my head it became all to clear. Roc and DJ had become pretty close with all the business they shared. Rhonda was always one to seek attention from all the guys DJ bought around.

I don't know what they see in him, what I do know is she saw Sidney and Roc on the side of the house the night of the party and she was not happy about it. Mia said

Sid and Roc I said more as a question. Where was Rickey at? She know she like to live dangerously don't she. I talked to her last week and she was crazy drunk or high, or both. She almost sounded suicidal. I asked her if she wanted me to come over or if she wanted to come over here, but she said she had to much to do.

What have you been up too lately she asked. It seems like we never get a chance to talk. How is my baby?

He's fine, demanding as usual. Remember Kim, I asked. Rhonda's friend

Yes, I think so, the pretty little chocolate girl with big ta ta's she said

Yea, that's her, she's been coming over lately. I didn't know if I wanted to share the fact that we'd made out. or that I kinda liked it. Or if I wanted her to know that she said she was in love with me Although I really needed someone to talk to about it, I wasn't sure if Tamia was that person, she wouldn't understand and would probably tell me I was crazy.

yea, we've got a lot in common was all I said. I haven't talked to Kim in days. There may not be a story to tell I had decided.

Didn't she have a baby recently? She asked

Yea, a little girl, she is so adorable, Mia you would just eat her up. she looks just like a baby doll.

So, are you going to bring Lil D to Mississippi, she said.

Probably not, I'm going to call DJ's mother and see if she'll keep him for me. Shoot, if this is supposed to be vacation. Then I am going to take full advantage of it.

Ok. Well, I have to go I'll call you tomorrow she said in a rush to hang up.

After I put Lil D down and took a hour long bubble bath I felt renewed. I had been working on the art of relaxing. Although I missed Kim more than I would care to admit. I refused to let myself worry about her. I never considered the fact that I was a person who liked women. I've always loved what men had to offer. Even if I didn't have a lot of experience. Maybe that's what I needed I thought. Some more experience with men. How would I know if I truly liked women, if I hadn't fully grasp all that men had to offer. I put on my long silk robe and went into the kitchen to refill my wine glass. On my way there the door bell rang. I looked at the clock and saw that it was almost midnight, and wondered who would be coming over here so late. I looked out the window to see Kim standing there. I opened the door not knowing what to expect. She stood there looking so pitiful. She had on a jean mini skirt and a vintage old navy tee shirt with some cloth wedge heels on.

Hi, she said smiling can I come in.

As she walked past me, I could smell the scent of peaches and liquor.

We just stood there looking at each other, until she spoke. How you doin? she asked.

I'm fine Kim, I'm sorry about the other night. I'm just not ready for all that. I've never been with a woman before. I don't even know how I feel about that.

No, Reece, I'm sorry she said. The last thing I want to do is push you away. I've never met anyone like you before. I feel so safe and understood here. I've never had that before. Friends don't come easy for me.

We sat on the couch until daybreak talking. I let her know that although I didn't want to go as far as she might have. I did enjoy the other night and didn't regret that. When the sun came up, and she got up to leave she came and gave me a hug. There goes the butterflies from the other night I thought as I hugged her back. She kissed me on my neck and left.

As I went about my day, I noticed that I smiled more. I found myself in the best mood I had been in for years. I decided to redecorate the house. The things that were in the house now where the ideas of mostly DJ, since he was the one buying it, he said that it was his choice. I was pregnant with DJ at the time and didn't have the energy to argue about it.

I felt like it was time for me stop living in the past and start rebuilding my life without him. I started with DJ's clothes. I put all of his things that I' hadn't been able to touch in boxes and sealed them. I made three piles. The biggest of the piles were all of his designer clothes and nearly new shoes. I thought that maybe I would give those things to Sidney for some under privileged children she came in contact with at work. The second pile, I would give to his mother. Trophy's and items I know she'd want of his. And the third pile which was the smallest was things that I would keep and put in the garage. Things that I would one day give to his son. And the things that I just couldn't part with, like the silk boxers that he wore on the night we were married, or the diamond cross he wore around his neck that I'd bought him for his birthday. I'd noticed that he'd stop wearing it some time ago.

I came across the brown bag sent home from the hospital from items he had on him the night he was shot. I still wasn't ready for that, I had yet to cry during this process and didn't want to start. So I put that in the smaller box too. Maybe one day I could open it. When I had finished getting all of his things sealed up, I put them in the garage with the exception of the things I had for his mother.

While I was in my closet, I pulled out all of the sexiest things I could find to take to Mississippi; this trip was just the thing I needed I thought. Maybe I would meet and have a fling with a nice country boy. I would defiantly need to go shopping I thought as I took a real look at my clothes. I hadn't been shopping for myself in ages. It was always for everybody else. I put everything back in the closet and decided to buy everything I would need for the trip. The insurance check had come in and it was time for me to recreate myself. The new Reece was here to stay. Kim made me feel like bad girl. I had never felt so much excitement for life. I was never one to take risk. I took the first boy who showed me some attention and married him. I dressed for him. I lived for him and what would make him happy. Then I had a baby for him and it became about him and the baby. And although it's still about my son, I would start living for me and what made me happy.

After I dressed the both of us, I called DJ's mother and asked her if she'd like her grandson for a couple of days. She was all to pleased that I had called her. Even though I wasn't leaving until Friday, I decided to take DJ over there today since I had a lot of things to do before the trip. Kim had called and was going to meet me back at my house after she dropped off Deanna to her mothers' so we could go shopping together.

Our day together was so relaxed, I had expected tension from the past couple of days to get in the way of our friendship, but it didn't. We shopped, we laughed, and we talked as usual. I bought everything from underwear to shoes. The clothes I bought, Kim helped to picked out. I never would have chosen the stuff she picked for me. I felt as sexy as Kim said I looked in my new outfits. Afterwards we went to Bones in Midtown and ate dinner. Kim told me while we ate that she'd only dreamed of eating at such a nice place. By the time we got back to my house it was after eleven and we were both pooped.

As I looked at her I thought how pretty she looked, even after a full day of shopping. Her halter dress she had on showed off her huge boobs. I could tell that she had just shaved her legs. They were smooth and shiny as silk. As I studied her more, I found myself wishing she would try to kiss me again.

Do you want a glass a wine I said snapping back to reality.

Sure she said taking off her shoes. she went over and turned on the radio. Welcome to my sex room by Ludacis was on.

I sat back down and handed her the glass of wine. We drank in silence the tension I looked for earlier was now like an elephant in the room.

Wanna smoke a blunt she asked, I think I have one in the car.

While she was in the car I sat while my mind raced. Just how far I was willing to take things with her?. I hadn't been sexual with anyone in so long; maybe I was just horny and was settling for a woman. Maybe I was really gay all these years. Maybe I'm putting too much thought in this. Would one time with a women mean I was gay I thought as she walked back in.

This time she sat on the couch right next to me with only room to breath between us. She almost kissed me but instead leaned back on the couch and lit the blunt.

After we smoked I felt higher than I ever had. Everything in the room was there but it seemed really far away. Ron Isley's body kiss song was now playing and it was making me more horny with each beat. The robe I had on was now too many clothes and I began to take it off. Kim just sat on the couch watching me with wanting eyes. I went over to her with the desire to see if her breast felt as good as they looked. I straddled her lap and undid her halter and let them hang. I was amazed at how firm they still hang to be so big. I rubbed them, and played with her stiff nipples like a kid in the candy store. As I sucked them she began playing in my hair telling me how good it felt. I went back up and met her mouth with mine. As we kissed the room was spinning. she got up and laid me on the couch and went to work. She kissed my entire body with such intensity that I thought I would climax even before she hit my hot spot. I had never experienced anything like that before. DJ rarely kissed me below my neck even when we were still having sex. Most time, he would climb onto of me and finish even before I realized we were having sex. We only had oral sex on special occasion nights.

Kim took her time with each kiss and lick she gave me. she took my body through feelings that I never knew I had. After she'd made me climax several times, which was something I had never done before, I was still just as horny as when we began. We moved into my bedroom and As she laid on my bed, I and looked at her perfect body. She had not only shaved her legs that day. She was hairless everywhere. As I stared at her and swayed back forth to the music, At that moment, I felt like a sexy super hero, like I could do anything. I danced around my bed teasing her body making her moan.

The next thing I remember was waking up with her behind me. I looked down to see that we were both naked and noticed the huge headache I had. She stirred and began feeling around trying to put her fingers in my hot spot. I jumped which made her wake up all the way. What's wrong baby she said.

What happened last night I asked her.

Baby, you don't remember she said kissing my shoulder.

I got off the bed scrambling to find my robe, as I began to rehash what happened the previous evening. Everything was a blank past us sitting on the couch drinking.

I knew you loved me she said. breaking my thoughts.

What was in the blunt Kim I asked suddenly remembering how high I was after smoking.

Just some ecstasy to help you to relax she said getting off the bed walking toward me.

X, Kim are you crazy, you drugged me to have sex with you.

No baby, it's not like that. I knew you wanted me too, but I knew that you would never let yourself go if you didn't have a little something extra to help you. It wasn't the first time you had some. She said.

So you thought you'd give me ecstasy to loosen me up. I screamed. How often did you give it me?

It was just a little bit both times Reece, look at what it did you for you. We had an amazing night.

Yea, an amazing night I can't remember. If it was just a little then why don't I remember anything. I remembered everything from the other night? but now I was unsure about even that

She stood in front of me and said. I never wanted to hurt you. I love you Reece. I would do anything for you. Hopefully everything will come back to you.

How could you I said looking at her in all her nakedness. I never wanted it like this. I'm not even sure if I ever wanted it at all.

Of course you did she said pulling at the towel I'd found to cover myself up. The way you made love to me told me that you wanted it as much as I did.

She started kissing my breast which made my body remember the passion from the previous night. I jumped away from her and just looked at her like she was crazy as the door bell rang.

On my way to the living room I found and put on my robe, I saw the mess we had left. Anyone who saw that room would know exactly what had happened the previous night.

Just a minute I said scrambling to erase last night. Kim had slipped on her clothes and joined me in cleaning up any evidence.

Rhonda was outside the door telling me to hurry up. She'd lost her key. What is she doing here I said out loud.

When Rhonda walked in you would have thought she'd seen a ghost when she saw Kim. What are you doing here she asked.

Just hanging out, how's school? Kim replied getting off the subject.

School is great. Hey sis she said giving me a hug you look great. she still had the look of confusion on her face.

Thanks, what are you doing here I asked.

I thought I'd go to the funeral with you guys and fly back to school from there. You think Tamia can get me a ticket to fly out with you guys.

There where? Kim said interrupting.

Mississippi, you know they found Roc's body week, their having him shipped home Rhonda said, suddenly saddened at the thought of Roc.

How long will you be in Mississippi she said more to me than to Rhonda.

Well I'll be there until Sunday morning she said.

Kim held her glare on me until I said I I don't know. I was afraid to say anything to her in fear that Rhonda would be able to tell somehow that I had made love to a women, even if I didn't remember it.

I'm going to go get dressed I said leaving the two of them. Kim would never tell Rhonda. Would she I thought. In the shower, just as Kim had said our evening started to resurface in bits and pieces. Well I wanted to experience new things and this was about as new as I could have ever thought. I said to myself laughing I was really glad that I was going away, I needed this time to think away from her.

On my way back to the living room to see if Kim was still there I passed Rhonda's room and heard her say. Either you tell her or I will.

I stood there suddenly interested in who she was talking to and what she was talking about.

Rhonda, please let me take care of it. it's complicated I heard Kim say in a pleading tone.

How complicated can it be that your baby is her dead husband's child. What are yall Bff's now or something.

I felt like a ton of bricks had just hit me. The same way I found out that DJ had another child. I was in the same spot finding out that the love child my husband had was Deanna.

I opened the door and just looked at Kim. No words would come out. I didn't know what to say to her. She had slept with my husband, had his child, came to my home with that child, she drugged me into making love to her, while telling me that she was in love with me. yea, that pretty much summed it up I thought.

Reece, I'm so sorry, she said tears streaming down her face. I wanted to tell you so many times. I hated what me and DJ did. I'm so sorry I'm so sorry she kept saying over and over.

Get out I said to her. This whole thing was a big lie. From the beginning, everything you said has been a lie. Did you planned this? I asked

No No No, please Reece can we go talk. Please can I talk to you alone.

Why do you need to talk to her alone Kim, Rhonda said. She told you to get out.

Please boo, let me talk to you.

Boo, Rhonda repeated what's going on with the two of you?

I figured I'd have to get this girl out of there or she started running her mouth and I knew that I was not ready to answer any questions yet.

Rhonda can you please excuse us. I need to deal with this.

Don't you want me to stay here with you? She asked

No, Rhonda I need to deal with this by myself. I knew DJ had a baby, I just didn't know who she was. And besides, you need to get with Tamia about a plane ticket don't you I asked her.

Rhonda looked at me shaking her head before she grabbed her purse and told me to call her if I needed her.

The thought came over me to kill Kim for how much she hurt me. I could probably claim temporary insanity. Not a jury in the world would convict me after hearing the whole sorted story. But then I would have to tell the whole sorted story and I wasn't ready for anyone to know my little secret.

I never meant to fall in love with you Reece she started. I came over here to tell you that first day, but we clicked so much that I couldn't. As the days went by, it became harder and harder to tell you. You have to know I never meant to hurt you.

You were sleeping with my husband. You had a child by my husband. Don't you think that that would hurt me?

I didn't know you then. DJ said that your marriage was over, he never wore his ring. He said he had been planning on leaving you. He had said he'd even went to a divorce lawyer. I love you Reece, I've never felt like this before. I didn't plan on falling in love. You have to believe me

As I listened to her ramble on and on. I was numb. I couldn't even cry. I don't even know if I wanted to. I had already made my peace with knowing that DJ had a baby outside our marriage. The fact that it was Deanna only put salt on a old wound. It barely even stung. I was hurt for many other reasons. I was confused and didn't know what to think less and only how to respond to the ultimate betrayal.

Baby, say something she said coming over to me.

I don't ever want to see again I said to her. All the countless talks we had, you could have told me if you really wanted to.

I wanted to so many times she said crying. I wanted to the other night. The first night we kissed. That's why I stayed away. I couldn't feel that way about you knowing what I had done. This has been eating me up inside. I didn't think I would fall in love with my baby s daddy's wife. You have to believe me Reece. Please forgive me.

Kim I need you to leave. I can't do this right now. I need you to get out.

Please baby, don't do this to us. I love you she pleaded.

You gotta go Kim,

Do you ever think you'll be able to forgive me she said gathering her things.

For what I said yelling. For sleeping with my husband. No No, Maybe for drugging me on more than one occasion, to sleep with me. Maybe forgive you for making me love your baby knowing she was the daughter of my dead no good ass husband. Just get the hell out Kim I said suddenly exhausted. My headache had now turned into a migraine. After she left I went and laid down, but not before praying to God for strength, peace and understanding. To my surprise, I still had yet to shed a tear.

I slept the entire day away. By the time I woke up it was 9 o'clock pm. I felt better but hungry

I looked at my phone to see that I had 12 missed calls. 10 of which, a voice mail was left. As I ate, I listened to them. Rhonda called 3 times, Tamia called once to tell me what time we were leaving and the rest were from Kim. As I listened to her begging and pleading for me to forgive her I began to wonder just how long were they sleeping together.

Me and DJ hadn't slept together for over a year. He had begun hitting me a few months before that. That first night he slapped me hurt the worse. He had come home drunk out of his mind. I told him I was tired and didn't feel like having sex with him. After he slapped me, he told me he was sorry, he even cried and said he would never do it again. When I still resisted having sex with him, he choked me and took it anyway. It was so harsh, it may have hurt worse because I was in no way wet, after having such a hard time putting it in, he spit on me and forced it in. He kept one hand on my neck the entire time. the next day when I started packing my clothes, the hitting started again. He told me I'd better not ever think I was leaving him. He'd said that the only way I would leave him would be in a box. I guess that statement turned him on, because he forced himself on me again.

We went on like that for about 2 months, and then one day after beating me and again struggling against my dryness to stick it in, he just went to sleep, and never tried again. In my mind, our marriage ended that first night he hit and raped me.

After packing all of my new things in my new coach tote I'd bought on my shopping trip. I laid back down. My thoughts went back to Kim, how she made my body feel. Never had I felt so much pleasure. I didn't even know what it felt like to have multiple orgasms. The irony of it all. the same women that used to pleasure my husband was the same women who made my body tingle at the thought of her. Could I forgive her for sleeping with my husband? Could I forgive her for drugging me and providing me the best night of passion I'd ever had. Can I get over the fact that Breanna is little D's sister. Am I even interested in continuing a relationship with her at all, not because of DJ, but because she was a woman. All of these thoughts ran over and over in my mind as I drifted back off to sleep.

The next day I pulled Rhonda aside before we boarded the plane and asked her to keep what had happened the day before to herself.

What happened she asked.

As soon as I'm able to figure out what's going on, Rhonda I promise you will be the first to know. But for now, please don't tell anyone about Breanna or Kim or anything. Ok

What's going on between you and Kim, she called me today, she was messed up. She kept saying she never meant to hurt anybody.

I can't go into that now Rhonda, just please keep this on ice.

Well I know this don't make you feel any better, but she only liked DJ for his money and the excitement he brought.

Much like why you liked Roc, I said. Yea, I know about you and him Missy.

She looked at the ground and said we'll keep that on ice too.

Chapter 7

TAMIA

After days of thinking about Mac, I needed someone to talk to. Although I wasn't sure if Sidney Rose was that person I went over her house anyway. She wasn't there but I still had the key, so I let myself in. I looked around the house and saw that she had not cleaned up in a very long time the house was a mess. There were dishes in the sink from what seemed to be a week old. It looked like she was sleeping on the couch from the covers all over the place. There was loose weed all over the table and several that were already rolled up. empty liquor bottles and glasses covered both end tables, along with empty pizza boxes and fast food containers, some with food still in them. Sidney was obviously going through more than she was talking to me about. She had never let things get this bad and her drinking looked to be out of control. I took off my shoes and began cleaning up. Just as I was done cleaning up the door bell rang. I opened it to see none other than Mac. He stood there looking like a million dollars.

Well hello there Mia'amore. What a pleasure this is he said smiling.

Hi Mac, Sidney's not home. I said quickly. A small part of me hoped he would have just turned around and walked away.

That's ok, you don't mind if I come in do you, he asked as he walked past me slightly touching me as he passed.

No, I was just cleaning up a bit.

What a good friend you are to clean up for her he said giving me just enough room to shut the door.

Well, I don't think she's been doing so well lately, I thought I would help out. I said trying to go around him to get to the couch.

Your good at running aren't you, he said pulling me close to him. I think it's time that I told you know that I can't think of anything but you. I crave you. I know how close you and Sidney are, and I know you probably see me as an old man. But I want you Mia'amore. I've wanted you for a very long time.

He smelled so good. His body heat was making my head spin. I don't think your old at all I said taking his smell in. he always smelled so good. I… I'm about to get married

So you mean to tell me that you don't want me?.That's not what your eyes say when you look at me. he said touching me gently all over my face. I could look into these eyes forever he whispered.

I I'm getting married I repeated as I looked at him. He looked like he could see straight through to my soul, I was mesmerized and couldn't pull away. He touched my face so gently, that he barely even touched it. he didn't say anything for awhile, he just stood there tracing my face with his fingers.

Mac, please don't I said finally, I'm getting married to. to… I couldn't remember his name for anything. I'm getting married to Lance I said like I had just won a prize.

He covered his mouth over mine and gave me a gentle yet passionate kiss. Please don't ignore this he said between kisses. He kissed my cheeks and my nose and my forehead before he moved to my neck. He kissed it and gently sucked on it which made my body soft as jello.

I had come to the conclusion that I wasn't going to fight it. I had to see what all this passion was between us. I would never be able to move on completely with Lance until I settled this. Even if I wasn't sure if I still wanted to move forward with Lance. He had become very hard to live with. He began trying to control everything I did, and when I didn't do something to his liking, he would say the most hurtful things to me. He was a ticking time bomb since the night of the shooting. He all but forbid me to talk to Sidney again. He had even threw my phone across the room when he saw her calling me one night. Each day that went by that he hadn't heard from Roc, became a reason to get drunk.

As me and Mac kissed, things began to heat up and we started to undress each other. His body was better than I could have ever imagined. He had six pack abs, and he had fine hair that laid on his chest that I found so sexy. Lance was hairless all over except for the hair I made him grow on his face. He picked me up still kissing me as I straddled him. He moved over to the couch and laid me down, he told me over and over how beautiful I was. All of a sudden he stopped. He got up and just stared at me. the only items I had left on was my blue jean shorts and a my bra. I just looked at him wondering if I had done something wrong.

I'm sorry, I can't. Not like this he said, I have wanted you for so long Mia that I am willing to wait until I can have all of you. I don't want you like this. I have to much respect for you. You don't belong to me yet. If we do this now, you will resent me if this stops your wedding. I don't want that. I want you to know for sure it's me you want and come to me.

I got up and put my shirt back on. I couldn't argue with that. I was wrong for allowing myself to cheat on Lance. Even though I wasn't all so sure if this wedding was even going to take place. I'd had my doubts about me and Lance for some time.

After we were both completely dressed, he walked up to me and grabbed my hands. Mia don't get me wrong, there is nothing I want more in this world than to make love to you. But when I do, it will be right. I've lived my life with the wrong woman for all of these years, I'm not going to do it anymore. I want to be with you. This is not a game.

Mac, I don't know what to say.

Don't say anything, if letting you go now means that you will come to me later than I'll have to let you go and take that risk; he said hugging me. he grabbed my hair in his hands and looked at me. I want you so bad he said kissing me hard before leaving out the door.

I sat down after he left and went over everything in my mind that had just happened. No man has ever walked away from me when we were about to make love before. I never knew that Mac wanted me. How could this be? I loved Lance I really did, he was perfect for me. we were just 3 months apart in age. He was gorgeous, he was wealthy and we were the perfect couple. We were getting the perfect house built, we were going to have the perfect children. So what that he didn't make my stomach do little flips when I saw him. He loved me. Even if I did think he was spoiled and acted like a baby whenever he didn't get his way. Or that he let his mother make most of the decisions about our relationship. We were perfect together.

It was obvious that Sidney was not coming home, so I finally left and went back home. I hoped Lance wouldn't be there because I could still smell Mac on me. The thought of him made me smile and my stomach do little jumps. One my way up the elevator to our house, my phone rang, it was a number I didn't recognize, but I answered it anyway. It was Mac. I wondered how he'd gotten my number because I didn't remember giving it to him. Hi beautiful he said.

Hi I said this is a surprise.

I just had to talk to you. I couldn't sleep tonight without knowing when I would see you again.

I was reaching my floor and knew I needed to wrap it up just in case Lance was home.

Before I could answer, he did. Have dinner with me tomorrow at my place at around 6.

No I said over and over in my mind. Yes was what I said to him. I'll see you at six I said just as I reached the door,

Until then Mia'amore he said hanging up. The way he said Mia'amore was a turn on in itself, I thought as I opened the door. Lance was not there so I ran upstairs and took a shower. I had to wash the day I spent about to sleep with another man off me.

Several hours later Lance came home. He looked like he had been working out, because he had on his gym clothes and he was sweaty.

He gave me a kiss on my forehead and headed to the shower. While he was in there his phone rang. I never answered his phone before, but whoever it was kept calling. Lance please and older man said when I answered, he was choked up and sounded like he could barely get those words out.

I went into the bathroom and handed Lance his phone as he got out of the shower, and went back to the living room.

After awhile, I went back into the bedroom to find Lance sitting on the bed with his towel still wrapped around him. he had his head down and he was crying.

What's wrong baby, I said sitting down next to him on the bed.

They found Roc dead, he said.

Oh no, baby what happened. I said tears had began to run down my face, partly because Roc was dead, but mostly because Lance was so hurt. He looked lifeless.

He was shot he said laying his head in my lap.

I'm so sorry baby was all I could say. I had never seen a man cry this hard before. I didn't know what to do but sit there and hold him.

I finally convinced him to lay down after what seemed like hours of sitting there, him crying off and on.

The next morning I got up and made us some breakfast and took it to the bedroom for Lance. He wouldn't eat, he wouldn't even talk to me. I left the food on the bed just in case he got hungry and went to the living room to give him some space. At noon when I decided to go get dressed, he was still laying in the bed. His back was turned and he wouldn't say anything, so I didn't know if he was awake or not. I went to the store and ran a couple more errands and came back a couple hours later. He was still laying in the bed, this time when I asked him if he was hungry, He yelled at me to leave him the fuck alone and get the fuck out. Lance had never said those words to me before. I knew he was hurting, so I was willing to overlook his harsh words. I left you some food on the table if you get hungry I said turning to walk out. What I want really from you is to Shut the hell and up and get out. He was really pushing his luck with me, he was hurting I kept repeating to myself. He would never say such words to me I thought. I had forgotten my purse in the bedroom so I went back in there to get. He had the nerve to throw a glass at me on my way back out. It missed my by mere inches.

Have you lost your mine, I yelled to him going back in the room. I know your hurting and all, but you trippin now. I'm gonna leave you to your thoughts, you better get your act together, because if you still have this attitude when I get back. I'm leaving and I won't be coming back.

Promises promises he said as I turned to leave.

What had happened in 24 hours. Roc's death had affected Lance in the worse way possible. I didn't even know who that man was I just left. Was this how the abuse started with Reece I wondered. I had still yet to talk to her about it. I drove around contemplating going over to my mothers, then to Reece's, I still hadn't talk to Sidney. I ended up over Mac's house we were supposed to be meeting there at six and it was only 5, I hoped he didn't mind. I just didn't have anywhere elseI wanted to go.

He opened the door with a look of surprise. Is it six already he said.

No, I'm sorry I'm early I said before I let all the tears out I had been holding onto all day.

Mac took me in his arms and listened to me tell him all about what had happened that day. When I was done, he didn't say a word. He just looked at me and stroked my face. I'm glad you came he finally said

We ate the dinner he had prepared and sat in front of the fireplace sipping brandy and talking. Mac's phone rang all the time, people were always stopping by too. I assumed it was people still mourning Ms. Lorraine because when they came their first words were always "I just heard" or "how you holding up". It was so much about him that I didn't know. He was fascinating. I always thought he was just a old hustler, but he'd actually gotten his masters in psychology. He was about to open up his own practice when his brother needed him one night to have his back during a drug deal and he never walked away. The money was addictive he said.

I wanted to ask about Ms. Lorraine but decided that I would let him come to me with that story when he was ready.

We talked for hours as I was in no rush to return home with that maniac. Who knew what he would do next. And I was not trying to find out. Maybe it was the brandy we were drinking or the soft jazz he had playing on his Bose sound system, it sounded like they were playing right there in his living room, it could have been the fire that seemed to move to the beat in the fireplace, but I could no longer resist touching the handsome man that sat beside me. it was me who grabbed his face this time and kissed him. We rolled around on his plush carpet kissing, hugging, laughing and talking. It was the best time without sex that I had ever had.

When I woke up, I was in a huge bed with a black leather head and footboard. The sheets on the bed had to be at least 2000 thread. I only bought 1000 and above thread sheets and knew exactly what they felt like. I was impressed that he used them too. I looked up to see him standing there looking at me with nothing but some black silk boxers on with the robe to match that was open, revealing his perfect body.

Good Morning beautiful. You want some coffee, he said. I just made a fresh pot

Morning, I repeated, what time is it?

A little after nine he said looking at his Rolex.

I guess I'd better get home. I said getting out of the bed going to the bathroom. I was glad that I traveled with my toothbrush, all those years from wearing braces, I spent terrified that I had something stuck in them, made me carry a toothbrush with me at all times.

You never have to leave he said suddenly serious. Stay here with me. I will buy you all new clothes, anything you need. Don't go back he said as he watched me wash my face and brush my teeth. I felt so comfortable with him that I didn't even mind. I contemplated what he'd just said. I really could stay there with him forever. As much as I thought I loved Lance, I now knew what it meant to be in love with someone. Me and Mac had a connection that I had never felt before. This was beyond the childhood crush I'd held for him for so many years.

I wish I could my darling I said. I must go and face the music, whatever it may be.

He gave me a long kiss, when he let me go he said. I'll be here when you get back.

Mac, I don't know what's going to happen with me and Lance, this thing between you and I is so complicated. You're my best friends uncle I said, how could we or would we explain this.

We don't need to explain anything to anyone. This is our life, he said kissing me again.

Lance just lost his best friend, and although I can't condone his current actions, I have to go back.

Baby, just tell me one thing before you go, he said playing with the top button on my shirt touching my breast just slightly.

What, I said, getting moist in my hot zone

This thing between us is real, right? I'm not dreaming am I?

I rubbed my hand over the fine hairs on his chest. Your not dreaming Mac. I don't know what will happen past today, but what I do know is that how I feel about you is real.

Call me or send me text me and let me know your ok. You say the word and I will be there to get you. That boy had better not put his hands on you Mia, you call me.

Mac, don't worry I'll be fine. I'll call you. Now where is that breakfast I smell.

I was impressed with Mac's culinary skills, they were almost as good as mine.

When we finished eating and I finally left. I felt brand new. Things with Lance up until recently have been good, but with Mac it was different. There was no pressure to be perfect. We hadn't even made love yet and I felt like we were more connected than me and Lance had ever been. I tried calling Sidney again to no avail. Where is that girl at I thought. She's been out of pocket for the past couple days.

It was almost noon and I didn't know what to expect from Lance. I had never stayed out all night before. I didn't even call and I didn't care. That would teach him to talk crazy to me I thought. As I entered the house, I could tell that Lance still hadn't gotten up. I went into the bedroom and just as I had suspected, he was still in the bed. When he heard me, he turned around. He looked terrible, never had he looked so bad. The hair on his face was a full grown beard, his hair had grown out of control and was now an afro. He looked like he smelled, which was bad. He looked thin, his face was sunk in and he his eyes had dark circles around them. He didn't even look like the same man I had fell in love with. I never expected him to go into depression this much. I knew him and Roc were close, but this was beyond grief. I didn't know what to say to him to make it better or even if there was anything to say.

Oh, your back he said turning back around.

Lance, I don't know what to do, I don't know how to help you out of this. Tell me what to do for you. I don't like to see you like this.

Well get used to it Mia, this is the real me. I'm not the perfect man you thought you had.

Lance, I know your not perfect. No one is. Once you realize that you really are human than maybe you'll be able to handle things that are beyond your control.

Mia, I was suppose to have his back. he said sitting up. I was suppose to be watching out for him. I promised him I would have his back he said, tears streaming down his face. It's my fault he's dead.

Lance, I said moving closer to the bed, it's not your fault. Roc lived his life the way Roc wanted to, you know that. He would never want you to blame yourself for this.

Mia, I'm sorry for the way I've been acting.

It's ok Lance, I know your hurting. Now can you please go take a shower I said smiling.

Roc funeral is next Sunday at home. I t hought we would go down on Friday and visit with my family. My mother wants to talk about the wedding.

Lance, about the wedding. I think we should post-pone it I said while I changed the bed linens.

He stepped out of the bathroom and looked at me. You don't want to marry me anymore? he asked.

Lance there is just so much going on with the shooting and now this. Do you realize that we only have 2 1/2 weeks to prepare. I just think that we need to wait.

After a few uncomfortable minutes, he finally said yea, I think your right. I need to find out who did this to my brother and make them pay he said with a far off stare.

What are you talking about, I said looking at him like he was crazy.

I'm talking about finding whoever shot Roc and making them regret the day they were born.

That won't solve anything Lance. That won't bring him back

Maybe it won't, but it'll make me feel better.

While he dressed my mind wondered to Mac. I wondered what he was doing and if he was thinking about me. I thought about last night and how great it was to just be me. I thought about the way I felt when he touched me, the feeling in my stomach began it's little dance at the thought of the kisses we shared.

Mia, Mia, did you hear me? said Lance now standing over me. I have to go. I'll be back later. As soon as he left, I called Mac.

Hey there Mia'amore he said picking up the phone sounding so very sexy, how did you know I was thinking about you?

I took a chance I said. smiling twirling my hair around my finger

How are you, that boy didn't trip on you did he? I'd noticed that he always referred to Lance as "that boy".

No no, I'm fine I said. I had a wonderful night last night. Thank you.

What are you thanking me for?

Just for being there for me. I know I was a mess when I came over.

Mia I will always be there for you, you don't have to thank me for that. Now when am I going to see you again?.

When would you like to I said smiling like a kid with a new bike.

Now, he said. I want to see you now.

I just left you,

Yes, and I want you back.

Ok I'll be right over. Let me get cleaned up. I couldn't believe that I had agreed so quickly.

After I showered and got dressed I was out the door back to Mac's. I couldn't help but to wonder what I was doing. I couldn't explain why this man had captured my heart in such a short time. Was I willing to give up my life with Lance for him? Is this just a crush that will pass?. I was so confused. The only thing I was sure about was that I felt better than I had ever felt. Lance hadn't even asked where I was last night. He's so hell bent on revenge. As I drove, I heard our pastor's voice in my mind talking about commitment and how the true test of that was through the rough times. Was I giving up on Lance when he needed me most. Is Mac just an excuse to not to deal with the rough times. I pulled over in the gas station to get myself together, my head was now spinning with all the thoughts and feelings of guilt that suddenly consumed me.

As I sat there with my head on the steering wheel, Sidney called

Where have you been I said answering my phone

Mia, everything is fucked up. Rickey left me for good this time.

That would explain her house I thought.

What happened Sid?

She began rambling, I could tell she had been drinking a lot already. I got caught up over Terry's house, I wanted to go home. Rickey wanted dinner, from the store. I forgot my panties again. Roc calling. The truck tint was dark. The drugs Roc is dead. And then she started crying.

Sid, Roc called you I asked. Sid, hello

Mia, he left me. I don't think he's coming back.

Sid, what did you say about Roc, when did you talk to him? I kept asking her. I didn't know how to tell her he was dead.

She was so out of it. nothing she was saying was making sense. I'm on my way I said starting the car.

No, Mia don't come over. I need to be by myself. No you don't Sidney, I'm coming over. I said hanging up before she could protest any further.

When I got to the house, I didn't try the door bell I just used my key to let me in. The house was dark and smelled like a night club. Liquor and weed smoke filled the air. Sidney was on the couch looking like Lance did earlier. I had never seen Sidney look so undone. She was eating something and most of it was on her lap and hanging out of her mouth. She looked like she had gained some weight since the last time I'd seen her which was only 2 weeks ago. She had on a long dirty sundress that she looked to be wearing for days. The house was still semi-clean in all the other rooms that I cleaned on my last visit, except for the vomit that was by the kitchen door.

She looked up when she saw me and tried to smile. Hi Mia, what are you doing here.

Sidney whats going on with you lately.

You'd never understand, here have a drink with me. she said handing me bottle of grey goose. Although I didn't think she should drink anymore, I took the bottle, I did need a drink.

I stayed there with her for over an hour drinking before I came to the conclusion that I wasn't going to get anything sane out of her. Nor was it a good time to tell her Roc was dead.

I cleaned her house back up. helped her get cleaned up and put her in the bed. I sat down on her couch and smoked a blunt and had one more drink before I left. I had had one hell of a day.

It was now going on 8 o'clock and I had completely forgotten about Mac.

When I got there, I expected him to be mad, but he only smiled when he opened the door and held out his arms for me.

In his arms, I felt so safe. Tragedy had struck my best friend and my finance in ways that I couldn't help them. Outside of feeling helpless I was exhausted trying to be there for everybody all the time.

Me and Mac cooked dinner together and ate. We had such a good time talking and laughing that when I looked up it was almost midnight. I knew that there was no way I could stay there all night again and that I would have to be leaving now if I wanted to avoid any trouble with Lance. I had to keep up appearances until I was sure what I was doing.

I have to go I said, looking at Mac. It's getting late.

Baby, how long are you going to do this? he said getting up walking towards me

I wasn't ready to answer all the questions he had for me. so I went up to him and started kissing him. That would shut him upI thought. And it did, he kissed me long and passionately. We stood there just kissing for what seemed like forever, until he went up the dress I had on and started fondling my breast. I thought I would go insane when my phone rang. there goes my baby came on and I knew it was Lance. I straightned up and regained my senses. We both just looked at my phone like it would answer itself until is stopped.

We both knew that I had to leave.

This is hard, he said putting his head down. I never thought it would be like this.

I'm sorry Mac, I'm complicating your life. This is not fair to you at all. I'm going to go on and leave now.

This time he didn't protest, he just looked at me. even sad, this man was sexy I thought as I walked to the door, I wanted him to stop me. I wanted him to tell me again not to go. To stay there with him forever and everything would be ok. But he didn't, he didn't even walk me to the door. I stood at the door with my hand on the knob. I just couldn't leave like that. I wanted nothing more than to fall in his arms and never go back to Lance. Even if I couldn't do that tonight. I could make him understand that I was falling in love with him.

Mac, I said turning around walking back towards him, please don't be sad. I just need some time. Please understand. This is all happening so fast between us. I have to settle things with Lance.

Mia, I've spent most of my life living for somebody else, first my brother and then Lorraine. I haven't done one thing that was the best thing for me. I'm not a young boy anymore and it's time to realize what it is I want and go after it, he stressed. What I want, is you. I want you all to myself. These past few days with you have been the best days of my life. I've never before felt the way you make me feel. I've never been in love before. I didn't know what to expect. I didn't even know how love felt until you.

Why me? I wanted to know

Why not you. You're a beautiful woman inside and out. I've watched you grow up and I know your heart. You give yourself fully to everyone around you with no expectations in return. I've never known anyone to do that. I see life through you, the way it's supposed to be. filled with peace and love. I've always wanted both of those things, but gave up on ever finding them until now.

The way he spoke almost made me cry. No one had ever expressed themselves to me like that before. The look of sincerity on his face melted my heart. He wasn't trying to be sexy, he wasn't trying to be cool. He just spoke from the heart.

His door bell rang and startled us both. He went up to the door and looked out the peephole and shook his head before opening the door. Was he crazy I thought, why would he run the risk of someone knowing I was here this late. Before I could complete my thought in walks Betty Reed. She was referred to as Betty Boop around the way. Because she had a shape just like hers including her big head. She was an attractive older lady who dressed way too sexy for her age, she was one of Ms. Lorraine's frienemys.

Hey there Mac she said as she swayed past him touching his chest, I thought I'd come and check on you in this big ole house all by yourself. Oh, I didn't know you had company, she said finally noticing me.

Hi, Ms. Betty I said.

Hi Tamia I didn't know you'd be here, where's Sidney is she here too?

I'm waiting on her to get back from the store. I lied. I knew if she didn't believe me, that I would be tomorrow's topic at the beauty shop.

Oh, that's nice she said tuning back to Mac, well I guess I need to make an appointment to see you these days. You haven't returned any of my calls.

I told you I've been busy. There's no need for you to worry about me Betty, he said, trying to keep his distance.

I looked at this lady try every trick in the book to get him to notice her. It was rather amusing what some women did for the attention of a man.

Well can I make dinner for you one day this week, asked Betty,

I can't get into that now, I have company and my niece is on her way back. I'm really going to be tied up all week, but I'll call you ok, he said walking toward the door.

Oh, ok then she replied sounding disappointed. On her way out the door, she leaned in and kissed his cheek. Call me

Mac closed the door and gave a sexy giggle, that woman is relentless.

Yes, appears so I said feeling a little jealous. I knew he wasn't interested in that woman, but it had just set in that Mac was a fine, wealthy, eligible widower. Of course he was going to be on the menu for a lot of single women. There were women lined up to get a piece of Mac.

By the time I'd left it was almost one o'clock and I knew I was surely in store for some serious questions from Lance. I decided on not calling him back, just showing up at home with a lost phone excuse or something.

I wondered how Sidney Rose always managed to juggle more than one man. This was hard. I now understood however how she could love two men. I never thought that was possible before now. As I rode the elevator up to our place, I got a whiff of myself and smelled again like Mac's cologne. Damn I thought, this is bad, if I can smell it I knew he would.

I opened the door quietly hoping not to wake Lance if he was sleep, but he wasn't even there. Exhale.

I jumped in the shower and changed in record time just in case he came home.

I called Mac and talked to him until I got too sleepy to hold the phone to my ear. By the time Lance came home it was after 3 in the morning. He came in loudly.

Mia, Mia you sleep.

I was I said trying to focus. I could smell he was drunk again.

I called you. Where the fuck were you?

What I said, not sure if I'd heard him correctly

I said, where the fuck was yo ass at when I called you he said slowly slurring every word.

When did you call me Lance, I said playing it off. In my sleepy voice.

Lance was in Tupac mode and I knew that it wouldn't take much to set him off.

Where have you been I said changing the subject. It's after 3 in the morning.

I was where I was at he said. These muthafuckas fuckin with the wrong one. All these fools will know my name he slurred.

What Lance, what are you talking about, your drunk.

You damn right I'm drunk. Im a grown ass man. I can drink if I want too.

He went on cussing and rambling about how he was going to kill them all while he went into the bathroom. I turned back over and tried to go back to sleep.

When he got out the bathroom, he got in the bed and starting yanking at my gown. Give me some of this pussy he said trying to snatch my gown off.

Stop Lance, your drunk stop. Having sex with him was the last thing I had on my mind.

This is mine, he said trying to fill between my legs. You can't tell me no. give me some head now.

Lance, if you don't let me go,

What Mia, what are you gone do. You always tellin somebody what to do. You ain't perfect you know. Look at Ms. Perfect he said standing on the bed.

Lance get down, you are really tripping.

Roc said you was a stuck up bitch, I should have listened to him. And now he gone he said sadly.

What ? I said, waking up. Lance I am warning you. You are really trying my patience.

Oooooohhh little Ms Perfect is warning me. what are you going to do Tamia Rose. That statement made him giggle so much that he fell on the bed.

I started getting up, but he grabbed my arm. Mia, I'm sorry, he said. don't leave. Please don't leave me, he said suddenly crying like a baby.

I just sat there looking at him. He was really getting on my last nerve. Was this the rough times the pastor talked about. How much of this was I suppose to take.

Before long, he had cried himself to sleep and I joined him. The next morning he was gone before I woke up. He didn't leave a note like he normally would or anything. A part of me was relieved, I no longer knew how to talk to Lance. It was like a part of him died with Roc. The best part.

I looked at my phone and saw that I had a text from Mac, a simple I love you. I smiled at the thought of him. He was one thing in my life right now that felt good.

I had a message from the wedding planner wanting to go over some of the changes we had discussed. I had forgot to call her and let her know that the wedding had been postponed. Maybe indefinitely.

She did not take the news well. She was able to relax once I told her that I would be dropping off full pymt for her services.

That was the easy part, I thought after leaving her office, the hard part would be telling Lance's mother that the wedding would not be taking place in the upcoming weeks as we had planned. Maybe I would let Lance deal with that, she was his mother after all.

I had talked to Reece and talked her into going with me to Mississippi, although I hadn't talked to Sidney yet, I assumed she would too. I decided to go shopping for some new things for the trip. Shopping always relaxed me and I knew that If I was going to be in the presence of Lance's parents, I would have to look flawless. They were such snobs. And would expect nothing less from their soon to be daughter in law.

After shopping I went over Mac's. not seeing him for a few days would be hard.

I called him first to make sure he was home. I could tell that he had had a couple of drinks. When I got to his house he opened the door looking sexy as ever. Here is my Mia'amore he said taking me in his arms pulling me into his house.

I want you so bad he whispered. Kissing me up and down my neck. We were interrupted by his phone ringing. He picked it up irritated.

From his conversation I could tell it was Sidney Rose.

They talked for a few more minutes before he hung up.

Baby I gotta go, Sidney needs me to come over.

Is she ok, I asked

I'm gonna go see, I'll call you later he said kissing me on my forehead.

I'm going to Mississippi tomorrow, I wanted you to know. Remember I told you Roc, Lance's best friend was killed.

How long will you be gone? he asked with a frown

The funeral is Sunday, we'll probably come back on Monday

I don't like this Mia, from what you tell me that boy has become unpredictable, do you think it's a good idea for you to go out of town with him?

Roc was my friend too. I have to go pay my respects.

Baby, when you get back, we need to talk about our future together. It ain't about to be to many more trips that you go on with some other cat. I don't like this shit at all.

I know baby I said. If only he knew that he was turning me on more than ever. He was staking his claim and I found that so sexy. Mac still had a frown on his face, so I thought now would be a good time to let him know exactly how I felt about him.

Mac, I said slowly looking in his eyes, do you know that I am in love with you too.

His frown turned into a smile instantly, you love me he repeated, sounding like a little boy.

Yes Mac, I love you. As I said it out loud it sounded right. I loved this man. He was the man of my dreams and that, I could no longer deny. I couldn't marry Lance. I was now sure of that.

You have just made me the happiest man alive. I will never forsake you. I will never hurt you, that is a promise.

I know you won't. I said letting him kiss me all over my face.

On our way outside the door, he pulled me close and said you won't regret loving me.

As much as I wasn't sure at first if I wanted to take our relationship to a sexual level and cheat on Lance, I was somewhat disappointed that we hadn't. I don't know how much longer I could leave from his house hot and horny.

If I made love to Mac, then I was cheating on Lance. If I made love to Lance I felt like I was cheating on Mac. This was beginning to be too much for me. I knew that I would have to end this with Lance once and for all.

Chapter 8

SIDNEY-ROSE

Rickey came into the house and wouldn't even look at me. He went up stairs for a few minutes and returned with his bag. I can't do this anymore Sidney. When you grow up call me.

Please Rickey, I love you, don't leave me I said crying. I never saw myself as the type to beg a man not to leave me, but here I was on my knees begging Rickey not to walk out on me. I promise Rickey, no more, I can be everything you want me to be. I can be perfect I cried.

Sidney, if only I could believe that.

You can baby, I love you I said holding onto him. I knew I didn't mean it as the words were coming out of my mouth. I just didn't like the fact that he was leaving me and it wasn't the other way around. The pain was different. My phone started ringing. I knew it was Roc calling me back after I had hung up on him. I knew he was not going to be happy. But I had to put out one fire at a time. I ignored the phone and continued to plead with Rickey not to leave.

He was almost ready to put his bag down, but my phone rang again and again.

You'd better get that, he said, walking out the door.

I sat there on the floor crying thinking about how I had made such a mess of my life I started growing more upset by the minute. That damn Roc, why did he have to keep calling me. he knew that if I wasn't answering the phone, that meant I couldn't. He is so selfish. I need to get him his stuff and break it off with him. I'm done for good. And this time I meant it.

When my phone rang the next time, I snatched it up knowing who it was. What, I screamed into the phone.

Bitch, you gone make me do something to you. Why the fuck did you hang up on me. I need my shit ole stupid hoe.

Roc, you better shut the fuck up before you don't get this shit. I'm sick of your threats. I'm doing your ass a favor, don't forget that.

Im not trying to hear that shit from you girl, I need my shit. You over there playing house with that lame ass nigga. I don't give a fuck about that fool. I need my shit.

Where do you wanna meet I said tired of arguing with him.

When I got to the seedy motel I was meeting Roc at, my phone rang. it was Tamia, I would have to call her back. she would kill me if she knew what I was doing right now. Lately every time I talked to her I felt like she was judging me for my decisions to deal with Roc at all. Of course little Ms. Perfect would never get caught up with more than one man. That would be unladylike, I said out loud mimicking Tamia.

Roc met me at the door looking like a madman. His hair had grown unevenly on his face and looked extra nappy, which matched his hair on his head. He had on a dirty white tee-shirt and one of his pants legs were pulled up with what looked to be a sheet around it with dried blood on it. Before saying anything, he grabbed his bags and searched the contents of the smaller one.

Well hello to you too. I said walking around the dirty room. The motel itself was old and nasty There were beer cans and philly blunt guts all over the place along with old food containers. It smelled like death in there. Clean much I said sarcastically.

There you go with that damn mouth, what the fuck took you so long, he yelled walking towards me. I started backing up unsure of his actions. Why you backing up acting like you all scared and shit. Girl, ain't nobody gone do nothing to you. But love you he said smiling revealing teeth that had not been brushed in what looked like weeks. Breaking it off with him was going to be easier than I thought. There was no way he was ever going to touch me again. Even if he did clean himself up. The image of him right now would be sealed in my mind forever.

Come here, he said holding out his arms, I know you miss this dick.

Yea, Roc that's what I want to talk to you about. I can't do this anymore. I'm trying to get my life together. This case we got lingering over us got me fucked up, and I just need to chill right now.

What the fuck is you talkin about, fuck that. bitch I ain't had no pussy in weeks, you gone give me some of that shit.

Roc, I'm out, you got your stuff. We're done. Don't call me no more.

Oh, you think it's gone be that easy. Bitch now you thinking you better than somebody, you wanna go live happily ever after with that ole country muthafucka.

This don't have nothing to do with Rickey, this is about me and you I said walking towards the door. Oh and I know you fucked Rhonda, you bastard.

Yea, I fucked that little bitch, she was throwing it at me. Her and her little homegirl that was throwing it at DJ. They was begging for it. You know how you women are. See a nigga with money and do any and everything you can to get a piece of it. What is it to you?

Nothing, I don't want anything to happen to her fucking with you. You seem to have that effect on people, everything you touch turns to shit. I knew I went to far when I said that, because his eyes got real wide and he rushed up to me. he was now in my face and I could get a full whiff of what he smelled like. As my stomach tried to keep everything down I'd eaten, my hands were trying to get his hands off my neck.

Bitch I can kill you right now. Don't nobody know where you at. By the time they find your body. I'll be long gone, he said. as he reached up my dress and tore off my panties. Stop, Roc, please don't do this. I said.

He had a wild look on his face that scared me more than his current actions. He pulled his penis out of his zipper area of his jeans and started trying to force it in me as I struggled to release myself from his grasp. During the struggle, my purse fell off my shoulder; I suddenly remembered that I never put the gun back in his bag. It was in my purse. I fumbled around until I got it out of my purse and put it against his side.

Back the fuck up Roc. That scenario goes both ways.

He was completely shocked when he looked down and saw it was a gun that I was holding. His gun.

He immediately calmed down and began to back up. Oh so it's like that, you gone shoot me now.

You was just about to kill me remember

Baby, you know I couldn't kill you. You know I love you.

Save that I love you shit for somebody who believes it. You don't love nobody but yourself.

So it's like that Sid, it's like that.

I was trying to hold the gun on him and open the door behind me when he came for the gun. It went off and hit him in the head as I lost my balance.

I stood there looking at his lifeless body in amazement. I killed him. I looked around the room for anything I may have touched and began to vigorously wipe down anything that may have had my fingerprints on it. I grabbed both bags I had bought in and my panties that were torn on the floor. I left the room closing the door with a napkin.

On the way home, I cleaned the gun and pulled over to the side of the road where I saw a river and tossed it in the water. My hands were shaking so bad, that I didn't know if I was going to be able to drive home.

Before I made to my house I had to pulled over twice to throw up. What had I done? Outside of the fact that I had just killed another human being, I could go to jail for the rest of my life. Maybe I should just go to the police, he was trying to rape me, it was self defense. Where did I get the gun from? How did I know where he was? What was in the bags? All questions I was not ready to answer. with that amount of money, no one would believe that it was an accident.

I needed a drink, so I pulled over and went to the liquor store for the biggest bottle of tequila they had. Normally I would have never been seen in public looking the way I did, but I didn't care that night. I ran into Rhonda's friend Kim while I was there. She was always so pretty to me. she had lost all of her baby weight, she was talking to some big dude, I was relieved so I wouldn't have to run frivolous conversation with her. I put my head down, grabbed my tequila and headed for my car.

I looked back in the store and noticed that the guy she was talking to was one of the guys from Roc's apartment that day. They were looking for Rhonda. I was glad that she was out of town, out of reach. Even though I never really cared for her grown ass, I didn't want anything to happen to her behind Roc.

I drove home in record time from the store and parked my car in the garage. I threw the big bag in my trunk and took the smaller one with the money and drugs in the house. I went and hid the bag in the back of my closet.

I paced my kitchen drinking the tequila from the bottle, wondering if I'd wiped off everything, wondering if anybody saw me go into the room. Wondering, If anybody heard the shot or If they had discovered his body yet.

I must have passed out because when I woke up I was on the floor by the couch. I felt like a truck had rolled over me. After vomiting my guts out, I went back into the living room with the blanket from my bed and figured that a blunt would help with my nausea. Two blunts later, I wasn't as nauseous anymore, but I was hungry. While in the kitchen waiting on my pizza to get ready, I looked at the calendar on the wall and for the first time thought about the fact that I hadn't had my period in almost two months. I just can't be pregnant I thought. That would be the worst thing to happen to me right now, outside of committing murder. As I ate my pizza and racked my brain about the last time I'd had my period, I was even more stressed. I walked back into the living room and picked my bottle of tequila back up, but this time, I used a glass.

The next couple of days mirrored that one. When I ran out of tequila I decided to get dressed and go get some more I put on a long sundress that was laying on my floor, put my hair in a ponytail and threw on some flip-flops and left.

This time I planned to drive to Conyers so I wouldn't run into anybody I knew. Conversation with anyone was not something I could handle. I had briefly looked at my phone to see that I had 10 missed calls. Without looking to see who the calls were from, I stuffed the phone back in my purse and went into the store. Without even realizing it, I had driven almost all the way to Covington Ga. After I left the store, I took the street way home, so I could drink while I was driving, somehow it seemed safer if I wasn't driving that fast.

By the time I'd made it back from my journey and got home it was getting dark out. I missed Rickey, he always turned the light on outside if I wasn't home when it got dark. The thought of Rickey made me cry again but was pleasantly surprised when I opened my door to see that my house was clean. Who did this. maybe Rickey had come home. I staggered through the house calling out his name. it wasn't until I looked in the refrigerator that I realized that it was Tamia who'd cleaned up. She kept the ketchup in the refrigerator, Rickey hated that. I loved and hated her for that, I loved her because cleaning up your house for you was the kind of thing Tamia would do. But hated her because everything always had to be perfect. My house don't have be to clean all the time like yours Tamia I yelled in the empty house.

How do I do this I began thinking, how do I live knowing I killed Roc. if I'm pregnant, then it could very well be Roc's child, and that would mean that I would have killed my baby's father. No no, I couldn't be pregnant I didn't even want to think about anymore. I'm just stressed is all. As the nausea came back, so did my need to smoke again. Passing out had become a regular thing for me, I never remembered where I laid down when I woke up. At least this time I wasn't in the bathroom I thought as I got up in from my bed barely able to stand. I didn't know what day it was or how long I had been in my house. I didn't know how much longer I could go on like this. walking seemed to much of a task, so I laid back down and went back to sleep. I had stopped trying it to making to the bathroom each time I vomited. And let it out wherever I was.

I clicked the TV on for sound and laid back down after smoking a couple of blunts.

After a couple hours of weather reports and other things I was barley paying attention to, I heard it: Today, a man's body was found at the state route 21 inside the Baytown motel. He was found by the housekeeper, he had been shot in the head. No word on who shot him or a motive for the shooting. He has been identified as 28 year old Rocston Davidson. I went numb. They found him. Did they know it was me. they said they didn't know who it was, they always say that though. The tears came and wouldn't stop. Everything that I had been through the past couple of weeks came down on me hard. My mind was racing a mile a minute. I went back into the kitchen to look for the only thing that helped me not to think about anything. I grabbed the bottle of vodka and sat on the couch and drank and drank and drank some more. I needed to talk to someone, so I called Tamia. She wanted to come over. The last thing I needed was her to see me like this. she would know, she could always tell when I had done something wrong.

I woke up the next day, again not remembering getting in my bed, this time I had on some clean pajamas and my house was again clean.

Knowing that someone loved me the way Tamia did made me want to love myself for her. I finally got up and after smoking a couple more blunts for the nausea that had become a regular feeling. I ran me a bubble bath and soaked until the water got cold. I looked in the mirror for the first time in weeks and didn't recognize who was looking back at me. my eyes had black circles around them. My hair was a disaster zone, my face looked fat for some reason, swollen to match my sore breast. First stop beauty shop, I thought as I put on some jean shorts a t-shirt and my tennis shoes that I hardly ever wore.

I sat at the kitchen table and wrote out a list of everything that I needed to do to re-join the living, and try to make some sense of my life. I now had the money to pay for the attorney, thanks to Roc. My next task was finding somebody who I could trust to get rid of the drugs. They had to be worth a lot of money. My door bell rang, I opened the door and there stood two detectives. Ms Stone the tallest one said. I was about to faint, but stayed cool. I couldn't believe that I picked today to be sober. Yes I said in the most calm possible voice. How may I help you? I said standing in the doorway.

I'm detective Moore and this is Detective James, may we come in? we have a few questions to ask you about a Rocston Davidson.

I moved aside as much as I could without throwing up all over the place and let them in. I decided to take a seat on the couch, standing up was just not working for me.

Please I said, sit. I knew that the only way I was going to get through this was to be cool. What can I do for you?

Do you know a Rocston Davidson, the shorter of the two said.

Yes.

When was the last time you saw Mr. Davidson?

A couple of Saturday's ago at a party.

The party where a shooting took place? 1502 Sherwood Lane

Yes. I had learned from my father that you only answer questions with a yes or no to the police without an attorney present.

So, he was at the party?

Yes I answered.

Have you seen or spoken with him since then?

No, I replied

Are you aware that Mr. Davidson was found dead on yesterday. Do you know anybody who may want him dead?

No, I said. I could tell that I was beginning to irritate the taller man with my one word answers.

What kind of relationship did you have with the victim?

We were friends. I stated.

Friends, the tall one repeated. What type of friends?

Friends. I said again, this time louder letting them know that I was also getting irritated. It had become clear that they had no leads to who killed Roc.

Well, if you can think of anyone who could help in the investigation, please give us a call he said handing me his card. On the way out the door, he turned around and said, you had a pending case with Mr. Davidson didn't you?

Something like that I said clearing my throat.

I guess him getting killed worked out in your favor huh? He said not waiting for an answer before he walked away.

I closed the door, watched them drive away and rolled a blunt. My nerves we completely shot and the nausea returned full force.

As I smoked, I started thinking, could this case work out in my favor with Roc now dead.

My first stop was to my attorney's office. He said that with Roc's death the case may go cold. They were after him for the drugs and was only using me to get him. But I still may have to answer the fraud charges. He said that he may be able to get me probation for that since it was my first offense.

Leaving his office things were starting to look up. that was the best news I had heard in weeks. It was going to cost me an additional 5k. Mr. Winters was the best attorney in Atlanta, but he came with a hefty price.

Once I counted the money and found out it in all there was seventeen thousand in cash. After giving Mr. Winters five of it. I was still sitting on twelve thousand dollars in cash plus the drugs that I had no idea what to do with. I smiled at the thought. Since I was probably fired for not working or calling them to tell that I wouldn't be working for the past couple of weeks. I would need the money to live off of for awhile. I didn't even care right now. I knew there was no way I could focus on that job. I had my own problems, how could I help other people with there's.

After I left the beauty shop, I called Rickey to see if we could talk. I had to admit to myself that missed him. I wanted our life back. I wanted him to come home. I didn't know if that was even possible, but I knew that I had to try. He didn't answer the phone, so I left a message. My next call was to Uncle Sid, he was the only person besides my daddy that I would trust helping me unload the white powder that was still a mystery to me as to what it was. And I could certainly not show my daddy what I had came up on. He would have had way too many questions. Uncle Sid would give a short speech, but he would give me a little more leeway than daddy did.

Uncle Sid said he would meet me at my house in a little bit. He sounded preoccupied. I usually talked to Uncle Sid about everything, but lately I haven't even seen him since the night of the funeral. I wondered if he was seeing a new woman, hopefully he'd gotten Tamia out of his system. He had no business liking her and I'd planned on telling him so when I saw him.

On the drive home, Flashes of Roc popped in my mind. It seemed like everyone I saw on the street looked like Roc. I kept blinking so they would go away, but he wouldn't. He was everywhere, in every car that passed me Roc was driving. I was losing it I thought. My plan was to go to the grocery store before I went home, but I stopped by the liquor store instead. I would replace Roc's face with that of Jack Daniels. When I'd made it home, I began to drink while thoughts of Roc lying dead on the floor flooded my mind. Go away I yelled. Leave me alone. Roc was hunting me for killing him and taking his money. Of course I thought, it wouldn't be Roc if he didn't.

The more I drank, the less I saw Roc's face. By the time Uncle Sid got there I was drunk and was starting to rethink my plan to sell the drugs. If Roc was haunting me, it would only get worse if I gained from his death.

Baby girl, I'm starting to worry about you Uncle Sid said when he looked at me.

I fine, I said giggling tripping over my shoe. I mean I'm fine.

You know you can tell me anything don't you.

I wish I could Uncle Sid, but some things are too awful to discuss.

Nothing you do can be too awful to tell me. I will love you no matter what you did.

I started crying and told Uncle Sid the whole nasty story. By the time I was finished he was drinking, and pacing the floor.

Shit he kept repeating, what did the cops say?

I told you, they just asked me about my relationship with him.

Are you sure he was dead when you left?

Yes, uncle Sid, I shot him in the head.

In the head, he repeated looking down, awwww baby girl.

Sidney-Rose

It was an accident Uncle Sid, I didn't mean too. He was trying to rape me.

Well he got what he deserved, now, where are the drugs he asked.

I stumbled into my room to retrieve the drugs, when I laid them on the table, his eyes grew wide. Damn baby girl, this is some weight you got here.

What is it?

He looked it over, stuck a pin in it and put it on his tongue. It's cocaine he said. Uncut.

He sat there looking at the bags for a long time, he then stood back up and paced the floor, then he sat back down. That's a lot of money.

Can you get rid of it? I asked

Baby girl, you know I haven't been in the drug trade for some time now. I've got some good things going on in my life and I can't take the risk.

You have to help me Uncle Sid, I don't have anybody else I can trust.

Sidney Rose, you know that I would do anything in this world for you, but I can't run the risk of going to jail at my age. This weight would send me to jail for the rest of my life.

But Uncle Sid, I don't know what to do with it.

Baby girl, I would love to help you, but I just can't. what I can do is put you in touch with my man, who would know what to do with this much weight. I trust him. He'll take care of you.

Uncle Sid, I've never known you to pass on this much money. What has you so good right now that you no longer care about money.

I've got all the money I need, baby girl. And it took me a long time to realize that some things are better than money

Like what, I said, since when

Since now, he said sighing

Is it Tamia I said in a serious tone.

What, he said startled that I asked.

I saw the way you looked at her at the party, I also know something happening the night after Ms. Lorraine's funeral

Nothing happened Sidney.

So you don't like her?

Of course I like her. She's your friend, I've always liked her.

You know what I mean Uncle Sid, Do you like her, like her I said getting up to pour me another drink.

Sidney Rose, you have bigger fish to fry than worrying about your old uncles love life.

Love life, so you do like her.

Sidney, I didn't say that and I won't have this conversation with you. he said sternly.

He told me what to do step by step, how to handle the police if they came back. told me to stop drinking so much and to be careful and he left.

After he was gone, my phone rang I looked to see it was Terry. I hadn't even given him a second thought since I left there that day. I wasn't sure if I wanted to be bothered with him today, but I decided that sex was just the thing I needed to get my mind of things.

As I took a shower I started to put on my channel #5, but when I opened it, the nauseas feeling returned. So I opted for something I had bought from Bath and Body works. I stumbled around my room looking for something sexy to slip into and found a short red lacy number. Easy access I thought. I opened the door wearing only that, Terry instantly got a hard on. Damn baby, it's good to see you.

Its good to see you too I said welcoming him in. he had never been to my house before, Rickey was always there.

As he sat on the couch, I pranced around in my nighty making us drinks.

The feeling of nausea was still there and I wanted to smoke, but I had never smoked in front of Terry, and don't know how he would handle that.

After a few more minutes of feeling like I was about to vomit. I pulled out one of the blunts that I had already rolled up and lit it.

I didn't know you drank, much less smoked. There is so much I don't know about you yet Sidney. His looked turned from lust to concern.

Yea, there is I replied not caring what he thought, he was there for one reason and one reason only.

Did you come here to judge me or make love to me?. As I turned to complete my sentence, he turned into Roc.

I jumped back and blinked my eyes real hard.

Are you ok Sid?

Yea, I'm good I said, now looking at Terry again. I needed more drinks.

I turned the stereo up loud and started dancing around, Terry could no longer contain himself and got up and grabbed me. my head did a spin from the movement. When it finally stopped, I pushed Terry on the couch, took his pants down and gave him the best head of his life. He returned the favor and blew my mind with his oral game. By the time we made it to my bedroom, we were all over each other. He turned me every which way but loose. One thing was for sure, he was an amazing lover.

When we were done, we laid there talking all night. I had never talked to him for that long before. I was always stealing time in order to be with him. Now that we had time to really get to know each other, I was intrigued. He was interesting. We had a lot of things in common that I never knew. He grew up in the same foster home as my mom, daddy and uncle Sid. He had no family. I found that very sad, I think that made me like him even more. He told me what made him become a firefighter in the first place and how had he not done that, he would certainly be dead right now.

I never saw him as a hustler, I always thought he was the book worm legal eagle type.

When I let him out in the morning, I ran to the bathroom to extinguish everything I had consumed the day before. Still no period I thought.

I would have to deal with that when I got back from Mississippi, I thought as I packed for the trip. Trying to figure out which man had possibly planted his seed gave me a uneasy feeling. I ran back into the bathroom and let out anything else that may have been left over. Before long, it was only the yellow stuff that taste like death that came out.

I called Tamia to find out that she had already purchased my ticket. Thank God for Tamia I said aloud. She always came through for me. I hadn't even thought about purchasing a ticket to get to Mississippi before today. I wanted her to come pick me up so I could ride to the airport with her, I didn't really want to be around Lance, but was willing to risk it for the ride. but she said she was also meeting him there. She said she had some last minute errands to run. They must have been some important errands for her to not give me and ride and have to meet Lance at the airport.

I thought about just driving myself, and parking my car over the weekend, but decided to call Terry instead, who was all too happy to take me. We had reached a new level in our relationship last night.

While I waited for him to get there, I ate everything in sight. I thought twice about having a drink afterwards, but decided that I would need something to calm my nerves so I polished off a couple drinks while I waited. Today would be first day that I'd seen Lance since killing his best friend.

Chapter 9

REECE

Once we got to Mississippi, I was glad that I had worn one of my new sundresses that Kim had picked out, the sun was unforgiving. You could barely breath in the hot humid weather. The dress was a perfect fit and I knew I looked good in it. Rhonda wore a khaki mini skirt and a button down short sleeve shirt. She looked like a naughty school girl. I'm sure that was the look she was going for. Lance's parents met us at the airport. I didn't know Lance's father was so handsome. He looked so dignified and sexy at the same time. There was something to be said about a powerful man in an expensive suit. We caught eyes immediately. The next eyes I caught were Mrs. Chapman's; she was a short thick little woman who looked like money. She held onto Lance like he was three years old. She gave Tamia a short hug and just slightly spoke to us. I now understood why Tamia needed us there with her. This weekend was going to be a long one even if this was supposed to be a vacation for me. I was going to have a great time even if it killed me. I couldn't wait to go to the hotel and get a glance at what Mississippi had to offer. We first went to Lance's parent's house for brunch. I knew Lance was wealthy, but had no idea just how wealthy they were until we got to the huge mansion on the hill. Dang Rhonda said, is that a hotel, or a house.

That's our home dear, Mrs. Chapman said, she seemed to had taken to Rhonda right away for some reason. She was the only one of us that she'd talked too.

Mr. Chapman insisted that we stay at the huge mansion, he didn't get any objection from us. Their house was like a luxury resort. It was better than any hotel that they had in that town. Sidney was the one who gave the most opposition. She really wanted to go to the Hilton like we'd planned. She sulked the entire time we ate.

When Mr. Chapman offered to show us to our rooms, she was the first one to jump up, and grab her bags. When I got to my room, Mr. Chapman took his time to show me all of the amenities of the room. It was a really gorgeous room, it had a king size bed, a chaise lounge and a huge entertainment center. All of the furniture looked to be expensive cherry wood. It even had a balcony past two glass and gold double doors. There was a second set of double doors in the room behind them was a huge bathroom with a garden tub and separate glass shower. I felt like I had officially stepped into life of the rich.

Thank you Mr. Chapman I said this is a beautiful home you have, thanks for letting us stay the weekend.

Please, Mr. Chapman is my father, call me Ross. And you're welcome to stay here as long as you like. He smiled revealing a perfect smile with the whitest teeth I'd ever seen. He'd taken off his jacket and vest and now only wore a white button down shirt and slacks.

Ok Ross it is I said, more seductively than I planned too.

Your name was Reecey right he said

Just Reece I said correcting him with a giggle.

Oh, Im sorry, Reece

That's ok I said interrupting him, I like the way you say Reecy.

What was wrong with me I thought? Here I am in Lance's parent's house flirting with his father.

Well then maybe I will call you Reecy, he said with a sexy grin on his face. I'll let you get settled in. When you're done, please join us for cocktails out by the pool.

I'll do that Ross I said returning his stare.

We sat out by the pool drinking expensive wine while the men drank scotch. I could tell that all was not right with Lance and Mia, besides at the airport they hadn't really said two words to each other, I looked at Tamia to see the signs of distress that she usually had when her and Lance were fighting, which wasn't very often. but the look was not there. She looked happy and content, even with Lance's mother shooting her dirty looks every chance she got.

Sidney looked like she was drinking for two. She had consumed twice as much as we had in the same amount of time.

After an hour or so we were all feeling good. A lot of Lance's family and friends had come over and before long it was a full house. I hadn't thought about Kim all day to my surprise. But now that I was feeling tipsy, I wanted to talk to her. I thought about calling her, but decided against it. I didn't want her to think she was off the hook or that I had forgiven her for anything she'd done. So I instead went and joined Ross who was sitting in a lounge chair by the pool. I'd nicknamed Mrs. Chapman chatty patty because she was walking around talking to everyone like she was going to lose her voice if she didn't use it.

Me and Ross talked into the night, it had become obvious that we were very attracted to one another. When I went into the house to find a bathroom, he followed. Like I knew he would. Instead of the bathroom in the hallway, I went to the one that was in the bedroom that I was occupying for the weekend.

Ross wasted no time coming over to me, once he'd locked the door. We kissed like there was no tomorrow. He moaned my name over and over while he kissed my neck and the part of my chest that was exposed. I want you, he said. You know you had me from the moment I laid eyes on you in the airport don't you? It's just something about you that I find irresistible.

Yea I know what you mean, I said moving my neck so he wouldn't miss any spots.

I'm going to hell for sure I thought as I let Ross take my dress off. I don't think he expected me to not be wearing a bra, because when he looked at me, I thought he was about to fall over.

Wow he said, you're so beautiful, your body is amazing. He had taken the words right out of my mouth, when he took off that shirt, all the feelings of guilt I had for being with him seemed to disappear. This old man had it going on. He obviously worked out faithfully. He had a better body than most men my age.

We went at it with so much intensity, that I was sure someone would hear us. He made just as much as noises as I did. I could tell it had been some time since he's had sex. Was this what I had missing wasting my life away with DJ?. I finally had someone to compare him too. And DJ had nothing on Lance's father.

When we were done, we laid there talking about what we had just done. He shared with me that he and his wife had not had sex in over three years, he said that she just wasn't interested in sex. And he had lost the attraction to her to even continue to try. The town was so small, that he would dare not have an affair with anyone there. So he didn't and just went without sex for the last three years.

I shared with him my tale about DJ getting killed, me in a coma and even the story of Kim, he didn't even flinch when I told him about our night together. I was so happy to have someone to share that with who wouldn't judge me. We started kissing again but decided that we'd better go and return to the party before we were missed.

It was hard to rejoin the party that had grown since we were in the house; I wanted to be back in that beautiful room with Ross. And from the look on his face as he sat with some of his friends he wanted the same thing.

I thought the feelings of guilt would show up again when I saw Mrs. Chapman, but they didn't. I had just sexed her husband in her house and was still able to give her the most humble smile that I had. I wasn't sure who I was becoming with this new body and new attitude. But, I was liking it. I wasn't the victim for a change.

That night after everyone had left and we had all went to bed. Ross came into my room. We made love until the sun came up. he had to sneak out of my room, because we had fell asleep in each other's arms, we were awaken by the sound of the housekeeper.

What will Mrs. Chapman say I asked as he put his pajama pants back on?

She had so much to drink last night that she was out like a light. She's probably still sleeping. We haven't shared the same bed in years he admitted.

After he left, I tried to go back to sleep, thoughts of Kim were now replaced with thoughts of Ross. His amazing body, the way he made love to me was slow and passionate. He had buns of steel. I had never done so many positions before and he was a great teacher. He took his time on everything he did to me.

When I woke up and got dressed, I joined the others downstairs for breakfast. Mrs. Chapman fussed over Lance which was a normal occurrence since we'd landed. I thought for a minute that she would start feeding him. They were talking about going to visit with Roc's parents. As soon as Sidney heard Roc's name, she excused herself and went to her room. Rhonda had decided to go with them; I still didn't know why she felt the need to go. Her relationship with Roc was apparently more to her than just a few good times. Her newfound relationship with Mrs. Chapman had grown in record time, much like my relationship with her husband. I thought I heard Rhonda call her mother as they walked out the door. Tamia decided to stay behind which didn't sit well with mother Chapman. She thought that Tamia's place was always by Lance's side. It surprised me as well that Tamia didn't go. At that point I knew something was wrong.

After the three left and me and Tamia were alone, she told me her secret. She was in love with someone else and had planned on leaving Lance as soon as we returned home. She didn't say who the man was at first, but that he was the man of her dreams. I was so happy for her. The way she looked when she spoke of him said it all. She really was in love. Even in the prime of her and Lances relationship, she never had that look in her eye. I wanted to know if I knew this man, I never expected her to say Sidney Mac. I sat there stunned at the news.

Sidney Mac was indeed fine as hell, but he was Sidney's uncle. She didn't feel good about having to tell Sidney the news, but knew that she wasn't going to be able to keep it from her for much longer.

I wanted to tell her about my night with Ross, but instead told her about the drama with Kim. She sat there taking it all in and waited for me to finish before she said anything.

Wow, I can't believe she drugged you. you did it with a girl she said busting out laughing. So Deanna is really DJ's she asked?

Yea, I guess so, that's what she said.

How do you feel about that?

I'm numb. I don't really care at all.

So, you said you like it. Does that mean that you're gay now?

No, Mia I'm not gay I said raising my voice, then whispering so one would hear me. I mean, I don't think so. I enjoyed being with her I guess, from what I can remember, but I also enjoy being with men.

What was it like? She wanted to know

I can't really explain it, all I can say is that it was different than being with a man....

Wow, you've come along way, she said giggling with her eyes open wide. Are you going to forgive her?

I don't think I can.

Well, people have done worse she said. I say just live each day, and don't try to push it one way or another. Your heart will tell you which way to go.

I never expected that response from her, she had changed over the past couple weeks, normally she would have been thinking about the consequences of it all. but today she laughed and made light of the situation, I could see the change Mac bought out in her. She was so carefree, she said she felt more love with him, then she's ever felt with anyone. Including Lance.

She also told me about how Lance had been treating her the past couple of weeks. You would have never known that she had been going through that with him. On the outside, everything always looked so perfect. I have something to ask you she said

What? She had gotten so serious all of a sudden.

Did DJ ever hit you?

What? I asked surprised at the question.

Did DJ ever hit you? She asked again

I didn't know if it was even worth lying, he was dead now. Yes, Mia, he had started beating me on a regular basis.

Why didn't you tell me, I could have helped you

What could you have done? You have your own life to live

I would have never allowed him to hurt you. I would have gotten you away from him.

Up until now, I didn't know if I could survive without him. He's all I knew. I thought that a good wife stuck by her husband through the rough times.

Rough times don't mean black and blue, she said frowning. That's what I thought about Lance. That we were just going through rough time. But when a man begins to disrespect you, it will only get worse. I'm getting out before the hitting starts.

Well he's dead now, and I will never let a man do that to me again. I'm glad to see that you know when to walk away. I enjoyed being able to share my secrets with Tamia again, we haven't really talked in so long. It felt good to just come clean about my life again.

When she returned to her room to make a call, I went looking for Ross.

I found him in his office. When I walked into the huge office, he was giving orders over the phone. I stood there watching him take control and felt myself getting hot. After his call was complete. I walked over to his massive desk, and stepped out of my clothes to reveal that I was wearing no underwear of any kind. He sat there stunned at my boldness, but turned on by it as well. He came from around his desk and we made love all over that office. He bent me in ways that I never thought my body could go.

When we were done, we went for a swim and was shortly joined by Tamia. I think during our swim she figured out that something was going on between us although she didn't know what, but she kept looking at the both of us with a raised eyebrow.

After the swim, Ross went back in his office to work and me and Tamia went and got Sidney so we could go sightseeing in town. Ross let us take his jaguar. We got looks from everyone we passed. I guess everybody wanted to know who the ladies were driving around town in the Chapmans car. It was only 4oclock but we decided to stop at a bar for drinks after we went shopping at Sidney's suggestion, That seemed to be the only thing to do in the small town besides the mall. The bar only had a couple people in there, looked to be regulars. The bartender was an old white lady with missing teeth and long stringy hair, she had so many wrinkles that I just wanted to iron her. All the people in the bar looked like life had passed them by.

Lances cousin Ray came in and immediately walked to our table. He was a short little man with a big gold tooth and bad skin. he must have worked on cars all day, because he was super dirty and oily looking. Betty give me a beer and give my friends some more of what their drinking.

How yall doin? He said with a huge grin and southern drawl showing off that hideous gold tooth

Good we answered in unison.

Ms Mia, he said looking like a predator, rubbing his hands together as he spoke. You shooo is looking good today. Where is that lucky cousin of mine.

He's over with Roc's parents, she replied backing up because he'd gotten in her personal space

He let you roam these here streets without him. He aint' too bright now is he? He said as Betty bought us our drinks.

Why is that she asked?

Cuz as good as you look, I would never let you out my sight.

Oh... well we gotta go, she said getting up downing her vodka and cranberry. We'll be seeing you

I shooo hope so he said watching her walk away. I don't even think he noticed that me and Sidney were there.

We all laughed once we were back in the car, it was a good day, me and my girls were together again like old times.

We were on our way back to the Chapmans and had stopped by the gas station when Sidney had some sort of breakdown. She wouldn't let us touch her, she just kept looking around crying. All we could do was stand there and wait for her to come out of it. The more we tried to help, the louder she screamed.

After a few minutes she seemed to have come out of it. she continued to cry, but at least she wasn't screaming anymore.

Tamia was the first to talk to her on the way back.

Sidney she said, Are you going to be ok? What's up with you?

Sidney didn't' say anything, she just sat in the back seat sobbing.

Once we got to the house, Sidney went straight to the liquor cabinet with a vengeance. Lance and the others came in shortly after us. You could tell that Lance was in a foul mood, he went right to his room and slammed the door. His mother went over to Tamia and asked her to go check on him. I find that it's best to leave him alone when he's like that, she replied.

That did not sit well with her. You know dear, a wife should be there for husband no matter what she said back to her. I sat there wondering how would she know. She wasn't there for her husband.

Tamia started to say something else but went upstairs anyway, when she came back down, she joined Sidney at the liquor cabinet.

I'd checked my messages and had two from Kim telling me how much she missed me and that she loved me and wished I could find it in my heart to forgive her. the second message she was a little drunker and told me exactly how my body made her feel. I thought I would feel something other than being irritated by her. I decided to go looking for Ross, he'd become my addiction. And I was I in need for a fix.

Mother Chapman was busy babying Rhonda so I slipped out to find her husband.

He was still in his office, this time he was laying the couch.

Want some company, I said walking in locking the door behind me.

Ummmm he said, your company is always welcome.

He was dressed down in some jeans and a t-shirt, he didn't' have on shoes, just white socks. He looked like he could have easily passed for 35 years old.

He began kissing me when someone knocked on the door. Ross are you in there mother Chapman said, why is the door locked. I ran into the bathroom while he unlocked the door.

Why is this door locked Ross? She asked again

Because I didn't want to be bothered he said, now what do you want. I was surprised at how he spoke to her.

I want you to go talk to your son, he is being impossible.

You need to stop babying him and let him grow up.

That is my baby, and he is grown up and you need to go talk to him.

That boy has you and his fiancé here. What do I need to talk to him about?

He's not taking Roc's death so good. I don't know what to say to him to make him feel better

Janice, the boy just lost his best friend, let him mourn in his own way.

Have I told you lately that I can't stand you. She said

Yes you have Janice, I am well aware that you can't stand me, he replied matter of factly

Why do you have to be such a heartless bastard?

This is what you made me he said, now please leave me alone. He was so calm and handled her perfectly.

She stormed out slamming the door.

I came out the bathroom with a smile on my face not knowing what to say.

I didn't have to say anything because he came and lifted me off my feet and carried my over to the huge leather sofa. We didn't speak at all. we let our bodies do all the talking for us.

Can I ask you a question? I said once we were done and laying on the couch in each others arms.

Sure he replied, you can ask me anything you want.

Why do you stay with her?

Because it's easier than leaving her.

But neither of you are happy.

Baby, she and I have never really been happy. Sure, there were a couple of years in the beginning that weren't the worst. But after Lance grew up and she found out she couldn't have any more children. She became bitter. She blamed me for her not being able to get pregnant. I've lived my life my life this way for so long, I had forgotten what it felt like to feel this good. To be able to live like there's no tomorrow.

Is that what your doing with me? Living like there's no tomorrow I said

You got it. he said, You make me feel alive again. I love the way I can talk to you about anything. I've never had anyone make love to me the way you do. Reece, I'd forgotten how to love, I thought these feeling were long gone. What you've bought out of me is priceless. I will never forget you.

You better not, I said teasing his chest with my tongue. I'd better go, before someone realizes that I'm not around.

How would you like to go out tonight after every ones asleep?

Yes, I said quickly where are we going?

It's a surprise, he said kissing me hard.

I went back to my room to take a shower and decide which sexy outfit I would be wearing tonight. I settled on a knee length A-line summer dress that tied around my neck. It was baby blue, which was my favorite color. I took out my thongs, but didn't think I would be wearing them.

I went in Sidney's room to check on her and she was sitting in the corner crying.

Sidney, you gotta tell me what's wrong. You know you can tell me anything.

I can't cried Sidney.

Yes you can Sidney, you know I won't tell anybody and you'll feel better if you tell someone.

No I won't Reece, she said drinking some more of her drink

Well Sid, you can't continue to live like this, your drinking is out of control. What are you going to do?

I don't know she said crying harder, please leave me alone right now Reece, I don't feel so good.

I left her room feeling so bad for her, something was terribly wrong with her. and It had to be really bad that she felt she couldn't talk about it. I wondered what it could be.

I passed Lances room and he and Tamia were having a heated conversation. I knew Lance was just digging a bigger grave for himself with her. She hates arguing. And from what I got from our conversation, she was done with him anyway.

At around 2 in the morning, Ross came and got me for our outing. We drove for about 30 minutes, I was so excited to see where we would end up.

It turned out to be better than I could have imagined. He pulled up to a port on the river where there was a boat waiting for us. We sailed around the Mississippi River that night talking about our lives, dreams and regrets. We made love on every inch of that boat. It was something about making love on the water under the stars that made that night magical. I didn't think it could get any better until he laid me down and showed me that his oral game was just as good. He took me to new levels of ecstasy. That I never knew existed. It was hard for me not to fall in love with this man who was old enough to be my father.

We returned back to the house just before daybreak. As tired as I was I couldn't go to sleep. My mind was racing at a mile a minute, so I decided to take a walk in the garden. When I got out there I could hear someone talking, I went around to where I heard the voices and saw Lance and Janine in an embrace. It looked harmless enough, so I turned around about to walk in the other direction until I saw them kiss, Janine then got on her knees and started giving Lance head. He stood there gripping the back of her head with his eyes closed. I tiptoed away, up to Mia's room. When I walked in, she was fast asleep.

Mia. Mia, I repeated. Come with me, your going to love this. I whispered.

Here she was trying to stay true to him even during his abuse until she broke it off and here he is getting head in the garden. I couldn't let him do my cousin that way. She didn't deserve that.

We tiptoed through the house as quietly as we could. And just as I had seen. Janine was still on her knees pleasuring Lance.

She just looked, she didn't say a word. I stood there ready for her to bust him out, but she didn't. she just watched until Janine was done. She then smiled and walked away. When we got upstairs, she gave me a hug and said thank you for having my back and went into her room.

By the time I made it back to my room, the sun was coming up and I was exhausted. The funeral was in a couple of hours and it was sure to be a very emotional day for everyone.

Chapter 10

TAMIA

I didn't hear back from Mac last night after his visit with Sidney so I took that opportunity to pack for the trip. I was glad that I did because as soon as I woke up, I received a text from him saying that he needed to see me right away. I rushed to get dressed, me and Lance had not said a word to each other all night. I didn't know what his issue was with me now, nor did I care anymore. I was tired of trying to make it work with him.

I have to run an errand, I will meet you at the airport. I said to him before I left

We ain't even packed yet. Where do you have to go?

Oh, I am packed and I have to go get some things for the trip that I forgot. You know we're going to see your mother. I have to have everything perfect.

He couldn't argue with that, he knew how his mother was.

Why did you only pack your clothes, give me a minute and I'll go with you and we can go to the airport together, no need in taking two cars. He said it with so much attitude, it was more like he was telling me what we were about to do instead of a suggesting it.

I had had enough of his attitude, No, Lance I didn't pack your clothes, nor am I about to. You're a big boy, you can handle it.

Mia, I said we're going together.

Noooo, you need to pack, I will go do what I have to do and meet you at the airport. He was not used to the opposition that I was giving him. Normally I would have just went along with whatever he said.

Those days were over. I grabbed my luggage and walked out without another word.

When I got to Mac's he still had on his robe, this time it was red and it matched his red boxers. That man was shear perfection I thought as I entered his house. I was met with the smell of bacon, eggs and smothered potatoes. He remembered I told him that was my favorite breakfast. He only ate fruit in the morning.

I had to be at the airport by 11, so I didn't have much time.

You look amazing he said looking me over. For the trip I had chosen my black pencil shirt, lemon short sleeve button down shirt and 3 inch Jimmy Choo sandals. I'd planned to curl my hair, but didn't have the time, so I wore it straight. Which I hardly ever did. It made me look like Pocahonas.

Thank you for breakfast baby, this is great I said eating as fast as I could.

When we were done, he got serious, This trip makes me uneasy. I think I need to go.

What? What's wrong I asked stroking his face. Nooooo, you don't need to go, I'll be fine.

I need you to promise me that you'll be careful and I need to you to watch Sidney Rose.

What happened yesterday, is everything ok.

Baby, just trust me, I need you to be on your P's and Q's this weekend. Don't let her out of your sight.

What's wrong Mac, your scaring me, what's wrong with Sidney.

Baby, he said holding my hands in his, I need you to promise me that you'll stay with her. Promise me Mia he said. the look in his eye was as serious as I'd seen him.

Ok, baby, of course. I'll watch her I said.

No, baby I need you to stay with her, don't let her get away from you, especially while she's around "that boy".

Here he go with "that boy" stuff again. What does this have to do with Lance I asked.

Baby, if he'll flip out on you, then he'll flip out on her too, you know how Sidney's mouth can be. I just don't want anything to happen to her

I won't let anything happen to her I promised.

After I promised, he began kissing me. Before long, we were on the couch, his phone ringing off the hook as usual. He could tell I was getting irritated, so he cut if off.

You don't have to do that for me I said.

There is no one I want to talk to right now. I have everything I need right here. Oh and Sidney thinks she knows about us he said matter of factly.

WHAT! What did she say? I said trying to sit up.

Relax, he said laying me back down. She just noticed the looks I gave you and something about the night of the funeral. I didn't tell her anything. Although I wanted too.

I just looked at him. He knew exactly what the look meant.

Ok, ok he said I'll let you handle that. but you better hurry up, because I'm ready to shout it from the mountain top for everyone to hear.

Even Ms. Betty Boop I said joking

Especially Ms. Betty Boop he said laughing.

I looked at the clock and saw that I had to go, it was already 10:45 which would only give me 15 min. to get to the airport. Mac lived 20 minutes from the airport.

Oh shit, I said jumping up. I have to go or I'll miss my plane.

I'll be waiting for you, Mia'amore, He said, please don't forget to call me when you get there. If you don't I will be in Mississippi. Don't play with me.

I didn't know if he was joking or not, so I just laughed. He didn't

Baby do you know how this is killing me that your going to Mississippi with "that boy"

I'm going to a funeral, that's all. I'm leaving Lance I blurted out. I can't deny that I love you Sidney Mac. I don't know what is going to happen in the future, or how Sidney Rose will take it, but when I get back, I'm going to be ready to share my life with you, if you'll have me I said.

We'll tell her together he said. and Thank you

Thank you for what I said looking at the clock

Thank you for loving me. thank you for having Faith in our love. Thank you for changing your life for me.

You don't have to thank me for loving you. I changed my life for me. I wanted to love and be loved completely, not for what I am on the outside, but for who I am on the inside. Now I gotta go, I will call you when I land. Give me some of that sugar I said kissing him on my way to the door.

I can't wait to make you Mrs. Stone.

Tamia Stone, I repeated as I drove away. It had a nice ring to it.

I had made my decision. I felt so good, knowing that I'm going to do something that I want to do, not because it looked right, but because it felt right.

Me and Sidney arrived at the gate at the same time, Reece and Rhonda were already there with Lance. Reece looked great, she's lost so much weight. She had on a cute little dress and she had on makeup, something I had not seen in a long time. When I walked up to them, before I could even speak to them, Lance grabbed my hand and pulled me to the side.

I know we have been going at it lately, but we need to put that aside this weekend and go back to being the happy couple my mother expects us to be.

Lance, we're not the happy couple anymore. the only reason why I'm coming is for Roc.

Mia, mother says that every couple has problems, that don't mean we don't love each other, it just means that we have to work harder at our relationship. we need to make some adjustments.

I wanted to tell him right then that I was leaving him, but I couldn't do that right now.

This is not love Lance. Let's just get through this weekend I said, walking away.

Reece I said approaching them, you look beautiful. I'm so glad that you decided to come. When I finished hugging her and Rhonda I went over to Sid who was standing far to the side.

Hey, Sid, why are standing way over there. Come over here, we're about to board the plane.

She dragged over to where we were like each step hurt.

During the plane ride, me and Lance barely said two words to each other. I spent most of my time talking to the girls and reading.

Lance's parents met us at the airport in a stretch limousine. His mother was so excited to see Lance, me, not so much. I could tell that he had the talk with her about the wedding. Of course she would automatically think I was the cause of that. Me and Lance had agreed to tell everybody it was because of Roc's untimely death. Especially since that was the only excuse I gave him.

His father looked like an older version of him, he was very handsome, he wore an expensive three piece suit with Italian shoes, he was a large man with a body that looked to still be in good condition. He was the only one that met me with open arms. He met Reece and Sidney the same way, unlike his mother, who just spoke while she looked them up and down. She had a way of making everybody fell as though they were beneath her.

On the ride to their house, I thought about Mac. Who could have ever known that a couple of weeks ago I would be hopelessly in love with Sidney Mac Stone. Sidney's beloved uncle. I couldn't wait to get somewhere so I could call him. I know he was waiting for my call and if he hadn't heard from me, he would surely be calling me. I still wondered what happened when he went to Sidney Rose's house. The look on his face when he asked me to watch her said that he was very worried about something. I can remember a time when I would be the one that knew all of Sidney's secrets, I could feel that we were drifting apart. I just hoped that when she found out about me and Mac that she would be able to accept it and we could still remain close. I also knew that I would have to accept it if she didn't. I was going to be with Sidney Mac no matter what.

Lance held my hand as we walked through his parents house, I couldn't bare his touch anymore, when no one was looking I let go. I didn't know if I was going to able to keep up this act for 3 whole days.

After we ate, Lance's father was all to eager to show the girls to their room. We had discussed going to a hotel, but he wouldn't hear of it. Their house had more than enough room for us all, he said. It'll be a welcome change to have some life in this house again. Mother Chapman was not all happy with that arrangement. She smiled and excused herself to the other room when they walked away.

We settled into Lance's old room, that they had redecorated since our last visit. I expected to see all of Lance's old childhood in that room, but his mother had another idea in mind for what that room should look like. Lance had a fit when he saw it. He stormed off yelling his mothers name. I took that opportunity to make my call.

Hey baby, I was starting to worry about you Mac said.

Hi, we're fine, we're getting settled in.

What hotel will you all be staying at he asked.

Well, actually we're going to be staying at Lance's parents house.

WHAT! He said

Well, when we told them that we were going to a hotel, they insisted that we stay here.

I don't like this Mia.

I know you don't baby, it'll be ok

Mia, I don't like this, please remember to watch out for Sidney Rose.

I will Mac, I promised you I would I said.

I miss you already he said in a much calmer tone.

I miss you already too.

I meant what I said, say the word and I will be there in a heartbeat.

I'll be home in a couple of days. I heard Lance and his mother outside the bedroom door, so I told Mac that I had to call him later.

He sounded so sad, but told me he loved me, then hung up. I wanted that man so bad it hurt at this point. Just as I was about to go meet up with the girls, Lance came back in the room, heated.

How could she change my room. He screamed. It's like I didn't even exist here. How could she do that to me.

Was he serious I thought. He was really having a temper tantrum about his mother changing his room. Lance I don't think she meant anything by it. she was just redecorating. I'm sure she didn't throw your things away.

That's not the point Tamia, he said looking at me, why do you always have to try to make light of everything.

Well I'm just trying to help Lance.

Why don't you shut up. I didn't ask for your help Tamia, I need your support

Support for your mother changing your room, how much support do you need for that. Grow up I said walking out.

I joined the girls out by the pool of their house, we sat and talked while drinking wine. It felt just like old times. Some of Lance's family and the neighbors that he grew up with came over, including Roc's sister Janine.

She was a tall slender girl, looked to be about 22. She was a prettier version of Roc, They were the same color and had the same big forehead. She was very friendly and like Sidney loved to party.

When Sidney came back outside and saw her, she cried even before she knew who she was. I hadn't realized how much Roc meant to Sidney until that moment. Me and Rhonda went to her trying to calm her down, people were starting to get concerned with her emotional outburst. Reece had went into the house about an hour ago and had not returned. I assumed she went for a nap after all the drinks we had consumed.

Lance and Janine seemed to be in deep conversation, I figured they were talking about Roc. Revenge seemed to be all Lance could talk about.

I slipped away again and called Mac, we ended up talking for an hour, until everyone had left and I heard Lance talking on his phone towards the room.

He was nice and drunk by the time he got there. Here we go, I thought. I tried to turn my back and make him think I sleep, but he didn't care.

Mia, he said shaking me, wake up. I need to talk to you.

What is it Lance I said turning around.

We need to start working on having a baby, he said.

What? A baby. What are you talking about now. This was sounding like the commands of his mother

We need to have a baby and I want to start working on it right away.

Your even more drunk than I thought.

What do you mean by that?

I'm not about to get pregnant because now you think you want a baby now.

My mother said that we need to start working on our family right away.

Oh, your mother said huh. Well if she wants to have a baby, she better get started.

What's your problem, we knew that we were going to have children. Why don't you want to have a baby with me all of a sudden?

Why should I Lance, to be honest with you, I don't want to do anything with you right now, less and only have a baby. One minute your yelling at me calling me names and the next you want to start a family. Your even crazier than I thought

What the fuck do you mean by that, he yelled

I mean that I won't be told when to have a baby by you or your mother. I don't even know what our future holds. Lance let's just get through the weekend ok.

Our future? What the hell are you talking about now, he said

I didn't' know what to say to that. I didn't want to lie, but I didn't want to end it this way before the funeral.

You hear me talking to you. He came around to my side of the bed and grabbed my arm. Let me make this easy for you. You ain't goin nowhere. You can get that shit out of your head right now. And mother said we need to get married as planned and I agree.

I don't care what your mother said, Let me go. We're not getting married on that day. We, meaning; you and I agreed to post-pone the wedding. Yo mamma ain't got nothing to do with this.

Mother has a lot invested in this wedding and she would rather not have to change all her plans.

Lance, I'm gonna need you to grow a pair, and let your mother know that we will not be getting married in two weeks. And that's it. and I promise if you put your hands on me again, it will be the last person you grab.

What makes you think this wedding is only about you. I've had enough of you telling me what your not going to do. And as far as your little promise, I will do whatever I want to you. We're in this for the long haul.

I've had enough of your temper tantrums. Just stay away from me.

Your going to regret talking to me that way.

Oh so, you threatening me now, I said becoming very irritated with this conversation.

Me and Lance went at it for about another hour before going to sleep.

That is until Lance thought he was about to get some. He started kissing me from behind. I laid there trying to play sleep, until he started trying to suck on my breast. Lance you have got to be kidding me, why are you touching me?

Baby, it's been awhile, I need this. don't you need some too? He whined

Lance, I don't care what you need. I'm not in the mood and…you make me sick. Now please get away from me.

Why don't you need some? You been screwing somebody else?

Lance, leave me alone I said getting fed up with his mouth

Who have you been with Mia, you better tell me

I haven't been with anyone ok. I screamed now leave me the hell alone.

Lance just stood there looking at me, he then got up and left the room and never returned.

The next afternoon after me and girls got back. Reece disappeared again. So I took that opportunity to talk to Sidney, she had just flipped out on us at the gas station and she was now drinking like there was no tomorrow.

Before I had a chance to talk to her, Mother Chapman called me in her study to have a "heart to heart".

She began by telling me that all couples go through their problems and that she'd heard us fighting last night.

I wondered how she managed to do that when her bedroom was on the other side of the huge house. I just sat there listening to her go on and on about how a good wife is seen and not heard. I wanted to shout to her that I'd had enough of her spoiled son and they could take that wedding she was planning and shove it where the sun don't shine. She then said that appearances are everything in her world and finding the perfect wife for Lance was not easy. I suddenly got the impression we were getting married because she said we should. Were we I thought. Would Lance had proposed if his mother hadn't told him too? Now I think we need to reconsider postponing the wedding.

Mother Chapman, I've given this a lot of thought and I just don't think now is the time for us to get married with everything going on with Roc and all.

What happened to Roc was bound to happen the way that boy lived his life. I'm surprised it took this long. We all knew that this day would happen. I don't see why we can't try to make light of situation with a beautiful wedding. She said

Well Lance is not taking Roc's death very well, I said and I don't think he's ready for anything else life changing right now.

Dear, I know what's best for my son, and what's best right now is for him to get married and began working on a family.

I'd had enough, she was relentless. I stood up and said Mother Chapman, I understand how you feel, but me and Lance have decided to put the wedding off and we're not going to change our minds. And with that I left the room.

I went looking for Sidney to have that talk with her but she was sleep.

Mother Chapman later on insisted that I go calm Lance down after his visit with Roc's parents. Little did she know that I was not about to go anywhere near Lance right then. I went outside in the back yard and called Mac instead.

When I did go up to the room Lance was not there. Thank goodness I thought, I had zero patience left for him and his mother. I called and talked to Mac until I went to sleep.

Reece came and got me in the middle of the night saying she had my out and I was going to love this. I didn't know what she meant but I was eager to find out. She had come out of her shell so much over the past few days, I had never seen her happier. Earlier while we were swimming with Lance's dad, I couldn't help feeling like a third wheel. I think he may have a little crush on Reece. who could blame him, being married to mother Chapman had to be a living hell. She was so frigid.

I had no idea that I would be looking at Lance receive head from Janine, Roc's sister. I was stunned, although I had no intention of continuing a relationship with him, how dare he. I hadn't slept with Mac out of respect for him and here he was cheating on me, while I was right up stairs. Talk about your disrespect. Reece was right, this was my out. I just walked away and went back to my room, I'd decided to hold onto that piece of information. Even though I was sure that I loved Mac and wanted to spend my life with him. Seeing Lance and Janine kinda hurt. For the first time in a long time, I cried. Maybe it was because I knew that the Lance era was over for good.

The next morning while getting ready for the funeral I went back to me and Lance's argument the other night when he asked me about a baby, Sidney rose, is pregnant I said out loud., She was so moody lately and she slept all the time, although that could be from the drinking, but she was obviously going through something heavy and what could be heavier than that. After I dressed in my black Donna Karen suit and new Prada heels I had just purchased, I ran to her room. She was in the bathroom vomiting. I knew it I said. that girl is pregnant.

When she walked out of the bathroom, I could tell she had been crying. She walked up to me and hugged me so tight, I messed up Mia, she said. I don't know what to do. I'm losing my mind.

I think your pregnant Sid, why don't we go get a test
I don't think I can go to the funeral she blurted out.
Why?, it'll be ok. I'll be right by your side I said rubbing her back.
I just can't go she said crying running into the bathroom to vomit again.

After talking her into going to the funeral, we joined the others. I had to admit that Lance looked so handsome in his suit. Even if I did hate him, he still looked good enough to eat. Janine had proved that.

The biggest surprise was Rhonda, she usually wore something short and tight everywhere she went, but today she had on a knee length black dress that wasn't even tight. Her hair was pinned up in French roll and she had on very little makeup. She looked very mature. You could tell that it was the work of Mother Chapman. They had spent a lot of time together. I think Mother Chapman missed having someone to fuss over and she was never able to have the girl she wanted to complete her perfect family. Rhonda was now that missing link, and she did not mind. It was a definite upgrade from her real mother. Don't you look nice Ms. Rhonda I told her. Thanks Mia, she said sounding like a little girl.

Reece walked in behind Mr. Chapman looking flushed. He looked very handsome as well, if I didn't know he was Lance's father, I would thought he was one of his friends. He looked more alive today then I had ever seen him. He smiled and tried make light conversation on our way to the church.

It was a closed casket, Roc's body was found days after he was killed and with the heat in the room, he had begun to decompose. Roc's father stood up to say a couple of words, and I guess it was the fact that Roc was the spitting image of his father that made Sidney faint.

We were in the limo when she woke up. The funeral was still in progress so we were alone in the car. She looked around trying to remember what happened, I told her she'd fainted.

Mia, you have to promise me that what I am about to tell you that you will never repeat it.

I won't Sidney, you know that.

Promise me Mia.

I promise, what is it? I said anxious to find out her secret.

I killed him, she said with her head held down. I didn't mean to she said as she began her story crying.

When she was done, I just sat there not able to believe what I'd just heard. I didn't know how to respond. What could I say? She was the one Lance spent all his time looking for.

She told me how she had been seeing his face everywhere she looked and about the money she went to his apartment to retrieve. She told me about two men that were there looking for Roc. When she was finished her story, the others were getting back in the car. Lance was noticeably shook up, tears were running down his face the entire way to the grave site. I felt so sorry for him, he was truly hurting at the loss of his friend. Sidney sat stone faced and passed on getting out the car when we reached the graveyard. I was eager to get some of the questions I had for Sidney answered and couldn't wait to get back to the house. That was the last thing in the world I expected was wrong with Sidney. She had been going through her own personal hell behind this. I thought about my own situation and thought how she was the cause of Lance's breakdown as well which aided in the demise of our relationship. I knew that I had to get her out of that house. I didn't think she would make it one more night before she had a total breakdown.

When we got back to the house, everyone went and changed so they could go to the family's house for dinner. The only ones who really ended up going was Lance, his mother and Rhonda again. Reece said she was exhausted and needed a nap and Mr. Chapman said he would join them later, he had a conference call he needed to make. As soon as they were gone, I got on the phone and tried to change our plane tickets to leave that night instead of the next morning. When I told Reece of our plans, she seemed extremely disappointed. she didn't understand the sudden need to leave early. I told her that Sidney was really sick and needed to go home.

Rhonda is gone with them she said, I can't leave without her. It's just a couple more hours she said, Sidney can make it a couple of hours can't she?

I didn't know the answer to that question. I didn't think a couple of hours would make a difference but who was to say. all I knew was that, I missed Mac, I wanted him to hold me and tell me that everything would be fine. I needed to feel his body against mine, and I too was ready to leave. I didn't know if I could take one more night with Lance each conversation led to him being more violent. And especially after seeing him with Janine and now with the knowledge that my best friend killed his. I was just ready for this trip to be over.

Chapter 11

SIDNEY ROSE

I didn't know how I was going to get through the funeral, I saw Roc's face everywhere in Mississippi. It didn't help that his sister looked just like him. I saw myself about to faint when she walked into the Chapmans house. I had tried to avoid Lance since we'd been there. I knew that something was going on with him and Mia, because I never saw them together since we'd gotten there.

Reece often disappeared throughout the day I didn't know what she was up too. She seemed like a new woman. She'd lost all that weight and her hair looked better than ever. She was even dressing differently. Who knew that her husbands death would be her rebirth. I was happy to see her so happy. She deserved it.

While we were at a gas station the day before the funeral, not only did I see Roc's face, but he spoke to me. He said that I would never get away with killing him. I had decided right then that I would not be going to the funeral, if he was talking to me at a gas station. What would he say at his home going services.

The more I drank, the more the guilt got to me. I needed to smoke a blunt, but left everything at home. For my nausea, I tried to drink and drink until I threw up and passed out.

The day of the funeral when I told Mia that I couldn't go, she insisted that I should and that everything would be ok. I knew she knew that something was going on with me, she came in my room that morning and wanted me to take a pregnancy test. Although I had thought about that, I wasn't ready to know for sure. I had to get through this trip.

At the funeral, just as I suspected Roc was everywhere, he even got up and spoke. The next thing I remembered was waking up in a limo laying in Mia's lap while she wiped my head with a wet cloth. I couldn't keep it from her anymore. I had to tell her and deal with the outcome. With Mia, you never know how she's going to react to something. She's usually so straight and narrow in her box, that she didn't understand things outside of it. When I finished with my story, she just sat there. She didn't say I was wrong or that I should turn myself in. She just held my hand and told me everything would be ok. She and Roc had a special friendship and I know that his death affected her as well. I got the feeling that she wanted to talk to me about something else, but everyone came back to the limo to go to the gravesite.

By that time, I had had enough, there was no way I was getting out that car to face Roc again.

Mia wanted to leave after the funeral, but after talking to Reece we ended up staying there until the next morning. I still don't remember Mia ever saying a word to Lance the entire day. Something told me she was more ready to leave than I was if that was at all possible. She only briefly hugged his mother and father before walking out carrying her own bags. Which was something I had never seen her do before, especially in the company of men not to mention the house staff.

When we landed Mia told me that she would meet me at my house after she took care of some business. She got there an hour later with a pregnancy test in hand.

My worst fear, outside of going to jail for murder, was now confirmed. I was in fact pregnant.

Tamia was the one who read me the results. She tried to cheer me up once she saw the look on my face. She had been great, she never left my side during our entire trip to Mississippi She had proven to me time and time again that she really was my best friend, and one of the most important people in my life. And telling her about Roc was one of the best things I could have done for myself, I hadn't seen Roc's face but once since we'd gotten home.

My first thought was go have an abortion, how was I going to have a baby, when I didn't even know who the father was. I may have killed him. Roc never used condoms and could have easily been the father. This is not the right time, I said to Mia, I can't a baby right now. I'm a mess.

Well she answered, there's nothing like a baby, to put a new spin on things.

I don't need a spin. I need a blunt to take away this nausea.

She thought I was joking and started laughing, but when her phone went off, she left in a hurry and I rolled a blunt. This time I threw up after I smoked. Maybe it's not working anymore I thought.

As I walked back into my living room, my phone rang. it was Terry. I had really missed him. We had gotten closer before I left and I called him every day on the trip, when I wasn't sleep or sick. We discussed moving in together again, and this time I agreed. I didn't have Rickey anymore, Roc was dead and it felt good to know that somebody still wanted me.

Hi baby I said answering the phone.

Hey, how are you? When did you get home?

Just now, Are you at work I asked. I really wanted to see him. I needed somebody to hold me. I thought about telling him I was pregnant, but decided to wait until I was sure of what I was going to do about it.

Yea, I'm at work right now, but I can come over in the morning when I get off if you want me too.

Before I could answer him the door bell rang.

Let me call you back I said to Terry, there's someone at my door.

When I opened it, Rickey stood there looking so good. He had on some Sean john jeans with a t-shirt to match. He had grown a gotee on his face and had a diamond earring in his ear, since when did he get his ear pierced I thought. It made me wonder who had upgraded him.

Hi, he said when he saw me.

Hi. Yourself

Can I come in?

Sure I said moving out the way for him to come in, he smelled so good, but his drakkar noir was making me nauseous.

We just looked at each other for a few minutes not knowing what to say. He was the first to break our silence. I came by yesterday but you weren't here.

Yea, I said I went to Roc's funeral with Tamia.

Roc was a sore subject with us, I hated having to tell him that I went to his funeral.

Yea, Lancetold me about that, did they find out who did it? he asked

I...I...I don't think so, I stuttered.

How have you been, you look good, he said

I'm fine. You look good too. Look Rickey I'm sorry about everything. I don't blame you for leaving me.

We sat down and had a real conversation for the first time about our relationship.

He got up and went to the bathroom and came out holding my pregnancy test. My eyes grew to the size of grapefruits. Rickey had the least chance of being this baby's father. We hadn't had much sex the past couple months.

So your pregnant?, he asked

I thought about lying telling him it was Tamia's test, but we were here because of all the lies.

Yea, it looks like it I said lowering my head.

That's great Sidney, I always wanted to be a father he said coming over and hugging me.

Baby everything is going to be alright, I'm sorry I left you. I love you and don't want to break up our family.

Our family I thought, he had to be wondering if it was his. I was so caught up with the fact that he wanted to come home that I just went with it.

But then I started to think about Terry, how could I tell him that it was over? I had a lot of thinking to do and I needed for Rickey to not be there while I did so.

Rickey I do love you, but when you left me, I went through a lot this past week. I realized that I needed to figure out some things. And now that I'm pregnant I need to think some things over about my future and the future of this child if I decide to keep it.

If, he said, what do you mean if?

I mean I don't know if I'm ready to be a mother, I've got a lot of growing up to do. I just found out about the baby myself, I need time Rickey.

I understand, but I want you to know that I am going to be for you every step of the way and you don't have to do this alone. I love you and I miss us he said kissing me.

When he left, I sat on the couch and began to think about my life. I reached for a bottle of vodka that I had on my table and poured me a drink. I sat the glass on the table and just looked at it. I thought about all the liquor I had consumed over the past month and how that may have affected my baby. My baby, I thought, was I really going to do this. Could I really be a mother? As I sat there looking at the liquor filled glass waiting on me to drink it, I saw the image of the cutest little baby girl. I realized that I now had something of my own. I lived in Tamia's house, what furniture she didn't buy, Rickey had. I drove a car that used to be my fathers.

The only thing I really owned were my jewelry and clothes. The thought of someone who would love me no matter what made me feel good. Someone always had to take care of me for one reason or another. It would be nice to have to take care of someone else for a change.

In the hours that I sat there in the now dark house. I had decided that I wanted my baby more than anything. I went and poured the drink that still sat on the table down the drain. I followed it with the rest of the liquor in the bottle. I was done with drinking, I had a baby to take care of.

I now had to decide if I wanted to share my life with Rickey. I knew if I did, then I would have to let Terry go. I was tired of juggling men. If I was honest with myself I did like them both, but I didn't really love either of them. They were both great guys. But when it was all said and done, Rickey was my rock.

I figured that if Rickey was willing to accept this child then I was willing to offer Rickey all of me this time, no tricks or other men.

In the weeks to follow, I did a lot of praying and soul searching. I continued to wake up throwing up. but it didn't even bother me that much now that I knew why. I'd went to the doctor and found out that I was further along than I thought. I only had 6 months left to prepare for my new little life. My entire way of thinking had changed, I'd finally stopped smoking and chose to eat crackers or lemon drops for my nausea. Since I stopped drinking I didn't see Roc's face anymore. I still felt guilty for killing him, but I had to realized that it was either him or me that night. I now had something more to live for. And I refused to let Roc control me anymore.

With the money I'd gotten from Roc, I redid my entire house. I bought all new furniture I decorated everything the way I wanted it to look When I was done and took a look around, I was pleased with my work. it was colorful and bright This house now said Sidney Rose.

Rickey called several times aday to check on me. He was ready to move back in and didn't understand why I still needed time.

I'd called Terry and told him that it was over and that I was changing my life and that I really did think he was a great guy, but I didn't think it would be fair to him to wait for me to get my act together. He told me he knew about the baby. I was about to ask him how he found out, but he bumbared me with questions.

How far along was I? Was it his? He even went as far as saying he wanted to marry me.

I told him that I needed time and space to wrap my head around this, but that I was sure that I didn't love him the way he deserved to be loved. He told me that if this baby was his, he wanted to be a part of his or her life. I promised him that I would call him in a couple of days. He would not have let me get off the phone without that promise.

I talked to Reece and told her about the baby, she was so excited for me. she told me that Rhonda planned on transferring to Mississippi state and was going to live with the Chapmans. Nobody saw that coming. But thought it was what Rhonda needed and she could have done worse than a rich surrogate mother figure. She always had Tamia's mom, but with Mother Chapman, she was like an only child, the baby girl she was never able to have.

Several weeks later when Rickey came by for dinner, he got down on one knee and proposed to me. This time I accepted. who was I kidding, I wasn't ready to have this baby alone.

Lance called almost daily looking for Tamia, she wouldn't accept any of his calls, she left him as soon as we returned from Mississippi. I'd asked her if she wanted to move back in with me like old times, but she said she had it covered. I assumed she was going to move into the house her and Lance had built. He refused to accept that she wanted nothing to do with him and he was now drinking heavily on a daily basis. He came over and helped Rickey move his things back in and he looked like a totally different person. He smelled like a distillery, His stomach that was once a six pack was now buldging out of his shirt. He's shaved his head bald and had let his facial hair grow into a full beard.

Although I felt sorry for him, I still didn't' like him and knew he still didn't care for me. Mia told me what he'd done with Roc's sister and how he treated her since Roc's death. I couldn't help but to wonder if I was the reason they broke up. if I never killed Roc, would they still be together? Since I didn't have anything to do with him and Roc's sister, I let that guilt go as well. She seemed to be dealing with it very well, she almost seemed happier lately. When he came or called I immediately got Rickey so I wouldn't have to deal with him at all. He told me he was glad me and Rickey had gotten back together and were going to have a baby. I think he really did mean that.

I was now showing and could no longer hide the fact that I was pregnant. Me and Rickey went shopping together for the first time for maternity clothes. He was so happy that we were going to be having a baby. and now, so was I.

I had finally got around to telling my mother that I was pregnant and about to get married. You would have thought she hit the lottery. Me and my mom were never close, but I'd planned on changing that, she wasn't getting any younger. My father's new wife had had a baby boy, I even went over their house to take little Pete Jr. a gift. They were both surprised especially when they saw my stomach.

My dad liked Rickey, he said he as a stand up guy. He was all too happy when I told him about us getting married. It was weird seeing my dad holding that baby, but I was happy that he'd found love.

On my way home, I stopped by Reece's house. She came to the door half dressed and out of breath, I looked past her into her house to see none other than Mr. Chapman, Lance's father. That would explain all the disappearing acts when we were in Mississippi. Before I judged her I turned around and told her to call me later. I would look forward to this story.

On my way home, I thought about how we'd put Lance through the ringer. I killed his best friend, Reece is sleeping with his father and Tamia left him high and dry.

I would be nicer to him the next time he stopped by, I decided. He'd had no idea the damage me and my girls put on him.

I couldn't wait to call Mia and tell her about her almost father in law. He sure was fine, if I hadn't been in my own personal hell that weekend I probably would have set out to sleep with him. But what was he doing here I thought and how long had he been here and what happened with Mrs. Chapman. were they still together? So many questions I thought. Since I no longer had daily drama going on, getting into someone elses was right up my alley.

That was until I stopped by my mother's house for one of my weekly visits to check on her.

We were sitting at the kitchen table eating some Fish, greens, macaroni and cheese and potato salad she'd made. I always left there 2 pounds heavier. When she said Sidney, there is something I need to tell you.

I thought it was about her new boyfriend she thought no one knew about.

Baby, Sidney Mac is your father not Pete. She blurted out

Mamma, what did you say. I couldn't believe my ears. What do you mean? I asked

Baby when me and your father first got married, he was never around, he was always in the streets. When I caught him with Lisa Reed I was distraught, I thought I would die. Your uncle Sidney was there for me. and we slept together. It was just that once, but I got pregnant. I never told your father about me and Sidney, at the time, he wasn't even an adult yet, and I knew what I had done was wrong. I wanted to again when he insisted I name you Sidney, but I just couldn't, he was so proud to have a beautiful daughter. He began to stay home, and he begun to be the husband I always wanted. I knew if I told him that you weren't his, he would hate me and your Uncle Sidney. We were all he had and I couldn't do that to him.

I thought I would be sick as I sat there listening to the story of my life. Everything I had known about my family was now in question. Did you tell Uncle Sidney that he was my father.

She just sat there quiet for a long time and finally said, yes baby, he's known from the beginning. He always wanted to tell you, but I wouldn't let him. It would have just killed your father.

My father I said. you mean my uncle I screamed. How could you keep this from me. how could you do this to daddy, I mean uncle I mean daddy. I don't know who I am anymore. at that moment I hated her. I wanted nothing more to do with her. I ran to the bathroom, the lunch I had just eaten was ready to make a quick exit.

When I came back out the bathroom, she was crying with her head down on the table. It was then that I realized how hard this has been for her all these years to keep this from me. maybe this was the reason, she was never able to look me in my face. I always thought it was because I reminded her of the husband she'd lost. I looked at her pain and it was then that I realized how much she meant to me. I guess becoming a mother soon myself. I was able to put myself in her shoes. if this baby wasn't Rickey's, would I tell him? That was a question I was soon going to have to deal with. Seeing the outcome of all the lies, made me think twice.

I guess that would explain why I look just like him huh? I said trying to break the ice with my mother

She got up and came over to hug me. It was the longest most meaningful hug she'd ever given me. We both cried.

When I left there, I went over my Uncle's house, or my daddy's house, this was going to take some getting used to I thought.

Mia's car was out in the driveway when I got there. What was she doing there I thought.

When he came to the door, and I stepped in I got my next big shock of the day. He was half dressed and flushed. Mia was on the sofa the same way.

Sid, let me explain she said getting up.

Before she could finish, Uncle Sid said Sidney Rose, I am in love with Tamia, and we're getting married, I know this a shock to you, but I need you to accept this.

Oh, accept it like accepting that you're my father, I screamed

You would have thought the h bomb was just lit, the way both of their faces changed.

What do you mean, your father? Mia asked

Oh, yea well your in love and about to marry my dad. She said matter of factly.

Who told you he said.

You knew she yelled.

Baby, calm down he said going over to her. let me explain

Yes explain how you knew all this time that you were my father and still managed to fall in love with my best friend. And Mia, how could you, you of all people you knew how much he meant to me.

I'm sorry Sid, I wanted to tell you so many times she said. I never planned to feel this way about him.

So your in love with him?

She shook her head like it killed her to do so.

I can't believe this shit, I said running to my car. I needed to get out of there and wrap my head around all the information I learned today.

Chapter 12

REECE

It was hard leaving Ross, we had said our goodbyes the night after the funeral. When everyone went to Roc's parents for dinner. Mia was ready to go back to Atlanta that night, but there was no way I was leaving there without a proper goodbye from my weekend lover.

I'm going to miss this I said when we finished making love. He was kissing down my back and said, you have no idea how much I'm going to miss you.

Maybe I could come to Atlanta for a visit, would you like that? He asked

Ross, yes I would very much I said, happy that this was just not a weekend thing for him. I didn't know if you could fall in love with someone over a weekend, but I was very smitten with this married man. I didn't want the weekend to be over.

After I got back home, and went and picked up my son. I got a call from Kim. She wanted to come over and talk. Even though I missed her friendship, I still couldn't get over the fact that not only did she keep such a big lie from me, but that she would drug me to have sex with me. I couldn't trust her. I knew that. it would never be the same with us again. Besides that, I was now sure that I wasn't gay. The time I spent with Ross made me realize that. I wondered if he had any idea how much this weekend really meant to me.

After I took a long bubble bath and put Lil D down to bed, he called. I was so excited to see his name come up on my caller id I almost missed answering it.

We talked for about 2 hours. He told me how much he missed me since I'd left and that he would coming to Atlanta sooner than he'd planned. That was the best news I had heard all day.

The next week when I got back from my walk with Lil D, my mother was sitting on my porch. What do she want I thought to myself as walked up to the house.

Hey mamma, I said irritated what are you doin here?

Do I need an excuse to come see my daughter and my grandson she said picking up Lil D. he didn't like the fact that this strange frail women had picked him up, so he started crying right away.

Mamma, he don't know you I said taking him out of her arms.

She handed him over with a sad look on her face. She appeared to be clean but who could tell with her.

Do you wanna come in? I asked, I was just about to make some lunch.

As we sat and ate, we talked. It had been so long since I'd had a normal conversation with her without her asking for more money that I'd forgotten how nice it was.

I talked to your sister. She called me and told me exactly how she felt about me. I always thought that once I got clean, that I would just be able to step right back into her life and be her mother again.

Well mamma, it'll take time, you hurt us, and Rhonda is stubborn just like you are.

Did she tell you she was moving to Mississippi to live with her ",mother" she said putting up the quote fingers.

Yes, I said I talked to her yesterday, and she told me all about her plans.

She went on and on about how rich they were and how much she's learned from her in such a short time. She said this Mrs. Chapman or whoever she is is going to pay for her entire college education. Why would this lady do that for a girl she just met?

I don't know mamma, they was together the whole weekend. I think Mrs. Chapman just needs somebody to take care of. and to be honest with you, Rhonda needs that. So I'm happy for her.

How could say you happy for your sister moving with a family she hardly even knows. What if those folks is crazy?. She said that the woman's married. What if he's some sort of pervert.

Pervert, your worried about him being a pervert, all the men that you had coming in and out of our house all the time. My first experience with man was given to me by someone you trading me for, a hit. At this point, I was screaming and about to start crying, Momma please don't get me started with you today. He's not a pervert I said thinking about Ross and the way he makes me feel. That made me smile.

What are you smiling for she asked.

Nothing, I replied coming back to reality, their nice people, and their richer than anybody I've ever known. Let's not forget that she's an adult now. If Rhonda wants to move there, then I'm happy for her.

What's gotten in you girl? You used to be so protective of yo sister. Now you willin to just give her to some family in Mississippi just because they got money.

Mamma, that's not why I'm happy for her, I love my sister, I always have, I was the one there for her since day one. Let's not forget. But that's just it, I'm her sister, and she's grown now. You gave us away, to Auntie Marie. And although she was the best aunt in the world, she still wasn't our mother. Rhonda has found a connection with this lady. She is the mother Rhonda always wanted and needed since you weren't there.

How could you be so cold Reece. I has a sickness, I never wanted to get rid of you and yo sister, going to live with Marie was the best thang I could have done for yall. Because I loved yall both so much.

Well mamma that was the chance you took. I don't mean to be cold to you or hurt your feelings, but this is a chance for Rhonda to be happy and to have something she never had. Your going to just have to live with that, the same we had to live with you leaving us.

My phone rang, and I saw that it was Ross. Excuse me mamma, I got to take this I said going into my bedroom to answer the phone. Ross told me that he just landed in Atlanta and was about to rent a car and would be on his way over. The inside of my stomach was doing the cha cha, I had to get ready. I was so sweaty from my walk and I had to get rid of mamma. I gave him the directions to my house and hung up.

When I went back into the living room, mamma was gone. I felt bad for her, but couldn't worry about that now, I had a lot to do to get ready for Ross.

I ran throughout the house trying to clean up, his house was so beautiful, I now felt like mine was a dump, even with all the redecorating I'd just done. Lil D followed me around the house messing up as he went along. I sat him in his hi-chair, gave him some cheerios, turned on the Disney channel and went to get dressed.

I didn't want to look like I was trying to hard, so I just put on a short, thin sleeveless grey dress. It made me look comfortable, but sexy.

When he got there, he swept me off my feet with a huge hug. I missed you he said coming in.

I missed you too I said giving him a long kiss. I missed those lips. He looked so good. He had on another one of his famous expensive suits, it was a dark grey color and he had on a deep red shirt button down shirt with a very nice tie that had red and grey in it.

He looked up and saw Lil D looking at him and immediately went over to his chair.

I think Lil D missed his daddy because he took to Ross right away. The look of them playing made my heart melt. I know my baby didn't understand where his father was, one minute he was there and the next he wasn't.

I like your house, he said walking around taking everything in.

That means a lot coming from you I said. your house is so amazing. It makes my house look like shack.

Don't say that, I love your house. He said hugging me from behind.

After I made dinner, we ate and put Lil D down for bed. We both couldn't wait to make love, the looks we gave each at dinner were electric.

We made love like it was our first time. We weren't sneaking, we weren't rushing we could just took our time and let our bodies get reacquainted.

It was the first time that we could wake up together and him not having to leave. After making love once more in the morning, we showered together. I washed him and he washed me and of course, we had amazing shower sex.

Lil D had taken to Ross so much that he wanted to be with him all the time. I knew how my son felt because I too wanted to be with Ross all the time.

We didn't even get dressed that day, we just laid around talking and relaxing and playing with Lil D who was having the time of his life.

Do you know how long it's been since I've been on any kind of vacation he said while we were watching a movie. I forgot what it felt like to just sit around like this.

Well I'm glad that your sitting around with us I said kissing him.

Let's go on a real vacation, to an island. How about Hawaii? He said, or Maui, or Aruba, he said getting excited.

That sounds great, I'd go anywhere with you, just say the word.

The word, he said laughing. Let's go next month.

I didn't want to put a damper on the day by mentioning the Mrs, but I had to know.

What is Mrs. Chapman going to say about all these trips of yours.

She's so happy that she has your sister there. I don't think she even realizes that I'm gone he said with a hearty chuckle.

We were making out on the couch when the door bell rang. it was Sidney I didn't mean to open the door so wide, but she saw Ross, the look on her face was priceless. I cracked up when she almost ran her pregnant butt back to her car. I knew I would be getting a call from her later. I thought that Ross would be upset that someone saw him there, but he wasn't he laughed when he saw her hightell it outta there like I did.

I told him that I thought he would have been upset, but he said he was not ashamed of being of me. That night he told me that he was falling in love with me.

I was happy and relieved at the same time, I thought it was just me that had fallen hard.

You don't know how happy I am to hear that, I told him.

I wanted to tell you in Mississippi, but I didn't want to come on too strong. And risk scaring you away.

I wanted to tell you too, I said but I didn't want to run you away

Ross stayed for three more days, we did everything in those three days. We took Lil D to the zoo and to the aquarium, we went shopping; he bought me everything I saw that I liked. Never in my life had a man taken me shopping.

He bought so many things for Lil D that he was going to be straight on toys and clothes for months, maybe even years.

I've been driving around in DJ's dope mobile since his death. it was a big tinted black Lincoln. It was nice, but it wasn't me at all. When Ross saw it, he frowned and told me he didn't like me in such a flashy car and bought me a new one.

I had never had a brand new car before all to myself. It was a little red convertible Bmw. He said that it matched me a lot better. I felt like I was in a fairy tale the whole day. At one point I just knew I was about to wake up and this would have been a dream.

When we got home from our full day and put Lil D down to bed, I thanked him properly for all he'd done for us. While we were in the middle of pleasing each other, my door bell rang.

I started not to answer it but whoever it was sat out there ringing the bell for like ten minutes. I snatched my rode off the back of the door and went to the door, not appreciating the interruption.

Kim stood at the door looking pissed off.

I just looked at her waiting for her to tell me what she was going there so late.

Why haven't you returned any of my calls? She asked

Kim, I can't get into this right now.

Why not? Do you have company or something she asked?

Well, I don't think that's any of your business I said ready to go and finish what I'd started with Ross.

It is my business, I love you.

Kim, this is not going to work between us I finally said.

What do you mean, I know you love me too she said, tears coming down her eyes

Kim, no I really don't. What you did to me I just can't get over it. I don't think I could ever trust you again.

I told you I was sorry, she whined

Kim I said interrupting her little speech, I have to go now, you take care of yourself.

Oh so it's like that she yelled. She went from 2 to 10

Ross came from the bedroom to see what all the yelling was about.

Kim looked stunned at the sight of him standing there half naked.

Is this why Reece, this old ass man got you dissin me. he's old enough to be your father.

I'm not going to have this conversation with you, it's over Kim.

Kim rushed past me and stabbed Ross. All I saw was blood and him fall to the floor. What did you do you stupid bitch I yelled tears coming from my eyes.

I bent down to see exactly where she stabbed him.

Why are you doing this to me. How can you choose him over me. I love you she kept repeating. She had went back down to a level 2.

Once I saw that she had managed to only stab him in his shoulder, I called 911 and went over and kicked her ass for old and new.

By the time the police and ambulance had gotten there, she was laying on the porch bleeding herself.

They were about to arrest me too. But in the end they said it was self defense.

They did take him to the hospital. I took Lil D over to his grandmothers and met them there. He had to have some stitches, but was told to take it easy and he should make a full recovery.

I'm so sorry I kept telling him. I felt so bad, it was my ex-friend who had stabbed him. He didn't deserve to get mixed up in my drama with that crazy girl.

You have nothing to be sorry for, he said. you got that good good he said laughing making light of it all. I love this man I thought as we drove back to my house, even if he was old enough to be my father.

I took pleasure in taking care of him, I had never enjoyed catering to a man as much as I did him. When it was time for him to leave, I cried like a baby.

He only had one arm, his other one was in a sling, but he gave me a big hug and told me that he would take care of everything for our trip, and that he loved me and he was gone.

I didn't know how much longer I was going to be able to see him leave me and return to his wife. It was so hard to know that he wouldn't be there when we woke up. Lil D, kept saying Ross all night. he was just learning words and the ones he knew he said all the time.

Ross called me when he made it home, and I let him hear Lil D say his name, he got the biggest kick out that.

He called every day after that. we were both excited about our trip. We decided to go to Hawaii, I'd never been on a island before. I always heard the most amazing stories about the beaches there. I never thought I would ever go.

I really needed to share this with somebody. And since I'd yet to tell Mia that I was sleeping with her ex's father. I went over Sidney's house, since I felt like I owed her an explanation after seeing Ross there anyway. This would be the perfect opportunity. I had been calling her and she hadn't returned any of my calls, so I figured I'd pop in on her the way she did me.

Ricky came to the door, I hadn't seen him since the hospital, he looked really happy.

Hey Reece he said hugging me, how have you been, you look great.

Thanks I said returning his hug. Is Sidney here I asked.

Yea, she's in the back in the bedroom, she sleeps all the time now. You can go on back, I think she's woke now.

Sidney was laying the bed watching TV when I walked in. I noticed that she had also redecorated her house. It looked like the Easter bunny house. She had a super big yellow sofa and two oversized chairs that where a purple color. The other rooms followed that color pattern with some green and blues here and there. It all came together nicely

She gave me the rundown on her recent discoveries. About how Sidney Mac was her father and how he and Mia planned to get married.

I knew Mia was seeing Sidney Mac, but had no idea that it was that serious. I wondered if it was too soon for her to start another serious relationship so soon after Lance, but I didn't share that with Sidney, she didn't seem to be taking the news of Mia becoming her Step mother so well

I shared my story about Ross and our upcoming trip. What is with you and Mia and peoples daddy's she said.

I thought she was joking at first but she had a look on her face that told me she was serious.

Well in Mia's defense, she didn't know he was your father.

She knew he was my uncle.

Yea, but what was so wrong with her being with your uncle? I asked

He's so much older than her, she said trying to think of more reasons why it was wrong for Mia to fall in love with her uncle/father

Age is just a number Sidney, and besides that, he's not that old.

I guess you'd know, she shot back.

Mia looks happier than she's ever been. Don't she deserve that. She's always been there for us even if she didn't agree with what we were doing. It's time for us to be there for her, I told her, trying not to let her attitude get to me. And don't you want the best for your uncle. Who can you think of that would be better for him than Mia?

Sidney's face softened at that thought. I guess your right. She's always had my back. But do you realize that she's going to be my mother.

That doesn't mean that she's going to stop being your best friend, I said to her hoping that she would come around.

By the time I left we were laughing and joking about everything. She said she was happy for me and Ross, but wanted me to be careful due to the fact that he was a married man, and Mrs. Chapman would surely kill me if she thought I was threatening her thrown.

On my drive home in my new convertible, I thought about Sidney had said, and as much as I had put it out of my mind, I did have to come to terms with the fact that Ross was married and that was not about change.

Chapter 13

TAMIA

Once we got home and found out that Sidney was in fact pregnant. I got a call from Mac. I made sure she was going to be ok and shot out there to go and see him. I missed him more than I thought I would. I would finally be able to tell him that me and Lance were done. Lance made it so easy to make that decision.

When I got there he was standing in the door waiting for me to get out of the car.

I didn't think it was possible for him look better. But he looked so good standing there in his starched jeans and yellow polo shirt, until now I had never seen him in jeans before. My stomach started it's dance as I ran into his arms to greet him.

Baby, I missed you so much he said carrying me into the house.

I missed you too. And guess what I said smiling.

What he said raising his eyebrow

I'm free baby, it's over

What do mean it's over, baby don't tease me he said with his sexy smile.

I mean I'm done with Lance, and I'm officially yours.

He just looked at me for a few minutes and kissed me, like it was our first kiss again. I wanted him so bad, we had been holding out on sex, until I was done with Lance, and now that I was. I wanted nothing more than to give him all of my goodies.

As we began undressing each other, somebody rang his door bell, go away he yelled.

The door bell continued to ring, so he got up and answered it. This time I just sat there half dressed, there was no reason for me to hide anymore. I hadn't told Lance I was moving out yet, but I think he got the hint when I let him have it at the airport. I told him that I did not appreciate the way he'd been handling me, I felt that his outburst were getting violent and that I would not be disrespected that way. my final speech to him was about the fact that I saw him and Janine and that I never wanted to see his face again. He was about to protest, but didn't. He just stood there looking at me like I'd lost my mind, He said your loss and walked away. That attitude only lasted until he reached his car and started calling me trying to explain about him and Janine. He said whatever he thought he could to get me to forgive him. Sidney sat on the passenger side listening to our conversation rolling her eyes, Lance had gotten on her nerves too, that was all too obvious.

At the door, stood Betty Boop with a tiny red satin dress on. Mac just looked at her like she'd stole something,

I thought I'd come over and make you some dinner she said. You never called me.

Betty, I didn't call you because….

Before he could finish I walked up behind him and put my arms around him and said, because he's with me now. Never had I been so bold. It felt good to stake my claim on him.

It was like I'd slapped her in her face, she got so red and just looked at us both.

Sidney, you need to ashamed of yourself, this girl is a baby. What do you want with this chile when you can have a real woman.

Before I could snap back at her he said, she's all the woman I need Betty and slammed the door in her face.

On our way to the bedroom; going at it like we were never interrupted, we smelled smoke.

Betty Boop had set his Tahoe on fire.

Mac was so mad. I had never seen him that mad before. Baby it'll be ok I said redressing while he called the fire dept.

One of the firemen was none other than Terry, Sidney's latest conquest. He came over and gave me a hug, Mac did not like that, he was already in a foul mood, so I stepped away. Who needed that drama over one of Sidney's men.

Have you heard the news he asked me

I thought he was talking about the baby, so I said yea she's going to make a great mother.

Sidney's pregnant he said, the look on his face and his reaction told me he didn't know and that I'd just stuck my foot in my mouth.

Oh. I said I guess that's not the news you were talking about. Sorry. Well, I have to go, you take care of yourself I said walking as fast I could to get away from him.

On my way back into Mac's house, my mother called and asked if I could come over, she needed to talk to me.

Sure, I said, I'll be over tomorrow morning.

No, I mean now Mia.

It was like the universe didn't want me and Mac to make love. When I told him I had to leave, he sulked like a baby. I told him that I would come back, I had no intention of going to Lance's until I was there I get my belongings, and even then I was not going to be alone.

Turns out my mother wanted to tell me that she had eloped. As surprised as I was. I was so happy for her. She deserved happiness and it was obvious that Mike made her happy. She said it was spur of the moment and she just went with it.

We talked for a couple hours like two school girls. I went on and told her about me and Sidney Mac, she wasn't surprised. She told me that she never thought I was happy with Lance, but she wasn't going to tell me that. I told her to always give me her opinions, they mattered.

When I left there it was almost 1 in the morning, I called Mac to tell him I was on the way, I could tell that that made him happy. His entire demeanor changed.

When I got there all of the lights were out. I rang the door bell wondering if he'd left. But he opened the door with a huge grin on his face. Inside there were candles lit everywhere, he had roses scattered around the house it was so beautiful.

You did all this all this for me I said smiling. Mac had changed into some silk pajamas looking edible.

He walked over to me, got down on one knee and presented me with a diamond ring. It wasn't as big as the one Lance gave me, but it was much nicer. While I stood there getting teary eyed, he went on to tell me how I was the love of his life and he wanted to spend every day showing me just how much I meant to him.

Will you be my wife? He asked

Yes baby I will I said I will I will I will. He put the ring on my finger and kissed me.

That night we finally made love. It was the most amazing sex I ever had. Mac kissed my body from head to toe. I took pleasure in returning the favor. It was a magical night. he didn't rush it, we took our time making every moment last. While he entered me, we looked into each others eyes and in that moment I knew this was the best decision I had ever made.

Over the next couple of weeks, me and Mac began to prepare for our life together. We'd went and got all my clothes from Lance's condo while he was out. I grabbed everything I could so fast, I was willing to buy whatever I had left. I never planned on going back there ever again. I left his ring and the key on the table and took one last look at what my life was and then looked at Mac at what my life had become. It made me realize that I was so caught up in appearances being with the "perfect man" that I lost sight of what was important.

Me and Mac would get a lot of stares and a lot of people would not understand our relationship, especially knowing that Sidney was his daughter. But that no longer mattered to me. I no longer cared what people thought. I lived my life trying to be the perfect daughter, the perfect friend, the perfect girlfriend because it's who I was or who I thought I had to be. but I'm not perfect, I make mistakes and it was time for me to start living my life for me.

Me and Mac went to the house in Gwinnet that was now complete. I had sent Lance a check for the money he'd put into the house. Mac was opposed to moving there at first, he said it was me and Lance's house not mine and his. Once we got there and he saw it and then I showed him the extra room that was now his, he came around. I told him that this house was built for love and that's what we had, so it would be our house, built on our love.

He wanted to know how I could afford such a big house, and I finally told him about my about my inheritance. He was the only person outside of my mother, Reece and Sidney that knew. I told him how I'd like to keep it that way. I liked the fact that he wasn't phased about the fact that I was very wealthy. He didn't care. I think I fell in love with him all over.

We broke the house in and made love in almost every room, the blanket we had in car from our picnic came right in handy that day. It was officially our house.

We spent the next couple of days shopping for the new home. He had become just as excited as I was about the move. He said it was time for him to leave that house that he shared with Lorraine for so many years. He was also glad that it was in Gwinnet, far away from everybody on the east side. He felt compelled to buy mostly everything for the new house, I think he didn't want me to think he planned on living off my money, because he kept making comments about how much the house must have cost to build. Mac had his own money, he didn't need mine. I knew that. but even if he didn't, I loved him with all my heart and was willing to share everything I had with him. I could never say that before. Lance never even knew about the money, he thought my mom was loaded and she took care of me.

We'd decided to tell Sidney about us the next day over lunch, but she stopped by and dropped the bomb. We were about to start packing up his house, but ended up making love on the sofa in the living room. That man had a huge sexual appetite. He said he was making up for lost time. When Mac opened the door, I hadn't quite gotten back dressed. The look on her face when she saw me there broke my heart.

She told us that Mac was not her uncle, he was her father. I felt uneasy about the fact that he knew this and didn't tell me, and the fact that I would be my best friends step mother.

Sidney was so hurt when she found out about us that she left with tears in her eyes. I wanted to chase her, but thought that I would let her get used to the idea before talking about it.

Mac begged me to forgive him for not telling me he was her father. He said he didn't know if it would ever come out, and he didn't want to put me in the position of having to keep such a secret like that from Sidney. Although I could understand his reasons, I was still uneasy with the fact that I was going to marry my best friends father. It made me feel dirty.

That night while we were in bed, we talked about it openly. I told him how I felt and he told me how he felt. it was the first time I'd had and adult conversation about my feelings with a man. Without feeling like I was going to hurt his feelings.

It was then that I knew that even if Sidney didn't approve, nothing was going to stop me from marrying him. The only thing I could do was hope that our friendship was strong enough to handle this.

The next day when I called her, Rickey answered her phone and said that she was sleep. She's back with Rickey, when did that happen I thought. Rickey told me that Lance was not taking our break up so well.

Well that's Lance's problem, it said he'll get used to it.

I heard that you were about to get married? Congratulations he said, maybe we can make it a double wedding.

You and Sidney are getting married, Rickey I'm so happy to hear that congratulation's yourself.

Thanks, he said it took awhile for us to get here, but when it's right its right.

Amen I said. I couldn't have said it better myself. I just wish Sidney could see that.

She'll come around, she's so emotional these days, I don't think she even realizes how she feels yet.

I didn't mean to hurt her Rickey. I would never want to hurt her.

I know that Mia, and she knows it too. Give her some time to get used to the idea, you'll see, Sidney has grown a lot since becoming pregnant.

I hope so, let her know I called and Thanks for the kind words. She's lucky to have you. I said before hanging up.

Reece called me while I was at the grocery store, I told her I would stop by when I left there. She said she needed to talk.

When I got there, she was on the phone grinning and playing with her hair. I wondered if it was Kim she was talking too. She only referred to the person as baby on the phone.

Hi there, she said hanging up the phone, don't you look nice. Did you change your hair or something.

No, Reece it's the feeling of being in love

I know what you mean, I'm in love too.

With the girl, Kim I said

Noooo, she said, you may want to sit down

With who I said, sitting down.

Ross Chapman she said slowly.

Who I said, not knowing if I had heard her correctly.

Ross Chapman, Lance's father.

Reece, tell me your joking

I wish I could Mia, but I can't. I'm head over heels in love with that man.

When, How, What? I said not able to find the right words.

She told me whole rundown of their affair in Mississippi and how he's just left and about her new car and about the upcoming trip. I was shocked beyond shocked.

Well is he leaving mother Chapman?

No, I don't think so she said sadly

So you went from a girl, to a married man. Reece what are you doing?

Mia, I've never felt this way about anybody, not even DJ. He really loves me.

Well if he loved you he'd leave his wife, I said.

Mia, you know it's not that simple. All that money they have invested in that marriage.

If he loves you, then it is that simple.

He does love me, and I love him. He even knows about Kim. She's in jail by the way for stabbing him.

What! I said louder than I meant too.

Yea, she came over one night telling me how much she loved me blah blah blah, and when she seen him, she stabbed him. It wasn't deep, they stitched him up and sent him home the same night.

Oh my goodness, I said, when did he leave?

He left a couple days later after that. but did you hear me say I'm going to Hawaii? She said excited

I wanted to be excited for her too, but the fact that he was married and that he was Lance's father concerned me. I hope you know what your doing. You know Mother Chapman will cut you if she ever found out. And… don't Rhonda live with them now. Don't you think that would put her in a uncomfortable position.

I never thought about that, she said, I guess it would

I don't mean to put a damper on things I said noticing that her mood changed.

No, I was so caught up in love, that I never stopped to think about what it could to to Rhonda.

Well I said trying to change the subject by showing off my ring. I'm getting married.

Yea, I heard she said. To Sidney's father she said snickering.

Oh, you heard I said.

Yea, I went to see her the other day, she is getting so fat. She told me her mother told her Sidney was her dad. I don't know what upset her more, the fact that Sidney was not her uncle or that your about to marry her father.

I know, she won't answer my calls. Did you know her and Rickey are getting married too.

No, she didn't mention anything about that.

Yea, Rickey told me today. I'm so glad their back together. He's good for her.

Yea, but does she love him enough to marry him and be faithful.

Well, she's about to have a baby, that changes things.

Lil D came and jumped in my lap when he came into the living room. He had gotten so big and cute as a button. I showered him with kisses.

Maybe you'll be having your own baby soon huh? She asked

Up until that moment, I had never even thought about kids. I didn't even know if Mac wanted kids. Maybe, was all I said answering her question.

When I finally left, I began to think about her question. Did I want kids? Did Mac? I couldn't wait to get home and talk to him about it.

When I got back to his house, he wasn't there. He didn't come home until almost midnight. I had a flash back of Lance coming home drunk and immediately got an attitude.

That night me and Mac had our first disagreement. I never did get to ask him about kids.

When he came back into bedroom, we talked about why I was so upset when he got home. I told him about the flashback I'd gotten. He told me to trust that he would never treat me that way. He said that he was over his brothers Pete's house visiting with him and their new baby. He wanted to be the one to tell Pete that he was Sidney's father before he heard it from someone else.

How did he take it? I asked

He said he had a feeling about it for some time.

Was he mad?

Not really, he felt like since it almost 30 years ago, there was nothing to get upset about anymore.

What about you sleeping with his wife? You were really young at the time weren't you?

I was 17 and He'd cheated on her with so many women, the fact that she cheated on him had to be charged to the game.

Wow, that was a mature approach.

Yea, we've been through worse. We'll get through this too.

I soften up when I heard that and felt bad for going off on him when he got home. I've never been the jealous type before, I didn't understand why I was I so insecure now. I put that thought aside, and thought it would be the perfect time to ask about our own babies one day.

What do you think about us having kids, I asked,

Hell yea, he said, the only child I had, I was never able to tell her, or be a real father to her. Lorraine never wanted kids. she said she didn't want to have to share me with no crying babies. So yes, my love he said, I can't wait to have a house full of children with you.

A house full I repeated, how many is that?

Well, he said taking off my gown, at least four.

Four I said, lifting my arms so he could have full access to my body. I didn't have the heart to tell him, that there was no way I was about to have that many children. What did I look like? A baby making machine.

Maybe even more he said laying me down, let's get started right now.

We'd decided to have the wedding at the house in Gwinnett, the back yard was so big, it was the perfect setting. And after all the wedding hoopla with Lance, I just wanted something small and intimate. Mac wanted a big wedding, so we compromised and settled on a guest list of no more than 75 people.

The next day, I went to the Target by the new house, in the next aisle over, I heard a couple having a heated conversation. I couldn't help but overhear them, as they weren't trying to keep it just between them. The woman kept saying how she was tired of sitting at home waiting for him while he was out playing house with "that bitch" the man just kept saying "it's complicated"

So complicated that you had to move out and move in with her? She asked

The man kept repeating that it was just very complicated.

The woman got louder when he said that and said what's so complicated, if he wanted to be with her, then it should be simple. She said that she had stuck by him for all these years and if he couldn't commit to her, then she never wanted to see him again.

The voice of the man sounded so familiar to me, but I couldn't place it, so I passed their aisle to get a view of the couple. The woman a short and heavy set dark skin woman, and the man was Rickey.

My mouth fell to the floor. I couldn't move, my legs would not let me walk away as much as I wanted them to run. Rickey has been having a relationship with this woman for years? How could this be?

The couple walked away in the opposite direction, while I still stood there in total shock. I didn't know what to do. Sidney wasn't talking to me as it was, how could I tell her this. She would be devastated. But how can I not tell her, she was my best friend, I couldn't let her marry this man. No one ever would have thought Rickey had been cheating on her for years. He never gave any indication that he wasn't faithful to Sidney. I gathered myself and followed them throughout the store, I thought about taking a picture of the couple and sending it to Sidney, but I couldn't let her find out that way. I could go and confront Rickey, and what, make him leave the her. But what would that do. Rickey had been cheating on Sidney for years with this lady. And although she cheated on him too, he put her through the ringer about it. I was so disgusted with Rickey. I wanted to call Mac and tell him, but he would kill Rickey and then go to jail and then I would lose him. I left the Target without buying anything, I needed to tell somebody, so they can tell me what I should do.

Chapter 14

SIDNEY ROSE

The baby kicked for the first time today. I wanted to tell somebody so bad, but Rickey wasn't home, I wanted to call Mia, but I still hadn't talked to her since the news of her upcoming nuptials. Reece made such a valid point when she said that Mia has always been there for us, no matter what.

I was tired of being mad at her, it took more energy to stay mad. Being angry with her, meant that I was also mad at my newfound father. They were two of the most important people in my life, not having them around to right now was just not worth it. I needed my friend. I needed my father. I talked to my daddy Pete, who had just found out himself, he was not as angry as I thought he would have been. Although he said at first he wanted to hurt my mother and Uncle Sid for keeping that from him for all these years. He told me that he didn't care what she said, he would always be my father. I agreed with him although I knew it would never be the same. I was always closer to uncle Mac, even as a child. He was around more than Pete was.

Me and Mia were both getting married and weren't even speaking, it just didn't seem right. I was about to have a baby and she and uncle Mac wouldn't be there.

That thought made me sadder than the thought of them two being together.

She really was happier than I'd ever seen her. She smiled all the time, she didn't even give me the legal eagle speech when I told her my secret.

I got dressed and went over there to make amends. It was time for me to grow up. this was their life, and I didn't have any business telling them who to love.

When I got to uncle Sid's there was a moving truck in front of the house, and men were walking back and forth putting all of his things in it.

I found Mia and uncle Sid in the house in an embrace. The house was nearly empty. Hey you two I said walking up to them. Mia had on some little jean shorts and a tight fitting t-shirt. Nothing like what the old Mia would have had on, she would have had on some perfect moving outfit, that she put together just for the occasion. She even had her hair in a curly ponytail. Who was this lady standing before me I thought. She looked so relaxed.

They both had a look of surprise on their face. Hi they said together.

I'm sorry you guys I said. I was being stupid. You two obviously mean a lot to each other, almost as much as you two mean to me.

Tears started running down Mia's face, which made me cry, we hugged and cried for awhile, before Uncle Sid came and got his hugs in. It felt so good to be there with them.

So, where are guys moving I asked.

To the house in Gwinnett Mia said

When is the wedding

A week from Saturday, Uncle Sid answered. You will be there won't you?

Wow that's so soon. I wouldn't miss it for the world. Did I tell you guys that me and Rickey were getting married too.

That's great baby, he said, when?

I don't know, we haven't set a date.

Baby, why don't you go with the movers and I'll meet you there. Mia said to Mac. Me and Sidney need to catch up. At the door, the way he looked at her, the way he kissed her said it all. They were meant to be together, I could now see that for myself. That also made me kinda sad. Me and Rickey didn't have that passion. Kissing him was a chore for me lately. As much as I tried I wanted to love him the way he loved me. but standing there looking at Mia and uncle Sid, it reminded me of what true love was. I wanted that.

When he left, Mia got serious. There something I want to tell you Sidney.

What is it Mia? I asked. Just then, the baby kicked again, feel this I said putting her hand on my stomach. Oh and let me show you the picture. I pulled the picture out to show her.

She was really excited. Do you know the sex she asked

Yes, I said smiling, it's a little girl. I'm having a little girl, can you believe it? Me and my daughter I said laughing. It sounds so weird. But I must say, she is the best thing that could have happened to me. I can't wait to meet her.

Do you have any idea who the father is? she asked

Well I pretty much know for sure that it's not Rickey's, although he is being so great about this whole thing.

About Rickey she said

Just then, I got the biggest pain I'd ever felt.

Sidney, what's wrong are you ok she asked helping me to the only chair left in house.

Ouch, I screamed oh my goodness, the baby, something is wrong. Mia something

is wrong I said crying.

Come on, let's go to the hospital she said helping me up to go to her car.

We made it to the hospital in record time. Once I was in a room finally relaxed, she and Uncle Mac came in to check on me.

How is the baby, she asked immediately.

She's going to be fine, I have to stay off my feet for awhile, and try to stay stress free but she has a strong heart beat see, I said pointing to the baby monitor.

Of course she is, she's a Stone, Uncle Mac said. Do you want me call Rickey he asked.

Mia face went from a smile to a frown when he asked that. So I asked her if everything was ok?

Yea, she said quietly you need to get some rest. We'll come back later, oh yea, I called your mom and she's on her way.

A few minutes later they were gone. I thought back to before I had my pains when Mia was trying to tell me something. I wondered what it could be.

Rickey got to the hospital about two hours later. My mom had just left.

Sid, are you and the baby ok, he said rushing to my side.

Yes, we're fine, it looks like I'll be on best rest though.

That's ok I'll wait on you hand and foot. Don't worry about nothin. I got you he said.

He was so sweet, the look of concern on his face melted my heart. Unfortunately not enough to make me love him.

Over the next couple of days, he did just that. He waited on me hand and foot. When he wasn't at work, he was at home taking care of me. He even had Lance bring me some food one day. I know I turned white when Lance walked into my bedroom.

Hey Sidney, he said, Rickey asked me to bring you some lunch. He gave me the key so you wouldn't have to get up. How you doin?

Im Im fine, I said thanks a lot. Lance looked like his old self again. He's lost the extra weight, and shaved the beard to a 5o'clock shadow. His head was still bald. He looked good. I had come to terms with what I'd done to Roc, and if I could help it no one would ever know it was me that killed him, except Mia and Uncle Sid that was. While we stood there running small talk, Mia walked in my bedrooom.

The last person she expected to see was Lance, I don't think she's seen him since the day we got back from Mississippi.

Hey Mia I said. look who's here?

Hi Tamia, he said grinning like the cat that ate the canary. You look terrific It's good to see you.

Hi Lance she said coldly, how are you?

I'm straight, just came to bring Sidney some lunch.

Well don't let us keep you, she said turning her back to him

Damn, is it like that? I got the check you sent for the house, you didn't have to do that.

I wanted to. I sold it.

I don't care about the money he said. I miss you Mia, do you think we can talk?

Lance we don't have anything to talk about she said.

I do, I need to apologize to you. I was such an asshole to you. I was just going through so much, I took it out on you.

She just stood there looking at him.

Do you think you can ever forgive me, he asked

Lance, I've moved on. I hope you can find the same happiness I've found. Now I'm sure it's somewhere you need to be. Thanks for bringing Sidney lunch.

Tamia, you can't tell me that you don't miss me.

Lance, I'm getting married, it's been over between us.

A ton of bricks had just hit Lance. Your getting married already he said. To who

Yes I am, She must have felt sorry for him because she softened up and said Lance thank you for apologizing we just weren't meant to be.

How can you say that? We were the perfect couple.

That's just it Lance, we didn't have anything past looking perfect together.

Don't say that he whined, we were perfect. I loved you Mia. I still do. Who is the man that stole you away from me

I sat there looking back from him to her enjoying the show. This was the most excitement I'd had all week since I'd been on bed rest.

Lance, no you don't, you love the way we look together. That relationship was never about me, it was about you and your mother. And he could have never stole what wasn't truly yours to begin with.

Tamia, I don't think we gave our relationship a chance, we were about to get married and spend our lives together. How can we just throw all of that away for some man you just met? Can we go talk, please just let me explain

Explain what Lance, how Janine was giving you head in your mother's garden. How your mother made you propose to me? And for the record. I didn't just meet him.

His eyes got super wide. He couldn't even say anything.

I think you should go I said to Lance, I'd seen enough and I know she'd had enough, and I wanted to hear the Janine story.

Lance turned and walked away without saying another word.

You sold the house I asked when we were alone.

Girl no, I wasn't selling my house, that's where me and Mac moved into. I just didn't want him to know that. So, do you do think you'll be able to come to the wedding? she asked

I hope so, I go back to the doctor tomorrow, can you go with me.

Sure she said, I have to go though I need to go check on a few things for the wedding. She kissed my forehead and was gone.

I could tell that she's wanted to talk to me about something, I would just wait for when she was ready. It was obviously something she couldn't talk about and I knew all too well how that felt. All I could do was be there for her and wait until she was ready to talk about it.

The wedding was beautiful, it took place at sunset, their backyard was transformed into the perfect wedding place. It was such a classy affair. Tamia had on an exquisite one of a kind Vera Wang wedding dress, it was the perfect ceremony. While they were exchanging vows, my uncle did something I'd never seen him do. He cried. Me and Reece stood up there with her, along with Pete/daddy. There was a lot of people there. Tamia didn't want Rickey to come, she said he would tell Lance about the house. Rhonda even came back for the day. She said she had to get back the next day. She loved living in Mississippi, she said it was like living in a fairy tale. She looked like she had matured so much. She was far from the little hoochie mamma we knew a couple months ago.

She couldn't believe I was about to have a baby. much like most of the guest there.

Everybody wanted to know where my husband was. I thought that I would feel ashamed to say that I wasn't married yet. But surprisingly I wasn't. only a select few even knew that I was engaged. This baby had bought about a different kind of strength in me, one that made me feel like I didn't need a man to complete me.

When Mia and uncle Sid got back from their honeymoon to Italy, Mia came right over to check on me.

Wow, you've gotten so big, she said when she saw me waddle down the stairs.

I know, I eat everything in sight.

She sure does, Rickey said from the kitchen.

I came to get you out of the house she said,. go get your stuff.

On the way to her house, she told my about her trip to Target and the couple that were having a heated discussion. She said that when she saw the woman, she didn't expect her to be as heavy as she was from her baby voice. I started laughing at the story, I had no idea that she was about to tell me that the man was Rickey. I wanted to scream at first, then I wanted to cry, then I wanted to kill him. Turns out, I didn't do any of that. I don't know if it was because I was numb or because I knew that something wasn't quite right with Rickey. I thought I needed him to help me raise this baby, so I dealt with him, I didn't love him.

I wanted to tell you so bad Sid, I didn't know if it would stress you out and hurt the baby. But I knew I couildn't keep it from you any longer

I laughed and couldn't stop, it was just my luck that the man I was about to marry had been cheating on me the whole time. No I wasn't mad. I wanted to get even.

Your laughing she said, I didn't expect that reaction.

Mia, look at my life these past months, I would have been worried if something like this didn't happen I said laughing again.

So, your not mad she asked. I would be pissed off. Ready to kill him. He's been messing around with this lady for years, she said.

I've been foolin around on Rickey since the first week we started going out.

Yea, but he left you for it.

It don't matter. It ain't about him, its about my Karma. I've put out so much bad Karma that it's just catching up with me.

Don't say that Sidney, you're a good person.

Of course your gonna say that, you love me. but look at the big picture.

The big picture is that this bum has been messing around with this lady for years. What if he gave you some kind of disease behind this. we don't know what type of person she is.

Mia I haven't had sex with Rickey in a very long time, and when we did, I made him use a condom most of the time, because I felt like I could. I couldn't get Roc too or Terry sometimes, but Rickey, he would just be so happy that I was giving him some, he didn't protest. Not that Rickey or Terry were any safer I said still laughing

So, your ok with this, she asked pulling up to their house.

No, I'm not ok with it. but it's time to get smart about a lot of things. Rickey will get his, I'm gonna get him. Have you told anybody else, and by anybody I mean your husband

Girl, are you crazy, he would kill Rickey, and be in jail. I need my husband.

Yea your right about that I said, Uncle Sid and daddy would surely make Rickey disappear.

Sidney, she said, what are you gonna do?

I don't know yet, but you'll be the first to know when I figure it out.

I walked into their house and thought I had stepped into a different world. Their house was gorgeous. If I didn't know Mia and Uncle Sid's taste I would have thought they hired a decorator to do their house.

Sidney Rose

You guys did a great job decorating, I said as I walked through the house.

Thanks, we spent a lot of time on it. Let me see if Mac is here.

As she walk around calling her husband, I began to think of ways to get even with Rickey for his dirty deceit.

Chapter 15

REECE

My trip was in one week and I had not talked to Ross in over 2 weeks, I'd called his phone, and just got his voicemail. I was about to go out of my mind. I didn't understand why he wasn't calling me, were we still going to Hawaii? Was he ok?

I thought about calling Rhonda and doing alittle research, but I really didn't want to involve her in any of this. and if I started asking questions, Rhonda would be sure to put two and two together as nosy as she was.

I tried to keep my mind on other things, Mia's wedding was going to be a good distraction. Sidney had finally come around about Mia and Sidney Mac. I was glad, all the tension between the two of them was starting to stress me out.

Kim was out of jail and back to calling apologizing. But now her apologies were for what she'd done to Ross. That girl was just bad news and now I was more sure than ever that I wanted nothing to do with her. I noticed that she had started sitting outside my house at night. She was so unpredictable, that I had no idea what she was capable of. I had started putting Lil D in the bed with me.

I had been going to visit my mother, she was keeping herself clean. Mia and Sidney Mac gave her a lot of furniture that they weren't taking to their new house. Her house almost looked better than mine. She was so happy. She said she'd never had such nice things, she started going to church with me and Lil D on Sunday's. She really was trying to turn her life around and I was really proud of her. In my entire life she'd never been clean so long. She'd done one week here, one week there, but never for months. She stood up with Auntie Marie when she got married. Auntie Marie had gotten her a job at the hospital in housekeeping and was even going to some of her meetings with her. She tried to call Rhonda and tell her of all the good things going on in her life, but Rhonda told her she was busy and would have to call her back, which she didn't. I could tell my momma's feelings were hurt, but she said she deserved it and that the lord would handle it and bring her baby back to her when she was ready. I was mad at Rhonda for treating momma like that. but I had to let Rhonda find her own forgiveness in her own time. Living in Mississippi had changed Rhonda so much, I thought she would now be able to handle a relationship with our mother, but I guess not

It wasn't until the day before Mia's wedding when Ross finally called.

Hey baby, he said like I'd talked to him last night.

Hey, I said not knowing if I was about to have an attitude

I know your wondering why I haven't called you. And I will explain everything to you when I get there.

When you get here? I asked

Yes baby, when I get there. I'll be leaving tomorrow and will call you when I get in.

But we don't leave for our trip until next week. Are we still going?

There is nothing that could stop me. baby we'll talk when I get there, I love you

I love you too, I said

When I hung up the phone it rang again, I didn't even look at the caller id, I assumed it was Ross forgetting to tell me something, but it wasn't Reece, a lady said when I answered.

Yes, who is this I said

It's Bernice Jones, Kim's mother

Hi, Ms. Jones, what can I do for you I said. Kim's not here, I haven't seen her.

Reece Kim killed herself today. She said crying.

What I said unable to comprehend what she had just told me.

Kim hung herself in the bathroom this morning. She left you a note. She said she couldn't face herself for the things she's done. And if she couldn't be with you, then she would rather not be here at all.

Ms. Jones, I'm so sorry I said tears started coming down that I didn't expect. I didn't want anything to do with her, but I didn't want her to kill herself either.

Is there anything I can do? I asked. I didn't' know what else to say.
Exactly what kind of relationship did the two of you have, she asked
We were or we used to be friends.
What happened that would make her kill herself? She wanted to know
I again didn't know what to say. was I supposed to tell her the truth, should I lie and tell her something different.
Please Reece, I need to know the truth she said.
Ms. Jones I'm going to come over, is that alright. I figured I owed it her to tell her in person.
Yes please do, she said.
When me and Lil D got to Ms. Jones house, she opened the door looking distraught holding Deanna who had gotten so big, she looked just like DJ. I got a big lump in my throat, but kept swallowing to get rid of it. Breaking down in front of this lady would do neither of us any good. Kim had said that her mother was a dopefiend, this lady didn't look anything like that. She looked wholesome. She put you in the mind of the mother on the movie soul food. This was obviously not a women who'd spent the majority of her life smoking a crack pipe like Kim told me.
I told Ms. Jones the story in it's entirety. Even when she stabbed Ross, she told her mother she was in jail for drunk driving.
I knew it was too soon she kept repeating aloud.
Too soon for what Ms. Jones, I asked.
Kim has always been troubled. I had her put in a mental facility a couple of years ago to get her some help. She's never been able to fully grasp reality. She seemed to be doing so much better after she had Deanna. I thought she was ok she said crying harder.
I went over and put my arms around her, she obviously needed a hug. I'm sorry she said.
You don't have anything to be sorry for.
Me and Ms. Jones talked for another hour about Kim's childhood and everything she put her mother through. I told her about my husband DJ being Deanna's father.
She asked if I knew where he was.
He was killed 3 months ago I told her.
You mean to tell me that this precious baby has no parents left she said looking at her.
I'm afraid not, I said sadly. If there's ever anything I can do for you and Deanna, please let me know.

I'm old Reece, I don't think I can raise this child. I don't know what I'm going to do.

At a loss for words, I shook my head and gathered up my son to leave. Please call me if I can help, I said walking out the door.

What did she want me to do?. Offer to raise the baby that my husband had by the woman who'd drugged me, stalked me and stabbed my man. I wanted to help, but it was still hard for me to look at Deanna, less and only raise her.

Mia's wedding was amazing, I pictured her wedding to be in some massive church with all the trimmings, but she had it in the backyard of her new home, by the lake.

It was the most beautiful wedding I'd ever been too. It was a lot of people there, but it was still an intimate affair. Tamia looked like a bride out of a magazine, and Sidney Mac looked as handsome as ever. They both looked really happy. I could only hope that one day I would find that kind of love and get married again.

Although I was happy about Ross's visit, I still didn't know how long I would be able to be the other woman. I've waited all my life to find a man who made me feel like Ross. It didn't matter to me that he was rich, or that he was twice my age. He made me feel so beautiful and wanted. a feeling that I had yet to feel since I was in high school. Kim said she wanted me too, but if was different. It was weird hearing her mother tell me how Kim had always been troubled in and out of mental facilities. As much as me and Kim talked she never said anything about that. it made me wonder if anything she'd told me was the truth. I remember feeling so connected to her, but it was all lies. I had to wonder if it was really a connection or if it was me needing to feel close to someone. I felt bad for her, and I felt bad for her mother, Kim had put her through the ringer and now she left her to raise her child.

I was glad that I'd met Kim though. I found myself again through our friendship. When DJ was killed, I had no idea what I was going to do, or how I was going to build myself back up and Kim helped me do that. I would always be grateful to her for that.

On the way home from the wedding, I told Rhonda about Kim killing herself. She didn't even seem phased. She told me she knew that Kim was crazy and she didn't really like her anyway. She sounded just like Ms. Chapman. you never told me the story between you too she said.

There's nothing to tell we were friends.

And that's it, Rhonda said giving me a look.

Yes, Rhonda that's it. We had gotten kinda close, she helped me to get over DJ's death. She was what I needed, when I needed it. That's all.

I didn't see the point of telling her about me and Kim's night together, Kim was dead and so was the memory of that night to me.

What time is your flight tomorrow, maybe you can go visit mamma. She has a real nice place and I know it would make her really happy to see you.

I had forgotten about Ross coming, Rhonda could not be there when he came. I was now in panic mode.

Maybe on the next visit, she said, my flight is at 8 in the morning. The car will be there to pick me up at 7.

A car huh? Must be nice. I said

Yea, like this new car of yours she said, when did you get it?

A couple weeks ago, I said smiling at the thought of Ross.

What's been going on with you lately, she asked, you seem giddy. It must be a man.

Why does it have to be a man?

Only a man can make you smile out the blue like you've been doing.

Well why don't you tell me about life as a socialite, I said getting off the subject.

It's great, mother Chapman bought me a new car too, a gold Lexus it suits me she said smiling, We go shopping almost every day, when I'm not in school. She introduces me as her daughter to everybody, and she gave me my own credit card and everything. Sometimes we sit up all night and talk and eat ice cream and stuff, we go and get our hair done and to the spa at least once a week. I had never even been to the spa before. She taught me how to spot fake jewelry and handbags. And she got me a piano teacher. Mother said that all ladies should have a talent. She's the best.

Wow, mother huh? That sounds really nice Rhonda, I'm so glad your happy. But you always talk about Mrs. Chapman, you haven't mentioned Mr. Chapman, do you spend a lot of time with him too? I had to ask

Well, sometimes we talk, he's always working or in his office. Him and mother have been fighting a lot lately. Mother thinks he's messing around with someone, she said he's always been distant, but now he was distant and happy.

By the time we'd made it to my house, we had talked about everything under the sun, it was nice to have my sister there, even if it was only for one night.

A tall white man came to the door right a seven on the dot. When she said car I pictured a town car, not a limo. Mrs. Chapman was really spoiling that girl. We hugged and promised to stay in touch more than what we have been. My little sister had come along way, walking to her limo, toting her Luis Vitan luggage.

A couple hours later Ross called to say he was on his way. When he got there I had forgotten how handsome he was. He scooped me up and gave me the longest most passionate kiss to date.

Sit down baby, he said leading me over to the couch. I have something to tell you.

I sat down without saying a word. I couldn't handle any more bad news.

Baby, I left her. I'm here to stay if you want me.

What? I said unable to believe what I'd just heard

I haven't called you in a couple weeks because I've been getting some things in order. I woke up one day and couldn't do it anymore. Life is too short to live the way I've been living. I've worked hard to make sure we had everything that life had to offer. But without happiness, it means nothing. You and DJ make me happy. I don't want to live another day without you he said, looking like a sad puppy.

So you left her? What happened? What did she say? I don't know how I feel about being the one to break up your marriage. You two have been married for so long.

Baby, slow down, he said your not the reason for anything but reminding me of what life is. I didn't call because I needed to know I was leaving her for me. I was suffocating in that house. Being with you means I can breath. You're my air.

By the time he was done, I was crying like a baby.

Don't cry my love, he said wiping my tears. You do still want me don't you he said smiling that perfect smile.

Baby of course I do, I love you. I'm crying because I've never had anyone to feel that way about me before, it's like I'm dreaming. And if I am, I don't want to wake up.

DJ walked into the room, when he saw him he smiled and started saying his name over and over.

As I watched the two men in my life roll around on the floor, I truly knew the meaning of happiness.

The next couple of days were some of greatest days in my life. Ross had unpacked his clothes and was officially living with me. He stayed on the phone a lot working. But I didn't mind, he was mine now. When he wasn't on the phone, he was playing with me in the bedroom, or playing with DJ. He was a great father to DJ, and DJ loved him some Ross.

One day Lance called and they had a huge argument about him leaving his mother. Ross said it was just something that had to be done. He never told Lance that he was in the same city as him. Not until that moment did I feel like a dirty little secret. I didn't want Lance to know either, but I didn't not want him to know.

Later on when we were in bed, I mentioned that I felt like a dirty little secret.

Why? He said sitting up in the bed

Well earlier when you were talking to Lance I couldn't help but notice that you never mentioned that you were here.

I'm serving his mother with divorce papers tomorrow, it's not easy for him, Lance has always been a mamma's boy. The less he knows right now the better.

Divorce papers already I asked.

Why wait, I'm not going back, there's not need to drag it out.

Well I figured with the amount of assets at stake, it would take awhile to figure out

I've set her up, she'll be just fine, I gave her the house and everything in it. She knows it's been over for some time. When I told her I was leaving, she told me not to let the door hit me on the way out. Now since she has your sister, she does not need me, nor does she want me anymore than I want her.

Well I want you I said, going down and giving him a serious blowjob.

Our trip to Hawaii was pure paradise. I had planned on leaving DJ with his grandmother, but Ross would not hear of it, he hired a nanny and we took him with us. Never in my life had I been treated the way he treats me, with such respect and care. He made me feel like I was special in so many ways.

On our way back we stopped at Publix, Ross was hugging me from behind while we were deciding what we were going to have for dinner. We ran smack dab into Lance.

Chapter 16

TAMIA

After the wedding, Mac and I went to Italy on our honeymoon. We had the best time, we ate the best food, which was my favorite part. We stayed in an amazing villa. When it was time to leave, we were both sad. That week was only about us, no one else. I wasn't ready for our fairy tale to end.

As soon as we got home, I went over Sidney's. Rickey was still there. I wondered what if anything Sidney had planned to do about him. She had gotten so big in a just a week. She seemed very happy though. They had started to buy things for the nursery, and get ready for the baby. Although I wasn't happy with what Rickey did to Sidney. He did love her, that was apparent. He waited on her hand and foot.

I finally told her about Rickey, she took it better than I thought she would have., I guess Rickey was right. She really was maturing with her pregnancy. It almost made me wish I had never told her. I wanted Sidney to have the same happiness that I had found. Rickey seemed to make her happy.

That night her and Rickey came over. Mac put us some steaks on the grill and we sat outside talking like the old days. She seemed to have accepted the fact that I was married to her father. It hit me that I was going to be a grandmother before I was even a mother.

Mac wanted me to be pregnant so bad. We tried several times a day. I told him that it would happen when the time was right. I didn't care. I was enjoying my husband.

Bittersweet

Mac and Pete had decided to open a restaurant. I had gotten used to having him around all the time, so when he wasn't around all time, I was lonely.

I decided to throw Sidney a surprise baby shower. The hardest part was finding people to invite. Sidney wasn't the most liked person. You really had to know her to love her. I had no other choice but to include her on the plans. She only had 2 more months before the baby was due. We were leaving the party city when we saw Rickey's truck parked next door at the Home Depot.

Since Rickey is a carpenter, we didn't think anything about it, that is until he walked out with a heavy set lady. I knew exactly who she was, she was the same lady that I saw him with at Target months earlier. Sidney all but ran as much as she could over to them.

Is this the bitch you been fucking with she asked. The fat lady was not having that. No. I'm the bitch he's married too, she said.

Married, Rickey is this true? She asked ready to hit somebody.

Sid, let me explain it's not what you think, he said getting between the two women.

She's pregnant the woman yelled. What the fuck is this about Rick? You told me she was unstable, you didn't say anything about her being pregnant.

Unstable, Sidney screamed. Oh I'm unstable, you aint seen nothing yet.

At that point I started to pull Sidney away, she was getting way too upset to continue this conversation. Let's go Sid, think about the baby.

Rickey stood there stuck on stupid. The lady hadn't stop cussing him out. I wondered how long she could go. She called him every name in the book.

Finally, Rickey spoke up, Mia, please take Sidney home, I will meet you guys there. Tanisha shut the hell up for a second. He yelled. You knew this so called marriage was a fluke from the beginning, don't sit up here and act like you're the victim. Please Sidney meet me at home. I will be right there and will explain everything, I promise.

When we finally made it back to Sidney's the door bell rang. I looked through the peep hole to find two police officers. Sidney it's the police I whispered. She got up and answered the door, may I help you she asked.

Sidney Stone, one of the officers said.

Yes, what can I do for you?

Your under arrest for the murder of Rocston Davidson We have a search warrant to search your home. Sidney all but fell over. one of the officers had to catch her from reaching the floor.

As they cuffed Sidney, more officers came in her house and began to search it.

I called Mac and told him what was going on. He coached me on the questions to ask the officers on Sidney's behalf until he got there. I was shaking so bad, I didn't know if I would even be able to speak. They had Sidney on the couch when two officers came from her bedroom with two big bags of what seemed to be cocaine. What the hell? I screamed more to myself than to anyone else.

Don't say a word Sid, I said. I repeated what Mac told me to tell her. What is your attormey's number. I remember her telling me that she had to go and make another payment to her attorney. The strange thing was, she didn't seem surprised to see the drugs, She gave me her attorney's number as they escorted her out reading her her rights.

While I waited there for Mac, wondering how this could have happened. Rickey came in looking puzzled. I explained to him what had just happened. He was as stunned as I was to see him with that lady that day in the Target. He just stood there not saying a word for about 10 minutes. What was Sidney doing with drugs. He asked. I hunched my shoulders not knowing what to say, I figured it was Sidney's story to tell him, not mine.

Me and Mac went down to the police station, but they would not let us see her. her attorney came out and told us that, she would have a hearing the next day, but that it didn't look good that she would be granted bail. But she's pregnant I said. won't they consider that? I asked him. He said that he would try everything he could.

Just as he told us, Sidney was denied bond. She was doing better than I thought she would be. They let us see her after her court appearance. She told us not to worry about her, she would be fine. I couldn't believe how strong she was. The old Sidney would have cried non stop. We left so Rickey could spend the rest of her visitation time with her.

By the time we'd made it back to our house, Mac looked like he'd aged. He was so sad, he didn't know what to say, or what to do. He told me that Sidney asked him to get rid of the drugs. He blamed himself for not doing it.

Bittersweet

Baby, you can't blame yourself you know how much I love Sidney, But she bought this on herself. I told her to get rid of those drugs. All we can now is pray for her. She knows we're here for her.

Mac held onto me like he didn't want to let go.

It had been a little over a month since Sidney's arrest when she went into labor.

She gave birth to a beautiful baby girl. She named her Taylor Carmela Stone.

We got the call about 3:00 in the morning. When we got to the hospital, Sidney was holding her staring down at her with tears in her eyes.

She's perfect Sid. I said looking at little Taylor. Just like her mom, Mac added.

I need you guys to do me a favor. Will you two raise her, she said through sobs. I'm looking at a lot of time for this. I may not be getting out. Sidney I interrupted, don't say that. You're going to beat this. Tamia, just listen she said. If this is my fate then so be it. Taylor deserves more, I want you two to raise her as your own. I don't want her to know that her mother is a murderer. I want her to have a chance at a happy life, coming to see her mother in jail is not a happy life. I can't think of two people who I would ever trust more to raise my baby. I know that you two will love her and give her the best possible life a little girl could have.

Sidney, I don't know what to say. you're the best mother for this baby. She deserves to know who her mother is. Don't deny her of that, I said. yea baby, your Taylor's mother Mac said.

Please you guys, do you love me? she asked

Of course we do we said together. Then if you love me you'll do this for me. you have to promise that you will raise Taylor as your own. Promise me, I won't be able to do this time without knowing that you promise me that you will raise her. please she said again. I'm begging you. This is the hardest thing I've ever had to do. I've spent my life being selfish, only thinking about myself. Let me do this for her. Say you'll raise her.

Me and Mac looked at each other, both of us were about to cry at what we'd just heard. Of course we will Sidney, I said. but when she gets older, I want you to reconsider telling her you're her mother.

No Tamia, she can never know. No one can. This has to be between us. I can't risk her ever finding out the truth. Look at her, she looks just like Roc. if I told her I was her mother, then I would also have to tell her that I killed her father. What kind of life would she have then? Promise me she'll never know.

Don't you think there have been too many lies about this, look at us. You know how you felt when you found out the truth about me. why would you want to put your baby through that? Mac asked

Yes, I know how I felt, and that's why I don't ever want her to know. It wasn't easy to accept the fact that you two were together, but looking at you tells me that the love you two have is just what Taylor needs. She could not have better parents then the two of you. My attorney will be bringing you guys some papers to legalize everything if you'll agree to do this.

Rickey came busting into the room before we were finished with our talk. Let me see her he said going over to Sidney's bed. She beautiful he said with tears in his eyes.

Rickey what are doing here? Sidney snapped

I wanted to see my daughter he answered

Rickey, she's Tamia and Uncle Mac's daughter, I've signed her over to them. Their going to raise her as their own so she can have a chance in life.

What do you mean, you didn't even talk to me about this. how can you just make a decision about our daughter without consulting me. I want to raise her.

Rickey, Taylor's not yours. You don't have any say in any decisions about her future. Deep down, you knew that. and your married remember.

Who is her father he demanded.

Her father is standing right over there Sidney said pointing to Mac.

You can't do this Sidney, I will fight you.

Rickey, it's already done. I've known from the start that Taylor was not yours. Look at us. Your married and didn't even tell me. What kind of parents would we have been to her. Neither one us knows what love is. We were never honest with each other. Our whole relationship was one big lie after another. I was never in love with you. And I don't think you were in love with me either. I want to give her a chance at happiness.

You two will love her won't you? He asked us

Of course we will Rickey I said sadly.

He told us all goodbye and walked out.

Three days later, we brought Taylor home. We went over to Sidney's house and picked up all of her things in the nursery beforehand. Her new room in our house looked like a room fit for a princess. I was nervous about becoming a mother. You usually get time to get used to the idea of becoming a parent, me and Mac had 3 days. I wasn't sure if I had the mother instincts to take care of her. We were both jittery the morning we arrived to the hospital to pick her up. They had already taken Sidney back to the jail. Taylor looked so much like Sidney that it brought tears to my eyes. I couldn't tell that she looked like Roc. She was so pink and tiny with wavy black hair.

To be so small, she had big lungs, in the beginning me and Mac both woke up with her when she was hungry. After 1 week of no sleep, we realized that we had to take turns. When Mac had to leave to take care of restaurant business, Reece and Ross came over and helped me. Ross's divorce had become final, and they were out in the open about their relationship. They both seemed to be on cloud nine.

Mac and I asked them to be Taylor Godparents, a title they were all too happy to accept. They said it was the first thing that signified them as a couple.

By the time Taylor turned 3 months I had the mother role down packed. Mac was a great father, he adored that baby as did I. Sidney trial wasn't for another 3 months. We sent her pictures of Taylor on a regular bases, until she called and asked us not to anymore, she said it was too hard right now for her to deal with. Taylor had become our life, I didn't know what to talk about if it wasn't about her. So Sidney called less and less. Her attorney said she wanted to plead guilty. He said that there was a good chance that her sentence would be much less that way. Mac would not hear of it. he couldn't understand why Sidney would plead guilty and risk spending the rest of her life in prison. He wanted to go and see her and talk her out of it. but when he got there, she refused his visit. He called on his way back home, I could tell he was crushed by her rejection. I knew he was hurting and wanted to do something for him. So I took Taylor over my mothers and cooked him a romantic meal. I lit candles all around the house, placed rose petals throughout and got the Jacuzzi ready. I pulled out my ace in the hole that I had for Lance and put up the pole. I had went and bought some 4 inch heels and some sexy lingerie for the show. When he walked in I could tell it was just what he needed. He couldn't believe I had learned to dance on a pole or that I had on such high heels. He was so turned on that we didn't even make it to the Jacuzzi. It had been so long since me and Mac made love. Having Taylor tied up most of our free time. When she was sleep, then so were we. As much as we enjoyed our evening together, we both missed Taylor and spent the majority of the night talking about her.

At Sidney's trial, Rickey and Lance were there. When Lance saw Mac, I thought he would shoot him on sight. He made a big scene in the hallway and had to be escorted out. He yelled that he should have known from the night of party when he saw that my new husband was none other than Sidney Mac. He said I betrayed him and that he would never forgive me. I didn't remember needing his forgiveness and told him so.

Terry even came to her trial. They had been talking since she'd been locked up and he was the one person besides her mother that she would allow to visit her. When they bought her out, she looked good, she had lost a lot of weight, and she looked healthy. her hair was in a pony tail, she couldn't wear weave in jail and it had been so long since I'd seen her real hair. She looked like a wholesome version of the old Sidney. As we were all seated waiting on the trial to begin, Mr. Winter's, Sidney's attorney got up and said that his client has agreed to plea deal. Mac and Pete both lowered their heads as he spoke.

Sidney was sentenced to 7-10 years in prison under her plea agreement. We were all devastated, but knew that if she had been found guilty she would have spent the rest of her life in prison. The sentence was bittersweet. She told us she loved us as they escorted her out.

Lance met us outside and had appeared to have calmed down. I need to ask you a question he said as we walked up.

Look boy, Mac said, There is nothing more you need to say to my wife. You better stay away from her if you value your life.

Oh, you gone kill me pops? I should have known, you were a killer like your daughter. Lance spat back.

Before he could even get that statement out Pete knocked Lance straight out. Lance fell to the ground hard. I found that so funny, but knew it was not the time for laughter. Rickey ran out to check on Lance while Mac told Pete to hurry and leave. Security has started walking our way. once we saw that Lance was still moving, we too left the scene.

Six weeks later, I found out I was pregnant. Mac knew before I did. He said he could look at me and see the glow. Taylor was almost 8 months when I found out. I was happy that I would be having my own baby, but was scared to death at the thought of having two children. When the new baby was due to makes it's arrival, Taylor wouldn't even be two years old. Mac calmed me down whenever he saw me in panic mode. I began to grow at an alarming rate. By the time I was 3 months, I could no longer where my own clothes. I was fortunate not to have experienced a lot morning sickness, but I felt hungry and tired all the time. Taylor was just beginning to walk and she was into everything all the time.

When we went for my 3month checkup, the doctor told us that I was pregnant with twins. Mac could have not been more ecstatic; he went around telling everybody. Anybody he came into contact with knew that we had a 1 year old and would be having twins soon. My mother was the second happiest person; she had begun to come over all time. She announced that her and Mike would be buying a house in Gwinnett to be closer to us. I was so glad, I would be needing all the help I could get. I hadn't talked to Reece much, she and Ross were traveling all around the world. He had proposed to her while they were in Costa Rica and they wed in the Bahamas. It didn't sit with me that she had eloped, but she told me that they woke up one morning and knew it was the thing to do.

When I was 7 months, and big as a house, Mac hired a nanny. She was a little Spanish lady with a thick accent. She was really good with Taylor and was excited about the arrival of the twins. We went to the doctor and found out that the twins were boys. It was my second time in months seeing Mac cry.

He surprised me one day with the nursery for the boys that he'd did all by himself. He shopped for everything without me ever knowing what he was up to and while I was over my mother's one day, he set everything up. The walls to the nursery were covered with basketballs, footballs, soccer balls and baseballs. He had two cribs fit for kings with the furniture to match, he even had matching rocking chairs in there. It was beautiful.

Once Reece was back, she called and invited me and Taylor over for lunch, I stopped by the store to get Taylor some more wipes, we ran into saw Lance and Rickey. It was Rickey's first time seeing Taylor since the day in the hospital, She so pretty, he said, she sho do look like Sidney. Lance just stared at me for a minute then said; so you can have a baby for that old dude huh, but when I suggested that you have a baby with me, you thought I was crazy.

Lance, don't start, I'm having these babies with my husband. Get over yourself. I knew I was just rubbing it in by telling him that I was having twins.

Babies he said, your having twins? I started to walk away when he stopped me. Did you know she killed Roc? he asked. Did you know your cousin was fucking my father? Neither of those questions was I about to answer. I didn't owe Lance anything I thought to myself. Taylor started whining which made Rickey tell Lance to leave it alone. Lance didn't want to, but walked away anyway. I'm sorry Mia, I told Lance to move on, but he can't and every time he tries, he finds out some thing else. He's hurting Mia.

Rickey I know that finding out Sidney killed Roc would hurt him, but I don't have anything to do with that. I really just want to get on with my life and wish he would too. Tell uncle Rickey goodbye Taylor. When I called him uncle Rickey, I could see that that brightened his day. He was so connected with that baby when Sidney was pregnant. I figured it was the least I could do.

By the time we got to Reeces' house, I was exhausted, from walking around the store carrying that load and emotionally from Lance rehashing the past. I knew that finding out the one person who he didn't like was the one who killed his best friend was devastating for him. I also knew that finding out Reece and his father were together was also a hard pill to swallow. I couldn't be there for him. I couldn't even act like I cared any more. I was sorry for the things that had happened, but there was nothing I could do about it.

I wrote Sidney and told her about the babies, I included pictures of Taylor walking just in case she was ready to see her again.

She finally wrote me back and told me how happy she was for us. She said that Taylor looked happy just as she thought she would. She told me that she missed me and our talks. She had been taking classes and going to church and felt like she was more at peace than she's ever been. She'd finally accepted that she would be there and told me to keep her posted on my delivery.

I missed her too, more than I would admit to Mac, the mention of her name made him sad, so I never really talked about her anymore to him. As fat as I had gotten Mac still always told me how beautiful I was, he had gotten back his sexual appetite, and so had I, it was a wonder I could still do it at all. my belly was the size of Kansas. The doctor said it was normal for me to be horny and that as long as it was comfortable, I should be able to still have sex up until the day I delivered.

That day came sooner than we thought. The babies came a month early.

We were sitting out in the backyard watching Taylor play on her play set when my water broke. I never knew pain until that day. I stayed in labor for 24 hours. Mac was a mess, I thought he was the one in labor, I had never seen him so on edge.

At 4:30 the next morning I gave birth to my identical twin sons, they were even smaller than Taylor was. We named them Jaden and Jordan. Jaden was slightly bigger than Jordan which was the only way we could tell them apart. The second day of their lives, the nurse had bought them to me so that I could feed them. I was there alone and found myself unable to breath. The doctor said that I had a panic attack.

When Mac got there I yelled at him for leaving me alone.

Baby, calm down, I went to check on Taylor and change clothes. He said smiling at me

It's not funny Mac, I'm scared. We have 3 kids now.

Mia'amore, there's nothing to be scared about. We have three beautiful children to share our love with now. Don't you see how blessed we are.

He hadn't called me Mia'amore in a long time. it took me back to our days before we were married when life was simple.

Chapter 17

SIDNEY ROSE

I think the real Sidney Rose Stone emerged the day I was arrested. I had just caught Rickey with his wife. All the while I was cheating on Rickey, he was cheating on me. He tried to tell me that she had gotten him drunk and took advantage of that. I thought about all the times I was drunk and even then would I have ever married somebody and then stayed with them. Rickey couldn't even admit that he stayed married because on some level he loved that girl. I didn't think Rickey liked big women, he always had something to say when we saw a heavy set woman out. He said he just couldn't get down with a women who didn't care enough about herself to be fit. I asked him how he intended to marry me while he was still married. He said that he was planning on divorcing her before that. He was so full of it.

My first night in jail it hit me. I didn't have Tamia there to tell me it would be ok. Rickey was not coming to save the day. I couldn't just call my father, or Terry to make this situation disappear. All I had was me. The first month I prayed for forgiveness, the second month, I prayed for guidance, it wasn't until I gave birth to Taylor, that I began to pray for strength. As I looked at her with that tiny face and button nose, I knew that she belonged to Mia and my father. I couldn't raise her from jail. She was so perfect. How could I subject her to a life of visitations and phone calls. I went to school with a girl who's mother was in prison. It made her grown up too soon. She didn't know life as an innocent 15 year old. she knew of the prison system. Her mother shared the only stories she knew, those were stories of other women's lives who'd ended up in prison. It was the hardest decision I'd ever have to make. I'd been all about me. I put Rickey through hell. Had I been faithful to him and just loved him, he never would have went in search of it. I put Terry through hell, I constantly lied to him, I still had yet to tell him that I lived with Rickey all those months. I made Lance's life hell by killing his best friend. I even changed Tamia life, although she would never admit that I was the demise of her and Lance's relationship, I knew I was. I even continued to drink and smoke when I knew there was a chance I could have been pregnant. I had not done one thing for anybody else. The best thing I could do for Taylor was to give her to the two people who had more love in their hearts than anybody I knew. She deserved the best that life had to offer, and I was not that. I knew that every time I looked at her, I would see Roc and be reminded all over of the hurt I could have bought to her life.

I didn't even want to see her again before they took me back to jail. It was just too hard, I had to get on with my life and if I kept Taylor on my mind I would never be able to began to work on myself. Giving her to them was my first step in my path to forgiveness. My second step was telling Terry the whole truth. My third was apologizing to Rickey. even with him being married, and although we all knew she wasn't his, he would have raised Taylor as his own. He never stopped being my rock. I would always hold a special place in my heart for him.

I had given Mr. Winters the rest of the money I had from the Roc fund to represent me. Even if I did get out of this, I knew that I would be broke. I also knew that if I didn't make amends for killing Roc, that I would never truly get over it. I had been able to put it out of mind for the most part, but reading the bible help me to see that until I was honest and atone for my sins, I would never be happy or at peace.

My first cellmate was an older lady named Ms. Jolene who had killed her husband, he beat her up real bad first and she was still healing. Helping her made me feel better. She didn't have any family and cried all the time. I read the bible to her every night. I told her that's how I was finding my peace, that maybe it would work for her too.

When it was time for her trial, she was scared, she said she was too old to go to prison and would surely die. When she came back and told me she was sentenced to 20 years, I cried with her. the night she was set to be transferred to prison, she died in her sleep. I guess she was right. She was the only person I had really talked to and losing her was a wakeup call.

My attorney came and talked to me a few weeks later. He said that he talked with the prosecutor and they agreed to a plea deal. If I plead guilty, they would only give me 7-10 years. That sounded a whole lot better than the 20 to life I was facing. I knew that pleading guilty meant that I would have no recourse for an appeal. But this was something I had to do. I did kill Roc and until I atoned for his murder I would never find the peace I needed.

When Uncle Mac came to see me, I knew he was going to try to talk me out of pleading guilty. When I talked to them over the phone, he said that I may be able to claim self defense, since Roc was trying to rape me. the only problem with that was. I got rid of the murder weapon, I wiped off everything in that room, I had a pending case with Roc, which would serve me better if he was dead and in their search for the weapon, they found what turned out to be two keys of uncut cocaine. It was a no brainer for me. I was not about to go to trial and risk my life on a sympathetic jury. It didn't work for Jolene and she had a 2 week hospital stay from the beating he gave her before she stabbed him. I knew that I hurt Uncle Mac when I rejected his visit, but I had to do what I had to do. I didn't feel good about it.

Mia kept sending my pictures of Taylor. When I gave her up, I had to detach myself from her. I had to forget that I was the one that carried her for 9 months. The only way I was able to sleep was knowing that she was with her real parents. I couldn't see pictures of her smiling or of her sitting up for the first time. I couldn't take seeing the pictures of her with her ears pierced. I had to let her go. I knew Mia couldn't understand that, but it had to be this way. I told her not to send anymore pictures, every time we talked, she talked about Taylor, or Taylor was in the background making noises. I had to get some distance from them. I loved them for loving me enough to raise my child as their own. But she was just that their baby. she wasn't mine anymore.

Terry had wrote me a letter. He wasn't asking me tons of questions, he didn't whine about what I'd did to him. His letter was just a friendly note from a friend. I appreciated that more than anything. I didn't want to talk about Roc, or Taylor or family, and he knew that. When he began to come visit me was when we talked about my case and the daughter I gave away. He was the one who convinced me to plead guilty. He said that 7-10 for murder was the best deal I would have every gotten.

I couldn't believe it when Mia wrote me and told me she was having twins. Mia having twins. I thought of how much her life had changed just as mine had. She enclosed a picture of Taylor walking. She said that she wasn't sending it for my benefit but she sent it because she was proud of their daughter and wanted to share that with her best friend. Leave it to Mia to put a spin on it I thought.

Taylor had even begun to look like the two of them. I could still see Roc in her, but it was very little. She was Mia's daughter and I could see that she loved her more than I ever could.

My fourth step to getting my life right was pleading guilty. I was sent to Pulaski prison to serve out my 7-10 yr sentence. It was the most depressing place I'd ever seen. The women in there were murders, child abusers, people who'd stolen everything from drugs to diapers. I was surprised at how many older ladies were in there. Some of those ladies could have been my grandmother. Some of them had recently gotten there, while others had been there for the majority of their lives. And there were some that knew that they would never be getting out. Looking at them made me realize how God was still blessing me. I knew that being there was the path that I had to take and I was now able to fully accept that path.

I grew up in that prison. My love for Terry grew in the prison. He stuck by me every day. He could have easily forgotten about me and moved on. I looked forward to his love letters and his visits. I knew what it meant to have those butterflies, Mia and Reece always talked about. It took me come to prison to realize that my true love was the one man I treated the worse.

I had come to understand that God put's people in your life for a reason, a season or a lifetime. I wasn't sure which category Terry was in yet. But I was now willing to find out.

Rickey also came to see me a couple of times, he told me that he saw Mia and Taylor in the store and that Lance is still not able to get over the fact that she left him and married Mac, or that I was the one responsible for killing Roc and now he was dealing with the fact that his new stepmother was none other than Mia's cousin.

I felt bad for him. Rickey said his wife was expecting a baby soon, and in the same breath told me he still loved me. he hadn't changed one bit. Except for the fact that he'd lost so much weight. He was no longer that big ole country boy. he was so small, that I wondered if he started smoking. I wanted to ask, but decided against it.

I'd taken up art classes and started going to church every Sunday. Mia wrote me and told me that she'd had the babies. Twin boys. She said it was hard. Even with the nanny they hired, she still never got any sleep. She told me that my father still wanted to make love all the time even before her 6 wk checkup. She was sure she didn't want any more children and wanted to hold off on relations until she was comfortably on some kind of birth control. She said if it were up to my dad, they would have more children right away. I wondered how my father still had the libido of a 20 year old man. I never imagined a life where I wasn't around when Tamia began having children, I always thought we would raise our kids together. And I guess I got it half right, our kids were being raised together, as brother and sister.

Mia told me that Reece and Ross had made it official, She had come so far from the overweight girl with no self esteem. If anybody deserved to meet and marry a millionaire it was Reece. I had to admit that when I first learned of their relationship, I was a little jealous. How lucky do you have to be to meet a man like Ross on her first time out as a single woman, fall in love and get married in the Bahamas. It only took her 30 years to find her happiness. A jealous heart was the old Sidney, the new Sidney wished them nothing but the best and meant it

Chapter 18

REECE

I got married on the beach in the Bahamas to the man of my dreams. I was so happy that it scared me sometimes. I would still wake up in the middle of the night and just look at Ross. He was so handsome and kind. He really loved me and my son. He wanted to start the paperwork right away to become DJ's father. When I told DJ's mother about my plans, she all but told me that I'd better not. She said that her son would be DJ's only father. I tried to explain to her that DJ would always be his father, but now I was remarried and we wanted to give my son our last name. She told me it was way too soon for me to get married anyway. She said that her son was turning over in his grave. I thought it was time for her to know the truth about her son.

After I was done telling her the whole story, even that she has another grandchild, she didn't believe me, she keep telling me that I was a liar, and that her son would have never done such things. After 2 hours of going back and forth, she finally came around. She said she wanted to know DJ's daughter and her mother. I told her about Kim killing herself and that Deanna was being raised by her grandmother. I gave her Ms. Jones telephone number so that they could talk. I know Ms. Jones would be happy to have some help raising their granddaughter.

Lance didn't take seeing us very well at the store. After he told Ross that he never wanted to see him again for what he's done to his mother along with some more choice words. He turned toward me and after calling me a home wrecking whore, he thought he was about to slap me. It was then that Ross grabbed him and put him up against a wall and told him that if he ever disrespected me again, that he would be making be the worst mistake of his whole spoiled life. I felt bad for coming between them. Ross said that Lance has always been an impossible child. His mother had led Lance to believe that he was inferior to everybody, even him.

When Rhonda found out about me and Ross, she like Lance also blamed me for breaking up her family. I had to remind Rhonda that I was her family, I was the one there for her since the day she was born. It was like she'd forgotten where she came from. After her rant, it was me that was mad at her. How dare she call me the names she called me. I raised that girl. I don't care how much she didn't approve of my relationship with Ross. I expected her to back me no matter what, the same way I've backed her up all these years even if I didn't approve of her decisions. Like the way she was treating our mother. She all but told her that she no longer existed in her world. Rhonda was becoming too much like Ms. Chapman, she spoke down to everybody. When she found out Sidney was on trial for killing Roc, she said that Sidney has always been trash, now she was amongst her true peers in prison. I had to remind her that Sidney was the one who made sure her hair stayed done, Sidney was the one who taught her how to apply makeup and even bought her her first makeup and she was also the one to take her to that abortion clinic that she didn't want me to know about. Rhonda had the nerve to say that was her old life, she was filling her life with a better class of people. I could not believe she just said that tome. When she first went to stay with the Chapman's I thought it was the best thing for her. how many girls get the opportunity she was given. But now I could see that Rhonda hadn't changed for the better, I didn't know her anymore.

As much as I loved Ross, I began to understand that being the wife of someone so powerful was not all it was cracked up to be. When we got back from our vacation Ross went back to work full fledge. He began making trips back and forth to Mississippi. I hardly ever saw him. When I told him that I missed him, he would stay home for a day or so then say that he had to go make the bacon. He told me to start looking for a new house. It was time to leave this life behind me. I was all too happy to start looking for a bigger and better house. Me and DJ went looking at hundreds of houses before we had 3 of them that we wanted Ross to look at. When he saw them, he didn't like none of them. He said that they were all kinda small and he had something else in mind. He gave me the listings of five houses. They were all very far away, most of them were past the Alpharetta area, there was one in Dacula close to Mia and Mac.

The houses were amazing, they were bigger than I could have ever imagined. Most of them had pools and in law suits in the back of them. As much as I liked them, I had to wonder if I needed that much house. Most of the time it was just me and DJ there and soon he would be going to school. When I told Ross of my hesitance, he told me that I would be too busy filling the house to get lonely.

We decided on the brick 6000 square foot home in Dacula. And just as he said I spent all my time shopping and decorating our new home, only to be there alone most of the time just as I thought. While moving I came across the box with the stuff from the hospital the day DJ was killed. Inside it was there was a bloody t-shirt, his cell phone and about 5 thousand dollars in one hundred dollar bills. Who walks around with that much money I thought as I counted it. There were also 2 rings, both of them were big and flashy with a lot of diamonds. Neither of them were his wedding band. Since I hadn't come across it with any of his other things, I assumed he'd gotten rid of it. Before I let myself get upset all over again, I put the money in my pocket and put the rings and other things back in the box. DJ was my past I repeated, Ross is my future. I'd decided that I would give the money to Kim's mother; I know she could use it, being that she was taking care of DJ's and Kim's daughter all by herself.

I had never realized that becoming the wife of someone so wealthy meant I would have to sacrifice being with my husband.

I went over Mia's to help her with the kids and vent about my marriage. I expected her to understand, since Mac had opened the restaurant, he also worked long hours sometimes.

Reece I'm going to need you to grow up. Look at your life now, look at all the things you have. When have you ever been able to say that you had a husband who respected and loved you more than anything, who gave up his life to be with you. So what he works a lot. You have everything a woman could want, and I promise you that there are woman who would trade places with you in a heartbeat. This is the life you signed up for, now enjoy it and stop trying to think of ways to be unhappy. she said.

As I sat there watching her with her twins, and her daughter I realized that she was right. I was so used to being unhappy that I didn't even know how to be happy. I complained to Ross all the time. When he came home, we spent more time arguing about the fact that he wasn't home, that I didn't enjoy the time he was. I was becoming Ms. Chapman all over again. That thought made me mad at myself.

When I got home, I was determined to make a better life for Ross, he had given me so much, the least I could do was be a good wife. When I told Ross that I wanted to have another baby, he told me that he'd gotten a vasectomy. I couldn't believe it. The reason why Ms. Chapman was never able to conceive was because he'd gotten fixed. How could you that to her I asked.

I didn't want any more kids with her. The way she raised Lance and didn't let me have any say on raising him. I was not about to go through that again.

But, now we can't have our own baby I said pouting. I think the fact that I couldn't have another baby made me want one even more. I couldn't think of anything else for weeks. I started doing research on getting his vasectomy revearsed. I had begun to pull away from Ross, but couldn't help it. I loved him more than anything, but I felt like I needed a baby to complete us. Ross said we were already complete with DJ and didn't need another baby to make us whole. As much as I knew he was right it didn't make me want a baby any less. The more I whined about it the more business trips Ross made. After awhile he was only home maybe once a week. I knew then that I was starting to lose my husband, not to another woman, or because he was abusive or because I was fat. But because of me. I had no body to blame but myself. Why couldn't I just be happy.

I began to fill my life with other things. I started a garden something I had always wanted to do and I went on and started school. I spent a lot of time at Mia's and we started working out together. Ross was still staying away from home a lot. When he was there, I would try to make the most of it. I wouldn't fuss about his absence, I wouldn't start an argument about us not being able to have baby. I just enjoyed him being home.

What I realized was, I had always looked for an outside source to make my happy. When it wasn't DJ, it was Kim, then it was Ross. I never took the time getting to know myself and what would make Reece happy. Ross being gone so much is what made me realize that. although

I missed him like crazy, I needed that time, I took that opportunity to get to know myself again, so I could be a better wife and mother.

It took awhile, but I got there and when I did my husband began staying home more. he moved most of his business to Atlanta and I fixed up his home office. We are now happier than ever. I have a husband that's home and loves me a beautiful son and I know that even if he's not there I'm still happy and complete.

Chapter 19

TAMIA

If someone had told me that I would end up a stay at home mother, I wouldn't have believed them. Instead of designer clothes and shoes, Mac and I both wore a tee-shirts with spit up on them most days. My hair stayed in a ponytail more times than I was willing to admit, and his was no longer perfect all the time either. I had started working out with Reece because I hadn't lost all the weight from the twins and had started to not care about the extra weight until she came over and made me stop and take a good look at myself.

She whined about her life and how Ross was never home, This girl came from a home where her mother sold everything they owned including her for a hit. Just a couple years earlier she was being beaten by her husband who cheated on her endlessly. She had everything we used to stay up all night taking about and she found every reason under to sun not to be happy. Sidney was able to find her peace in prison. There was no reason why she couldn't find it with her wealthy handsome husband.

It made me think. We can all find things to complain about. Life is what we make of it. No one is perfect, but our faith is.

At the end of the day, I have a wonderful husband, 3 wonderful children, and a family who loves me. That's my life and I wouldn't trade it for anything.